## Praise for *Telegraph Days*

"McMurtry balances his fast-moving romp of a story line with unexpected disturbing scenes . . . Nellie's amorous high jinks may seem over the top, but McMurtry is just pulling readers' legs a little. The light-hearted humor adds to the novel's fun."

*—Chicago Tribune*

"*Telegraph Days* is a picaresque and entertaining ride."

*—USA Today*

"It's a darn good read: an entertaining spoof about the Wild West that brings alive the romance of outlaws, gunfighters, and shootouts."

*—The Washington Post*

"Nellie Courtright is brassy, sassy, classy, looking for love anywhere, anytime. She's got a memory that won't quit. And, with a money-back-guaranteed, knee-slapping, jaw-dropping, eye-popping tall tale on every page . . . It's hard to imagine anybody having more fun than McMurtry while he wrote this—unless it's those who read it."

*—New York Daily News*

"Readers won't be able to help cracking a smile."

*—Publishers Weekly*

"An easy, breezy read."

*—Kirkus Reviews*

"Nellie Courtright is just what readers have come to expect from the author: a spunky protagonist of the American West, making short work of the villains who come along and, it seems, opening her arms to the charming ones."

*—Rocky Mountain News*

"Good news for the legions of McMurtry fans."

*—Library Journal*

# Telegraph

## LARRY

# Days

*A Novel*

# McMurtry

Simon & Schuster Paperbacks
*New York   London   Toronto   Sydney*

 SIMON & SCHUSTER PAPERBACKS
Rockefeller Center
1230 Avenue of the Americas
New York, NY 10020

First Simon & Schuster trade paperback edition June 2008

SIMON & SCHUSTER PAPERBACKS and colophon are registered trademarks of Simon & Schuster, Inc.

For information about special discounts for bulk purchases, please contact Simon & Schuster Special Sales at 1-800-456-6798 or business@simonandschuster.com.

Designed by Karolina Harris

Manufactured in the United States of America

10  9  8  7  6  5  4  3  2  1

The Library of Congress has cataloged the hardcover edition as follows:
McMurtry, Larry.
    Telegraph days : a novel / Larry McMurtry.
      p. cm.
    I. Title.

PS3563.A319T38 2006
813'.54—dc22          2005057458

ISBN-13:  978-0-7432-5078-8
ISBN-10:      0-7432-5078-8
ISBN-13:  978-0-7432-5093-1  (pbk)
ISBN-10:      0-7432-5093-1  (pbk)

# Contents

# Telegraph Days

# BOOK I

---

# Yazee Days

# 1

"I HOPE YOU'RE carpenter enough to build an honest coffin," I told Jackson, my younger brother. About an hour ago, I would guess, our father, Perceval Staunton Courtright, had foolishly hung himself from a rafter in the barn.

From the rope burns on his hands, it seemed likely that Father changed his mind at the last minute and tried to claw his way back up to the rafter, where he might have rid himself of the inconvenient noose—last-minute mind changes were a lifelong practice of Father's. In this case, though, the mind change had come too late, meaning that Jackson and I were faced with the necessity of burying Father in windy No Man's Land, a grassy part of the American West that, for the moment, no state claimed.

My younger brother, Jackson, was just seventeen. Here we were, the two surviving Courtrights, having already, in the course of our westering progress, buried two little brothers, three little sisters, an older sister, three darkies, our mother, and now look! Father's tongue was black as a boot.

"I'm a fair carpenter, but where will I get the lumber?" Jackson asked, surveying the vast grassy prairie. We were just south of the Cimarron River, in a part of the plains populated by no one, other than Jackson and myself—and I, for one, didn't plan to stay.

"Use some of this worthless barn," I told my brother. "It's only half a barn anyway, and we won't be needing it now." Father had first supposed that the prairies beside the Cimarron might be a good place to start a Virginia-style plantation, but he wisely discarded that notion while the barn was just half built. Now, with Father dead, we were down to Percy, our strong-minded mule, and a flea-filled cabin with glass windows. Ma had insisted on the glass windows—it was her last request. But she was dead and so was our gentle, feckless father. We had no reason to linger on the Black Mesa Ranch—the name Father had rather grandly bestowed on our empty acres.

I was twenty-two, kissable, and of an independent disposition. My full name was Marie Antoinette Courtright, but everyone called me Nellie. Mother told me I got named after Marie Antoinette because Father happened to be reading about the French Revolution the night I was born—my own view is that he anticipated my yappiness and was secretly hoping the people would rise up and cut off my head.

Jackson began to rip boards off the barn. He handed me a pick and a spade, implements I accepted reluctantly.

"Being a lady, I try to avoid picks and spades," I mentioned.

"I guess you've kissed too many fellows to be calling yourself a lady," Jackson remarked, picking up a crowbar—or half a crowbar. At some point, mysteriously, our family crowbar got broken in two; this setback annoyed Father so much that he threw the other half in the Missouri River.

"It's not my fault you're off to a slow start in the kissing derby," I told him.

"Where would I get a girl to try and kiss, living way out here?" he asked.

For once Jackson had a point. My various cowboys could always slip away from their herds long enough to provide me with a spot of romance, but very few young ladies showed up on the Cimarron's shores.

"I expect you'll get your chance once we get settled in Rita Blanca," I assured him.

Jackson looked a little droopy as he laid out Father's coffin. We Courtrights are, in the main, not a very sentimental lot. But burying brother after brother, sister after sister, and now parent after parent, as Jackson had been required to do, was the kind of work that didn't put one in the whistling mood. I marched over and gave my brother a big hug—he didn't sob aloud but he did tear up.

"I expect I'll miss Pa more than you will," he said, with a catch in his voice. "Pa, he always had a story."

"It's just as well he didn't hear you call him Pa," I reminded Jackson.

Father had no patience with abbreviation, localisms, or any deviation from pure plantation English; but Jackson was right. Father always had a story.

When we were at home, he was always reading stories to the little ones, but once we left Virginia and headed west, the little ones soon commenced dying—a common thing, of course, for westering families, but a heavy grief nonetheless. It broke our mother's heart. All along the Western trails, in the years after the Civil War, families that got caught up in westering died like gnats or flies. Santa Fe Trail, Oregon Trail, California Trail—it didn't matter. The going was deadly. The brochures the land agents put out made westering seem easy—sparkling water holes every few miles, abundant game, healthy prairie climate with frequent breezes—but in truth, there were no easy roads. Death traveled in every wagon, on every boat. Westering made many orphans, and picked many parents clean.

Jackson and I were young and healthy—that was our good fortune. Neither of us shied from hard work. I set aside being a lady and had the grave half dug by the time Jackson finished the coffin. We buried Father in a buffalo robe he had bought from an old Osage man. Then we rolled him in the coffin and eased the coffin into the earth. Dust was on its way to dust.

"We ought to sing a hymn at least," Jackson suggested.

Hymn singing makes me mopey—I have a good voice but a poor memory for the words of songs. Since Jackson and I had not been churchly people we could not quite string together a whole hymn, but we did sing a verse or two of "Amazing Grace," and then we sang "Lorena," in memory of the thousands of fallen heroes of the South. Since our vocal chords were warmed up we finished with a rousing version of "The Battle Hymn of the Republic." It was a Yankee hymn, of course—Father, who fought with Lee at the Wilderness and elsewhere, might not have approved, but Father was dead and his fight was over. Maybe it was time to let bygones be bygones—singing one another's songs was a start.

Across the Cimarron, to the northwest, the July sun was shining hard on Black Mesa, the only hill anywhere around. Rita Blanca, the little town we had decided to head for, was more than thirty miles away. Percy, our strong-minded mule, hated long stretches of travel and would balk and sulk most of the way. But Percy would just have to put up with a lengthy travel, since neither Jackson nor I felt like spending another night in the flea-filled cabin.

"Let's go partway and camp," Jackson suggested. "It's a full moon. It'll stay light till almost morning."

Having no one to keep us, or say us nay, that is exactly what we did.

# 2

In early July, along the Cimarron, the summer sun takes a good long while to go down. Percy began to pretend he was worn out before it was even good dusk. Fortunately we struck a little trickle of a creek, whose water was a good deal less muddy than what could be had from the river itself.

Seven or eight buffalo were standing around a wallow, and one was even wallowing in the dust, exactly as he was supposed to. Jackson and I had with us all the Courtright weaponry: Father's old cap-and-ball pistol, and a ten-gauge shotgun, and a rusty sword. Jackson had killed three geese and a turkey or two with the shotgun, but neither of us had ever fired the pistol.

The buffalo stared at us, and we stared back at them. Percy indicated, by a series of snorts, that he didn't care for their company.

"Buffalo liver's said to be mighty tasty," Jackson observed.

Of provisions we had none.

"I suppose we could bring one down with Father's pistol," I said. "But I don't know that I fancy trying to cut up a buffalo this late in the day."

"Be bloody work, wouldn't it?" Jackson said, in a tone that was none too polite.

I had long ago learned to ignore impolite remarks, and I ignored Jackson's pettish tone.

"I suppose you're afraid that if you ride into Rita Blanca all bloody, that sheriff you're so keen on might not want to marry you, after all," my brother said.

The sheriff he was referring to was named Bunsen, a sturdy young man about my age. Sheriff Bunsen had ridden out to propose to me half a dozen times.

Each time I politely turned him down. One of my grounds for refusing Ted was that he sported a silly-looking walrus mustache that I suppose he probably thought made him look important—ignoring the fact that it tickled when he kissed me. Of course, if Teddy Bunsen had been really important he would have been sheriff of a town better than Rita Blanca, a dusty place on the plains where people stopped when they just absolutely didn't have the strength to travel another step toward Santa Fe or wherever they thought they wanted to get to.

Father had hoped to hire a full complement of servants in Rita Blanca—after all, what plantation lacked servants?—but nobody in that miserable community even came close to meeting Father's standards. We were servantless our whole time on the Cimarron, which was probably a good thing, since it forced Jackson and me to acquire skills such as gardening and carpentry which we never would have been allowed to use if we had been stuck in Virginia, being minor gentry.

Be that as it may, we were, for the moment, camped on the prairie with nary a bite to eat.

"There's bound to be prairie chickens around here close," I told Jackson. "If you were to hurry up before it gets dark you could probably knock one over with a rock. If you do, I'll cook it."

"I'm a near orphan now," Jackson said, plaintively. "If you marry that dern sheriff I'll have no family at all."

"Wrong, you'd have more family—a new brother-in-law," I pointed out.

But Jackson was just in a mood to be gloomy—after all, we had buried Father that day. The buffalo had drifted off in the dusk. I walked over toward the river, armed with a couple of good rocks; within five minutes I had knocked over two slow-moving prairie hens. These I promptly dressed and spitted.

While we were finishing off the birds, that huge yellow prairie moon came up, and soon the coyotes were making their yippy, rackety music. Jackson hobbled Percy, a mule that could not be trusted. After supper, I suppose, I must have nodded off. When I woke up my little brother was curled up in the buffalo wallow, snoring like a sow, and that moon that had been so big and yellow was high up in the sky and white again.

# 3

THE NOT-SO-DISTANT booming of a buffalo gun brought me out of my restless slumber, though it failed to wake up Jackson, who could have slept through Shiloh. We got on our way in time to observe that the buffalo we had surprised at twilight didn't make it much past dawn.

Father's good friend Aurel Imlah, the smelly but neighborly local hide hunter, killed every one of the buffalo while they watered from the Cimarron. Two of them, both bulls, had actually fallen in the water, which presented something of a challenge for Aurel's two-man skinning crew. They were muttering and upbraiding one another in a language I could not understand.

"It's Polish," Aurel informed me, when I inquired. Aurel's beard was so long and filthy that I wouldn't have been surprised to see a small bird fly out of it. Aurel's brother Addison was the postmaster in Waynesboro, Virginia, ancestral seat of the Courtrights. The actual "seat" was a big yellow manor house whose fields hadn't been properly tilled since before the war.

I like Aurel Imlah, though I did my best to stay upwind of him when he came to play chess with Father. He had gentle eyes and a bemused expression.

"Mr. Imlah, Pa hung himself to death!" Jackson blurted out, at which news Aurel frowned.

"Damnit!" he said. "I expect you'd welcome breakfast."

Looking at the eight skinned corpses of the buffalo dulled my appetite for a minute—the poor dead beasts looked so nude somehow, now that their skins were off.

"I suppose you've heard about General Custer," Mr. Imlah added.

"Georgie Custer, what about him?" I asked.

"The young fool overmatched himself, finally," the old hunter informed us. "He was wiped out with some two hundred and fifty men at the Little Bighorn, which is a creek in Montana, I believe."

"Who got him?" I asked—I was not at all surprised that someone had.

"A huge passel of Indians got him," Aurel told us, before turning his attention to his Polish skinning crew. One of them was waving a knife in a manner that his boss did not care for.

"Poke a hole in that skin and you're fired," he told the man.

The Pole looked defiant for a moment, but then thought the better of it and finished his task without comment.

"Georgie Custer is dead?" Jackson asked, shocked. "Why, he used to come around plenty, courting Nellie."

I took the news about Georgie Custer in stride. Georgie had always been the soul of recklessness—why the army had let him ride off with two hundred and fifty men was a mystery to me.

All I could say about his courting was that it was crude at best. He was apt to corner me on the staircase and subject me to big sloppy kisses, which I declined to enjoy. Then I discovered that he had also been kissing my big sister Millicent, who now lies in her lonely grave near Council Grove, Kansas. I was not about to share Milly's menfolk—Georgie Custer never caught me on the staircase again. Being dead probably served him right, though of course it didn't serve his soldiers right.

"We could sure use breakfast," Jackson admitted. "You wouldn't have any buffalo liver, would you?"

"Son, I don't," Aurel said. "My Poles gobbled those livers down before sunrise. But we might have a few tongues left—and if you'd not acquired a taste for tongue I can chop off a tasty rib or two."

Neither of us much cared for tongue, so Aurel did chop off some hefty ribs, which he soon had dripping over a fire.

The Poles, now laggards, had already loaded their small hide wagon and set out for Rita Blanca.

Aurel Imlah seemed a little surprised that neither of us was very upset about the fate of Georgie Custer.

"It's a big thing," he said. "A big thing! I expect for the Indians it'll be the last big thing!"

He shook his head grimly, as if puzzled that such a tragedy could happen. "He shouldn't have underestimated the Indians," he added.

"Seems to me the army shouldn't have overestimated Georgie," I added. "Cuts both ways, don't you think?"

Mr. Imlah looked at me solemnly, for a long time.

"You're smart, Nellie," he said. "That's good."

The old hide seller had always been especially fond of Jackson. Since the Cimarron was only a short walk from our place, he often took Jackson fishing, and taught him how to make fish traps, which he considered more reliable than the pole and the hook. Mr. Imlah had been raised on the Chesapeake Bay and often talked to us about what delicacies the Chesapeake terrapin were. Our old darky woman Della was said to be able to make a fine dish of terrapin but she passed away on the boat between St. Louis and Westport. Jackson caught plenty of turtles in his trap, but none of his catch resulted in wonderful meals.

"I expect you'll be needing a job," Aurel said to Jackson, as he was getting ready to lope off toward Rita Blanca—Percy's pace was far too slow for Mr. Imlah.

"Come see me at the hide yard," he suggested. "I can usually find work for a stout young fellow like you."

Jackson, I could see, was about to burst out with thank-yous—but I had other plans for my little brother. Working with hides was smelly and I couldn't hope to stay upwind of a brother all the time.

"That's most kind, Mr. Imlah," I said. "You're a true gentleman. But the truth is, Jackson's already secured employment—I believe Sheriff Bunsen means to make him his deputy."

Aurel Imlah was hard to surprise, but Jackson Courtright had his mouth so wide open a bat could have flown into it.

"If this mule don't fail us my brother hopes to start work tomorrow," I continued.

"That is fortunate . . . I consider Sheriff Bunsen a fine man," Mr. Imlah said.

Then he tipped his cap to us and rode off east.

"What are you talking about, Nellie?" Jackson asked. "I haven't been offered a position with Sheriff Bunsen."

"No, but you soon will be," I assured him. "Have a little faith in your big sister."

With that, we pointed Percy east and got started.

# 4

Prudes and other censorious folk might consider it a bad sign when—as was the case in Rita Blanca—the most impressive building in town happened to be the jail. The founding fathers of this little community knew what they were doing in that respect, at least. The jail was a sturdy two-story building built of thick, mud-colored adobe. A lynch mob would have had to chisel half the night to break through those muddy-looking walls.

There was a long platform extending out from the second floor, boasting a well-built gallows, from which the more serious miscreants could be efficiently hung.

Rita Blanca, at this stage of its existence, was a disorderly straggle of buildings, perhaps twenty at most. Some of these had already been abandoned and were in the process of falling down. Beauregard Wheless's general store was a happy exception—it was a sprawling frame building, in good repair, with a small undertaker's office off to one side. Beau Wheless, the father of Hungry Billy Wheless—Jackson's one friend in Rita Blanca—was the busiest merchant in town. When he wasn't selling firearms, or dry goods, or hardware, he was usually in his carpentry shop, hammering together coffins as fast as he could in order to keep ahead of the deaths, no easy task in a place where life was cheap.

"I see Hungry Billy," Jackson said, as Percy plodded doggedly into town. "He's wasting time, as usual."

Hungry Billy Wheless had once got lost while on an antelope hunt. He had been forced to wander the prairies for three days, living on grass and weeds, or so he claimed. When he finally located Rita Blanca he eased his hunger pains by eating a whole goat, which, had it been a small goat, would have been no special feat. Locally there was much disagreement about the size of the goat. Those who couldn't stand Hungry Billy claimed that it had been merely a tiny kid; but others, such as Sheriff Ted Bunsen, who liked to keep in with the Whelesses, claimed that it had been a fairly hefty specimen of the goat tribe. I suppose people in remote communities need things like that to quarrel about. Anyway, the nickname stuck.

A central feature of downtown Rita Blanca was its three dilapidated saloons; the three were crammed together right across the street from the jail, which was convenient for Sheriff Ted Bunsen when it became time to collar the drunks.

In fact, when we rode up to the front of the jail, Teddy Bunsen was just in the process of releasing his catch of drunks from the previous night. Most of them still had sleep in their eyes, although it was nearly noon, and three of the men only managed to stumble a few steps into the street before collapsing in the dust. Most of the other slowly sobering drunks—about fifteen in all—staggered to the safety of the saloons across the way. Two looked as if they might be Mexican but the rest were white.

When Sheriff Ted Bunsen stepped out the front door of the jail, he was pretty surprised to find Jackson and me standing there, with Percy, our mule, burdened with all our worldly effects.

I gave him no time to preen, but he did manage to quickly tip his hat.

I saw no reason just to stand there, letting time pass.

"Hello, Teddy," I said. "Father suicided himself yesterday and Jackson and I have abandoned the Black Mesa Ranch."

"Oh Lord!" Ted said, looking shocked. He was a man of few words, as well as tickly kisses.

"We've moved to town," I added. That fact was obvious, but you don't ever want to count on a male to spot the obvious.

"Jackson needs a job," I said, pressing right on. "Do you think your budget could accommodate a deputy? He's prepared to work cheap."

It's likely that my forward way of doing things startled Ted Bunsen a good deal. He was, of course, a bachelor, and cautious to a fault. Maybe he was beginning to suspect that being so rash as to allow a woman into his life meant that she'd soon start putting onions in dishes he'd rather not have onions in.

Still, the man had ridden out six times to propose to me, and now opportunity was knocking on his own front door. I didn't look at Jackson during this negotiation. No doubt I was embarrassing him half to death, but embarrassment is only a temporary thing.

A deputy's job, which might mean he could board in a fine adobe jail, was not something Jackson could afford to pass up.

On his various visits Ted Bunsen had barely taken notice of Jackson—he had been too busy taking notice of me. He finally looked at Jackson, who was blushing fiercely in his embarrassment.

"I suppose it is about time I got me a deputy," Ted allowed. "What kind of things can Jackson do?"

I looked into the street, where three drunks were still snoring peaceably. Anyone hurrying through in a fast wagon might well run over them.

"He can remove public hazards," I pointed out. "Like those three drunks in the road. Suppose someone came along in a heavy wagon and ran over one of them. Such an accident might result in the loss of a limb, which could even prompt a lawsuit."

"A lawsuit?" Teddy asked, nervously. "Who would the one-legged fellow sue? No one around here can even figure out which state we belong to, or if we belong to any. There's no county. The town don't even have a mayor.

"Some think this is Texas," he added. "Some think it's Kansas, and a few favor the theory that it's New Mexico."

"Let's start with the simple fact that it's got a sheriff, whether it belongs to any state or not," I advised. "Drag those three drunks out of harm's way, Jackson—and show a little charity."

"Charity?" Jackson asked.

"Dump them in a shady spot, if you can find one," I explained. "We wouldn't want them to incur sunburn. And be careful. Don't let one of them wake up and shoot you."

"Oh, they're not armed," Teddy informed me. "I generally don't dole out the firearms until the middle of the afternoon. By that time they're usually feeling pretty tame."

Jackson soon had the drunks piled under a tree not far from the blacksmith's shop. By the time he finished I believe the notion of having a deputy had begun to grow on Teddy Bunsen.

"A deputy just might come in handy," he remarked, several times. "I guess he could bunk in one of the cells."

He said it in a slow, foot-dragging way, though. If there's one thing I can't tolerate, it's an indecisive male. I decided it was time to dig in the spur.

"If you're doubtful, Sheriff," I said, "we'll just let you be. Fortunately Jackson had another offer of employment. Reliable young men don't grow on trees around here."

I believe Teddy knew me well enough by this time to grasp that my loyalty to my brother could well affect other things—kissing, for example, or even, at a stretch, matrimony.

"Can you shoot a pistol?" Teddy asked Jackson, more briskly.

"Never tried," Jackson admitted.

Teddy sighed, and bit the bullet.

"I rarely shoot a pistol myself," he admitted. "Mostly the job just consists of walking the drunks across the street and packing them in."

The upshot of this tedious interview was that Jackson got hired, at a salary of fifteen dollars a month and board.

# 5

ONCE TEDDY BUNSEN reconciled himself to the fact that he now had an active deputy, he began to feel so generous toward us Courtrights that he even offered to stable our mule for free—a handsome gesture under the circumstances. After all, Percy had to live somewhere.

Then Teddy's mind seemed to go clickety-click as he thought of tasks he had been putting off and could now assign to Jackson, his useful deputy. Some of the locks could use a squirt of oil, and many of the cells needed a thorough sweeping—most of their occupants were not exactly tidy souls. And there were the long-neglected gallows, which could clearly use a coat of paint.

"I can handle all that, yes sir," Jackson said, relieved. I believe he feared that his first job as a deputy would be to arrest the biggest killer in the vicinity. In fact, Jackson could probably have arrested some pretty bad killers—he just didn't know it yet. My brother had abilities that he had no suspicion he possessed—though, at the moment, what he really needed to locate was a broom, a paintbrush, and a can of paint.

"I can't find the broom—or the paint either," Jackson admitted to Teddy, who got a kind of embarrassed look on his face.

"Golly, I forgot. Mexican Joe stole the broom—that's why you can't find it," he admitted. "I fear we don't possess a paintbrush, or a can of paint, though we might have some linseed oil somewhere."

"This is a fine kettle of fish," I told Teddy. "This jail seems to suffer from a dire lack of equipment."

Teddy didn't deny it.

"There's a well-stocked general store right down the street," I reminded him. "I bet they have a fine selection of paints, and probably even brooms and paintbrushes."

Before I could say more, the very thing that I had predicted happened. A wagon with a wild-looking old man on the wagon seat came racing hell-for-leather right down the middle of the road, where, a few minutes earlier, three drunks had been reposing. But for my brother's timely work all might have sustained a good trampling.

"I don't know where that old fool is going in such a hurry," I said, "but I hope you will agree that it was a good thing that Jackson cleared the street."

I can't say that my remark was well received. Ted Bunsen didn't enjoy my having an idea that he should have come up with himself. Besides, there stood Deputy Courtright, unoccupied due to a shortage of equipment. It all added up to a kind of pressure Teddy Bunsen hadn't had to experience when he was running things all by himself. He had a kind of crease down the middle of his forehead that I had not observed before.

"Sheriff, are you all right?" I asked. It's odd how it can take but a second for things to get out of kilter in this life.

"It's rare that I have this much opportunity for conversation," he admitted.

The old man in the wagon was nearly out of sight to the east.

"Who was that old man?" I inquired—it seemed about time to change the subject.

"Never saw him before," Teddy said. "Out here on the plains people just come and go."

"Is your credit good at the general store?" I asked. "Deputy Courtright is itching to get to work. I'll go fetch the stuff, if you'll allow me. It won't take a minute."

"It'll take a minute if you pass in earshot of Hungry Billy," Ted said. "That boy's got a wagging tongue."

But then Teddy's mood seemed to lighten—maybe he was contemplating the possibility of kissing, or more.

"It's a pretty day," he said, "and the jail's empty. Let's all go together and get the paint."

So off we sauntered, watched by two or three of the newly released drunks, who were sitting outside the saloons, warming up for their day by drinking beer.

# 6

HUNGRY BILLY WHELESS was a slouchy youth with buckteeth and a flagrant cowlick. He looked glad to see us and probably was—a day in Rita Blanca would make any decent person welcome the arrival of any other decent person, in my opinion.

Hearing that Jackson had become a deputy sheriff gave him a start, for sure.

"Why'd you want to be a deputy?" he asked. "Now all the killers will be after you, lickety-split.

"Especially Mexican Joe," he added.

Jackson looked taken aback. I don't believe it had occurred to him that being a deputy could be hazardous to the health. And all we knew about Mexican Joe was that he had stolen a broom.

I confess I hadn't given much thought to the possibility of killers. The Black Mesa Ranch, as Father had called it, was so remote and so poor that no killer ever bothered with us.

"Oh, now Billy," Teddy put in. "Jackson's just going to paint the gallows and help me collar the drunks. I'll look after him. I'd hardly let anything happen to Nellie's little brother."

Teddy, I suspected, still had his heart set on matrimony. He wanted me to believe that Jackson was perfectly safe, but burying six siblings, plus some darkies and our parents, had long ago convinced me that no one anywhere was perfectly safe. My own thought about Jackson was that at least he was living in the best housing in town. The jail was a fortress, and besides that, cool in summer, thanks to those thick adobe walls.

Hungry Billy was wound up on the subject of all the killers who were said to be roaming around No Man's Land: he mentioned Alex

Groat, Irish Roy, the Skivvy Kid, and several others of note. Jackson began to look a little peaked at the realization of what his big sister had got him into, but I got tired of listening to it all and wandered off to inspect the frocks. It occurred to me that the good citizens of Rita Blanca might want me to start a school, or be mayor, or something—anyway, I was in dire need of new frocks. Ted Bunsen trailed me like a puppy but I ignored him. I heard someone muttering and noticed an old woman sitting at a low table counting piles of pennies and nickels.

"Don't rush me, I'm working as fast as I can," she said—the poor old thing's eyesight was going. I suppose she mistook me for her boss.

"It's Mrs. Thomas, she's nearly blind," Hungry Billy whispered to me. "She's Pa's old nurse from Tennessee. He lets her count the small change to give her something to do."

I thought that was commendable on the part of Beau Wheless, who came bustling in from his coffin shop with curlicues of wood shavings clinging to his pants. Jackson had found the paint and the paintbrushes by this time, and I had my eye on two or three frocks. Teddy mostly stood around looking left out.

"Why, hello," Beau said. "Damned if we don't nearly have a crowd in this store, which is how I like it."

Beau was not entirely pleased, though, to hear that we had buried Father in a homemade coffin. It meant that he had missed a sale, but he was merchant enough to move right along to the next opportunity.

"The deputy will need a pistol, I'm sure," he said. "Fortunately, we have a good sturdy revolver available for purchase."

He put the good sturdy revolver on the top of the counter, when, to my shock, my brother flatly rejected it.

"That's just a plain pistol," he said sullenly. "I want that Colt with the pearl handles—it's just like the one Bill Hickok carried.

"It'll do me fine," he added, pointing to the fancy gun, as if the matter was settled.

It was the old Courtright need for elegant goods surfacing just at the wrong time.

"Ignore him, Mr. Wheless," I said at once. "The plain revolver will do."

My brother's face swole up like a toad, a thing that often happened when he was thwarted.

"Jackson, don't you burst out!" I warned him. "You're far too young to require a fancy firearm."

Teddy Bunsen looked as if he might be about to have a stroke. Ted might not be the sharpest knife in the drawer, but he was attentive enough to notice that expenses seemed to be mounting.

"Here now, Beau—one thing at a time," he remarked. "We came here to buy a broom, a can of paint, and a new paintbrush. Deputy Courtright has never shot a pistol—the deacons would probably fire me if they hear I've bought a firearm for a deputy whose main job is to sweep the cells and paint the gallows."

Then he turned to me, the girl he hoped to marry.

"Nellie," he said, "would you mind picking us out a broom?"

"Do I look like a janitor to you, Theodore?" I asked him. Using his formal first name was meant to signal that I was annoyed, though possibly he would have sensed that even if I hadn't called him Theodore.

"Do I look like I spend my time sweeping the porch?" I added, to make my point even more forcefully.

But Jackson, who knows me better than Teddy, saw that I was working up a full head of steam and he climbed down off his high horse and grabbed the broom himself in hopes of saving the situation.

"It's all right, Nellie," he said. "This broom's as good as any."

Teddy Bunsen quivered a little, but wisely held his peace.

Since Teddy was, for the moment, subdued, I turned my attention to Beau Wheless.

"Do you really think somebody might shoot Jackson just because he's taken a job as a deputy sheriff?" I asked.

Beau Wheless had more polish than Teddy, and evidently, he wasn't afraid of girls.

"Well," he said, "we are out here in No Man's Land, where killers like to congregate, mainly because there's little law to disturb them. The Yazee gang has been spotted not one hundred miles away, and of course the Yazee boys will shoot at anything that stirs.

"Any of us are apt to be shot any hour of the day or of the year," he added. "Lawmen are just a little more unpopular with killers than us common folk."

"You're right. I'll buy the plain pistol," I said. "But I expect the town to pay for the holster, along with the broom and the paint and the paintbrushes."

Beau didn't waste a minute. He got busy writing the invoice, which upset Teddy Bunsen, I could see. He began to turn red.

"You'll buy the pistol?" he said, glaring at me. "That pistol's a revolver. It won't be cheap. Here you are squandering money, and you don't even have a proper roof over your head."

"If she needs a room Mrs. Karoo has one available," Beau said, not bothering to slow his arithmetic. "I've just been working on a coffin for that Yankee lawyer who boarded with her. He finally drank himself to death last night.

"That fellow had money," he added. "He wanted his coffin velvet-lined."

"Mrs. Karoo's will be my next stop, then," I said. "Heft that pistol, Jackson. See if it fits your hand."

One of the reasons Father couldn't claw his way back up to the beam was because he had forgotten to take off his heavy money belt— he wore that belt day and night, January to December. I doubted that he had been wholly serious about suiciding himself since he kept his money belt on: after all, he wouldn't need money in heaven, or the other place either. He left Jackson and me in a bad situation, but he didn't leave us destitute. That money belt was crammed with double eagles.

"You oughtn't to be squandering money, Nellie," Teddy repeated, more weakly, when I handed a double eagle to Beau Wheless.

But he didn't offer to pay for the pistol himself, or even chip in half. Teddy had no reason to know it yet, but stinginess is one of the qualities I can't tolerate in a fellow. A man who can't be freehanded with you in a store is likely to backhand you, somewhere along the way.

Teddy Bunsen wasn't smart enough to know it, but he lost a step or two, in the romance department, that afternoon.

# 7

JACKSON DID AS I instructed: he hefted the pistol several times. It seemed to fit comfortably in his hand.

"Aim at something," I told him. Unfortunately Mrs. Thomas, Beau's old nurse from Tennessee, popped around a corner just in time to see Jackson aiming a Colt revolver at her. If it fazed her she didn't show it, but Jackson was embarrassed.

"My Lord, what if I'd shot her?" he asked.

"Oh, you couldn't have shot her, because your gun's not loaded," Beau pointed out. "However, I could offer you a few boxes of top-of-the-line ammunition. After all, you'll need to practice, I'm sure."

Beau had seen the money belt—visions of double eagles dancing in his head.

"Just hold your horses, Mr. Wheless," I said, giving Teddy Bunsen one of my firm looks.

"It seems to me I've spared the community enough expense. Supplying a deputy with ammunition is surely a civic responsibility. Don't you see it that way, Sheriff?"

Instead of answering Teddy Bunsen turned and walked right out the door. When he agreed to take Jackson on as his deputy he surely had no inkling that his own job was going to get so complicated so quickly. He thought, in his idleness, that he could make me his blushing bride, but Jackson and I had scarcely been in town half an hour and had already created problems that Ted was neither trained nor equipped to deal with.

Jackson quickly handed me the pistol.

"I think I better get over to the jail and get busy," he said. "I don't want the sheriff to fire me before I've even swept the cells."

He took the broom, the paint, and the paintbrushes and soon caught up with Teddy, who was walking stiffly.

I turned my attention back to Beau Wheless and his invoice.

"Most people who buy a pistol expect the holster to be thrown in," I told him. "I hope that's the case today."

Beau, as I said, had polish. He knew perfectly well that I had never bought a pistol and had no reason to expect a free holster. But he also knew we Courtrights weren't broke. And we had just arrived in town with the intention of staying. Any day I might find myself in need of curtains, or rose water, or a thimble, or a frock. Why lose a passel of sales over one holster?

"Of course the holster's thrown in, Miss Courtright," he said, meanwhile slyly setting two boxes of ammunition on the counter.

"That ammunition is what my brother needs to protect the citizens of this town from murderous killers," I proclaimed. "Why shouldn't the town pay for it?"

"I'll give you no argument there," Beau said. "Of course the town should pay for it, which doesn't mean it will."

"Who's the boss of this bunch of hovels?" I asked. "The sheriff mentioned some deacons. Who would they be?"

"Well, there's Joe Schwartz at the livery stable, he's one deacon," he said. "Aurel Stein's a second, and I'm a third. Old George Murray, who has a spread about twenty miles out, is more or less a deacon—but George is out of sorts right now. In fact he's Sheriff Bunsen's number one problem."

"I know Mr. Murray, he was a good friend of my father's," I said. "Is he a killer too?"

"Not by trade, but he's cranky," Beau said. "Cranky old men can kill you just as quick as the professionals."

"That's not many deacons," I remarked.

"I forgot Leo Oliphant. He owns the three saloons," he said, sliding the pistol into its nice free holster.

The two boxes of ammunition were still sitting there, in plain sight. It seemed we had come to an impasse. Beau wasn't willing to give them, and I wasn't willing to buy them.

"Do any of the deacons have credit with you?" I inquired.

"All except Leo Oliphant—being a saloon keeper means he's a bad credit risk," Beau said. "Few saloon keepers live to enjoy old age."

"What about Sheriff Bunsen—how's his credit?" I asked.

Beau winced at the question.

"I should not be talking ill about our gallant lawman," he said, "but getting blood from a turnip would be a whole lot easier than extracting cash money from Ted Bunsen."

"I see. If I put those shells on the sheriff's bill you'd be hard put to collect—is that right?"

Beau nodded.

"He's known to be a slow payer," he allowed.

"Here's my compromise," I said. "My brother, Jackson, is a hard worker, and honest as the day is long. He's a wage earner now—no reason he shouldn't pay for his own ammunition, is there?"

"No reason unless he gets plugged by some killer first," Hungry Billy remarked. He had wandered in and was standing around exercising his ability to waste time.

"Son, go saw a plank," his father said. "Now that the sheriff has taken a deputy, maybe the killers will spare us their attention for a while."

The upshot of the matter was that two boxes of high-grade ammunition got charged to Deputy Jackson Courtright.

"What do you think about George Custer getting massacred?" I asked while Beau wrapped my purchases, which grew to include a pretty cotton frock and several hair ribbons I had succumbed to.

"Oh, I try not to think of things like that," Beau said. "Daily life is hard enough to survive, in these parts."

He got a sad look in his eye. I suppose the thought of all those dead boys near a creek in Montana put him in mind of his own pretty wife, Glenda, who passed away less than a year ago, from the bite of a copperhead snake. Most people can survive a copperhead bite, but Glenda Wheless had been in delicate health to begin with. The snake got her while she was picking snap peas from their garden—she sat down by a bush, and before anyone missed her she was gone for good.

"I'm sorry about your father," Beau said. "I liked the man, but I could never understand why he chose the frontier life. He didn't seem to be the frontier type."

"He read too many brochures," I explained, before I headed across the street to give my brother his gun and ammunition.

# 8

MY BROTHER, JACKSON, had already done admirable work with his broom. When I walked into the jail he was just sweeping a substantial pile of litter out the back door, where the wind would soon scatter it over thousands of miles of prairie. The debris consisted mainly of cigar butts, though I did notice a dead rat or two in the pile.

"You're a wage earner now," I informed him at once. "The gun and the holster's on me but the ammunition is charged to you. Where's Teddy?"

"He's upstairs napping in the big cell," Jackson said. "I don't think he wants to be disturbed. He might have a toothache."

"I'm curious about something, Jackson," I remarked, snooping around the jail and looking in drawers, as women will.

"What?"

"This fellow Mexican Joe, who is supposed to be a bad killer, I guess, came in the jail and took a broom. Why would a murderous killer take a broom?"

"I don't know and I hope you're not thinking of waking Sheriff Bunsen up to ask him," Jackson said. "I expect he needs his rest."

"His rest from me, is what you mean," I told him. I could tell that my little brother was soon going to take against me and defend his fellow male. Jackson was plainly nervous about my snooping in drawers, but I didn't let that stop me. Teddy Bunsen had proposed to me six times, and was probably working up to a seventh try. In my view that gave me every right to snoop—after all, he could have a locket with another woman's picture in it. The fact that I had no intention of marrying him didn't mean that I had no right to be curious about what other ladies he might have in his life.

"I hope you don't think I'm too hard on Teddy," I said, with a grin.

Jackson just sighed in a tired way, as if the whole subject of myself and Ted and Father's death and the move to town had worn him to a frazzle, on the inside at least.

"You'd better get on up to that rooming house," he said. "What if somebody else rents that room—then where would you sleep?"

He squatted down to prise the lid off the paint can and looked at me with one of those lonely looks that never failed to touch me. Father's foolishness with the noose was forcing Jackson to have to grow up, and at a rapid pace. Father wasn't coming back, and even when he was alive, he had been only occasionally helpful. Father looked to his own needs, and expected the whole family—a shrinking company—to look after him too. If anybody raised Jackson it was me—except for a dance or two back in Virginia, when I stayed out all night kicking up my heels, Jackson and I had never spent a night apart. But here we were in Rita Blanca, faced with the necessity of sleeping under different roofs for nearly the first time in our lives.

"Jackson, are you sorry we moved into town?" I asked him.

"I don't know yet," he said, "but I like this jail—it feels peaceful. I just wish you could stay here with me, Nellie."

"Out of the question," I said. "But I won't be far."

Jackson managed to get the top off the can of paint and was staring into the white paint as if he wished he could drown in it. Young men are just moody—there's not a woman alive who wouldn't testify to that.

Then another thought crossed my mind.

"Is it Virginia you're hankering for?" I asked. "Is it that you'd rather just give up on the West?"

Jackson had found a stick and had begun to stir the paint, which was going to have to be thinned a good bit before it could be slapped onto those dry-as-a-bone gallows boards.

I suppose I was asking myself the same question I had addressed to Jack, my brother.

"Do I have to answer right now? I need to find paint thinner," Jackson said. "I sure don't want to be quitting Sheriff Bunsen until I at least get those gallows painted."

"I wonder if the criminals will feel any better about being hung once they notice that at least the gallows have been newly painted," I said.

Jackson was trying to be serious about his job—he didn't particularly appreciate my small attempts at wit.

But the Virginia question was a big question and we both needed some time to think it over. Should we just go home?

"Tell Teddy I hope he enjoyed sweet dreams," I said. "Right now I guess I'll take your advice and head on up to the boardinghouse."

"It's the one with the hedge around it," Jackson said. "They say the woman who owns it used to be a slave."

"How'd you get to be so expert on boardinghouses in Rita Blanca?"

"Hungry Billy told me, the know-it-all," Jackson said.

"You mean Mrs. Karoo is a darkie—and they let her run a boardinghouse out in this wild man's country?" I asked. "From what I've seen of No Man's Land so far a darkie would be lucky not to get dropped from those gallows you're about to paint—maybe with an anvil tied to her ankle."

"That's not all Hungry Billy said," Jackson confided. "He says some people think Mrs. Karoo is a witch."

"Yes, and some of the people might even think I'm a witch—which I'm not," I said.

Then I left Jackson to get on with his new job.

# 9

JACKSON WAS RIGHT about one thing: Mrs. Karoo's boardinghouse had a hedge all the way around it, with an opening in the front and another opening in the back. It wasn't a tall hedge yet—it came about to my waist—but Mrs. Karoo was out watering it when I walked up. If she kept at it the hedge would be a fine windbreak in another few years. Just seeing it made me feel better, because it meant that at least one other person in Rita Blanca had forethought enough to plant a windbreak. Civilization had made a start in No Man's Land, with the help of a tiny darkie woman barely five feet in height. She was the color of coffee that had a splash or two of milk in it, and she was expecting me, not because of any witchery but because Beau Wheless had rushed up to tell her to hold the newly vacated room—a neighborly act but also one that meant Beau was hopeful of tempting me to make a few more sales. He had also taken the liberty of telling Mrs. Karoo that Father had suicided himself—this I didn't appreciate.

Mrs. Karoo had deep gentle eyes; a smile was usually lurking around the corners of her mouth.

"Why don't you settle down here and be the mayor?" she suggested, two minutes after we had met. "A smart mayor is just what Rita Blanca needs."

I hardly knew what to say because the same thought had occurred to me.

"I doubt these ruffians would ever have me," I told her. Mrs. Karoo just smiled.

The room was a little bleak, but at least it was clean and airy. There was an overabundance of sunlight, but some good heavy curtains would solve that problem. Mrs. Karoo had had the forethought to put a few sprigs of sage in a little vase, to brighten things up. Out my window I could see over Aurel Imlah's hide yard, and on across many thousand acres of prairie. The rent was fifteen dollars a month, the same as Jackson's salary. Breakfast and three meals a day came with it.

A shaggy old hunter was snoring loudly on the back porch.

"That's Josh," Mrs. Karoo whispered. "He's an early riser and likes his naps."

I knew Josh, a little. He was the mail runner for No Man's Land. Once every two weeks he'd hitch up his wagon and go north to Rabbit Gulch, where he met the trail. Then he'd come by the Black Mesa Ranch, drop off the mail and magazines—I could not do without my magazines, and neither could Father. Sometimes Josh would consent to spend the night.

"A hanged man doesn't lie easy," Mrs. Karoo remarked to me in passing. "You're not through with your father yet."

"Do you know that because you're a witch?" I asked her. I suppose it was an impolite question, but Mrs. Karoo didn't appear to be offended—if anything my question amused her.

"If a woman gets a little uppity and there's a man around, pretty soon all the gentlemen will be calling her a witch," she said.

I knew what she meant, though I was too young yet to be thought a witch. If Ted Bunsen had had to come up with a word to describe me when he walked out of the general store, I doubt it would have been a very nice word.

Of course, she was right to mention that I wasn't through with Father. On our slow trip to town several big storms of tears came over me at the memory of Father. He was a fine fiddler, for one thing—his eyes would light up at the pleasure of his music; and if he wasn't fiddling he might be reading us some Walter Scott. No one that I knew ever thought of Father as anything but a gentleman. If only he hadn't read those cursed brochures and got a vision of Western paradise in his head. And then he promptly lost his wife, six of his eight children, and all the servants. I suppose that much loss would cause any man of gentle temperament to start thinking of the noose. He even lost his fiddle, which fell out of the wagon somewhere west of Westport. On the boat from St. Louis Father had played it frequently, and I danced with Bill Hickok as often as I could coax him onto the floor. Wild Bill

Hickok had never seemed wild to me, though it had to be admitted that he took a long time with his dressing—he'd show up well past the end of breakfast, in a boiled silk shirt and a velvet coat and a fine hat and yellow boots, his collar fastened onto his shirt with pearl studs.

It was a mystery to me that folks called him Wild Bill. He was far from being the best dancer I ever danced with, and not once did he try to kiss me—I don't believe I would have objected if he had tried. Certainly he was more of a gentleman than Georgie Custer ever pretended to be. Sometimes Billy Hickok would clap his hands to Father's fiddling—that was about as excited as the man ever got. Thinking of Father undid me—right there in Mrs. Karoo's kitchen a Mississippi of tears flooded out of my eyes. The tears fell like a waterfall. I tried to push my way outside but instead I stumbled into the churn. It was the thought of Father fiddling and Billy Hickok clapping that undid me. I guess my sobbing woke up Josh—by the time I caught my breath and dried my eyes on a dish towel the old mail rider was gone and I was sitting in the rocking chair where he had napped.

When I was steady enough not to spill liquids on myself Mrs. Karoo brought me a large mug of tea. In Virginia we drank tea every day, but we had long since run out of the substance on the Black Mesa Ranch.

It had been a while since I had tasted anything as good as Mrs. Karoo's tea.

"Thanks," I said. "I can't remember when I've cried that hard."

"People who make it as far as No Man's Land often have many loved ones to cry for," Mrs. Karoo said.

"Most of that cry was for Father," I told her. "I regret that you never heard him fiddle."

Mrs. Karoo stood by her back door, looking out at the hot flat distance.

"My father was a hanged man too," she said. "Only he didn't hang himself. We worked for the Choctaws then. One evening the night riders came and took him, and the next morning we found him hanging.

"He didn't settle easily, though," she continued. "Some people don't settle easily into being dead. My father was partly with me for a long time—he hadn't been ready to go."

# 10

I DRANK THREE MUGS of Mrs. Karoo's strong sweet tea before I more or less gathered my wits about me and hiked it on back to the general store. While recuperating with the healthful tea I had scribbled down a list of things I'd need: a settee if one was available, a small chair, a bureau, some material I could convert into a bedspread, a couple of fans, some candles, and a small picture of *The Stag at Eve,* which reminded me a little of Walter Scott.

While Hungry Billy got my purchases together and was preparing to load them in a wagon I thought I'd nip across the street and have a word with my brother, but before I got far a horrible screaming suddenly issued from a little house I hadn't noticed—a small frame house set back from the street. Hungry Billy paid the screaming not the slightest mind.

"That's Doc Siblee's office," he informed me. "He's more or less a dentist, but right now he's setting the leg bone of a cowboy that got kicked by his horse."

"Oh, is that all?" I said. "At least I'm glad to know there's a doctor in town. Now all you need to find is a mayor and a schoolmarm—I suspect I could fill both roles, if anyone asked me to."

Before Hungry Billy could comment on my suitability as a mayor and school marm, a wild fusillade of shooting broke out from the direction of the saloons, at which point Beau rushed out and pulled me into his store, where he insisted that we crouch behind a keg of nails. While we were hunkering the gun battle slopped over into the street, which seemed to be full of men shooting off guns. Then horses began to whinny, and some of the combatants mounted in a hurry and raced away, while the fighters that happened to be on foot blazed away at the horsemen until they were out of range, which was soon.

Only one man was down, that I could see, though another was hopping around on one foot—evidently he had been shot in the boot. Beau Wheless was eyeing the fellow stretched out on the ground—no doubt he had a coffin sale in mind—but before he could make his move the man sat up and two others began to drag him off in the direction of the doctor's shack.

"People here don't seem to be very good shots," I said. "All those bullets flying, and nobody dead?"

I remembered Bill Hickok, back on the boat, telling me that he had achieved his fame, such as it was, by being a fair pistol shot.

"What do you mean you're only fair?" I asked. "Nobody's got a bigger reputation."

"Pistols are dern hard to shoot with accuracy," Bill insisted. "I'm fair, at least I am at close range. The reason I have the big reputation is because everybody else is terrible. Jesse James couldn't hit a house at ten paces with a pistol, and neither could any of the Earp boys."

"What about Billy the Kid?" I inquired, a question that caused Bill to frown. I had already learned that he was vain as a prince, and was hoping to tease him a little.

"I have no reliable information about that young scoundrel," Bill said. "You can't depend on much of the talk that comes out of New Mexico."

I let the matter drop. It seemed to me that Mr. Hickok might be a little jealous of Billy the Kid.

As for the poor shooting in Rita Blanca, Beau Wheless had a simple explanation.

"Those were not the gunslingers," he told me. "These were just cardplayers, with maybe a cowboy or two mixed in. You can't expect accurate marksmanship from a bunch of drunk gamblers."

I looked over at the jail. Neither Jackson nor Teddy was in view. A can of paint was sitting on the gallows, but nobody was painting, just not at that time.

# 11

MRS. KAROO HAD an old cowbell hanging on her back porch, which she rang when her evening meal was ready. Her big table sat twelve but only eight showed up that first evening: Jackson, myself, Joe Schwartz from the livery stable, Aurel Imlah, Hungry Billy Wheless, Doc Siblee, Preacher Milton, and Mrs. Karoo herself, who presided. Josh was outside cleaning his rifle—he declined to join us.

I had put on one of my new frocks, which needed hemming, and had scrubbed my face and tied a nice red ribbon in my hair. In Virginia that much primping would have got me a proposal, probably, but at Mrs. Karoo's table it only produced a request to pass the sauerkraut to Joe Schwartz, a large man who looked neither left nor right when there was food in front of him. Besides the sauerkraut we had roast goat, snap peas, spuds, biscuits, corn, brown gravy, and vinegar pie for dessert. The drink was buttermilk and the meal was served expertly by Pete and Pat, both girls and both Choctaws, who lived in a small room off the back porch.

Though I enjoyed the tasty food, I was sorely disappointed by the total absence of conversation. In Virginia supper might take two hours at least, because of all the talk that accompanied it: there was bound to be plenty of general gossip, and talk of politics or novels. When the plates were cleared the gentlemen smoked and drank brandy, while the ladies, in good weather, would drift out onto the porch, to rock in rocking chairs and spout more gossip.

At Mrs. Karoo's supper table there was no talk—the only sound being the slurps and belches that accompanied the multiple mastications. Within ten minutes Joe Schwartz, Hungry Billy Wheless, Doc Siblee, and Preacher Milton had all pushed back their chairs, complimented Mrs. Karoo on the vinegar pie, and were swiftly out the door. My brother, Jackson, showed signs of wanting to go with them, but I grabbed his sleeve and kept him in place.

Aurel Imlah was also through eating, but he busied himself with filling a short clay pipe, while Mrs. Karoo produced a long-stemmed brown pipe of her own and joined him in a smoke.

"Where's Sheriff Bunsen? I thought he ate at this boardinghouse," I inquired.

"The sheriff's got a toothache—he asked to be excused," Jackson said.

"I see you're handy with a paint can, Deputy," Aurel told him. "Those old shabby gallows have never looked so good. It's bound to be a consolation to those who find themselves getting hung."

He chuckled at his own wit, and blew a smoke ring.

I suspected that there was more to Teddy's absence than a toothache. My arrival in Rita Blanca as a resident had put him off his feed. Perhaps he had realized he couldn't marry me and keep me at a safe distance too. A dilemma of that sort probably contributed to his toothache.

"So will you really be staying with us for a while, Miss Court-right?" Aurel asked.

He didn't appear to be studying me, but I had the feeling that he didn't miss much, and the same could be said for Mrs. Karoo, though she smoked her pipe and kept her thoughts to herself.

"I can't speak for Sis but I'm sure not going back," Jackson said. "If I was to, one of my uncles would pop me right in school."

Jackson was right about that: the Courtrights had an innocent trust in highfalutin education—Greek and Latin and the like. If the uncles got hold of Jackson he'd be in Harvard College so quick it would make your head swim. Or if it wasn't Harvard College, it would be somewhere else just as stuffy. Maybe there wasn't much to be said for Rita Blanca, but nobody could mistake it for a stuffy place. I was a little startled that Jackson had been so forthright about his plans—usually he cleared major decisions with me before announc-ing them. I guess being a deputy sheriff for one day had been enough to render him independent, a happenstance I was of two minds about.

"I won't be going back either," I said, not to be left out. "In the course of walking up and down the street I noticed that the telegraph office is closed. Is that permanent, or temporary?

"A town without a well-functioning telegraph office is never likely to amount to much," I added. I thought I'd hit them with a blunt opinion before springing my surprise.

"We had a telegrapher till last month," Aurel said. "His name was Zeke Ryan. But then Zeke took himself a Comanche bride and is farming weeds somewhere down by the South Canadian.

"Your point is on the nose, though," he added. "The hide business is hard on knives—we use 'em up at a terrible rate. If the telegraph was working I could replenish my knives in an efficient fashion, which presently I can't."

"Why, Nellie can work a telegraph lickety-split," Jackson said. He was on his way out the door but paused long enough to put a plug in for his sister.

"Uncle Grandy taught her," he added, and then he left.

"I seem to remember that your uncle Grandy was a particular favorite of General Grant," Aurel Imlah said, in a light tone. "Didn't he lose a leg or something?"

"At Antietam," I said. "He was the only one of the uncles to fight for the Union side. And he was General Grant's personal telegrapher for most of the war."

Mrs. Karoo got up and went to a small cupboard—she returned with three small glasses and a bottle of rum. She poured each of us a little, and I was glad to be included, although I did not often partake of spirituous liquors.

"I suppose there was some bitterness, after the peace," Aurel remarked, sniffing his rum.

"Yes, there was," I admitted. "So much bitterness that Uncle Grandy had to move to Louisville, Kentucky. But he was my mother's favorite brother, war or no war, so I was able to visit him in the summer."

In fact Uncle Grandy had been a wonderful man, with a white tapering beard and a gift for watercolors. He taught me to play checkers when I was two—if I saw he had me cornered I'd push his hand away.

"You're in this game of life to win, aren't you, missy?" he said to me with a chuckle. I don't think he ever made it up with his brothers, but then ours was hardly the only family that bitter conflict divided.

"I may be a little rusty with my codes at first," I told the two of them. "It's been a while since I tapped a telegraph key. I'll soon improve and be reliable. Does anyone have a key to that shack of an office?"

"I'd be surprised if it's even locked," Aurel said. "And I'd be surprised if you don't find a snake or two on the premises."

"What would I get for a salary?" I asked, finishing my rum.

That stumped the two of them. Neither of them had any idea what a skilled telegrapher might be worth to the community of Rita Blanca. There was only the group of deacons Teddy Bunsen had mentioned, a loosely organized bunch, at least by the standards of Virginia small towns, where city fathers are thick on the ground.

"If you need me to send an order for some skinning knives I'll do it tomorrow," I told Aurel. "We can figure out the salary, I expect. My younger brother is making fifteen dollars a month as deputy sheriff— and I'm well ahead of him when it comes to education, so I expect a little more than that."

Aurel Imlah seemed amused. It seemed to me that Mrs. Karoo got a special light in her eyes when she looked at him.

Since there was still a little light left in the summer sky I left the two of them to their pipes and strolled down the street to my new place of business, the telegraph office. It wasn't locked, but it was snaky. I had taken the precaution to borrow a spade from Mrs. Karoo, and I used it to ease two bull snakes and a small copperhead out the door. Of course, bull snakes won't tolerate rattlers, so there was none of that breed to be seen, though I did have to mash a bunch of black widow spiders and one sizable tarantula. There was the dust of the ages on the windowpanes, but the most important thing of all, the telegraph key, seemed to work fine. Zeke Ryan had been thoughtful enough to cover it with a snug leather sheath.

Impatient as ever, I immediately sent a wire to Dodge City—I wanted to wake them up to the fact that there was a working telegrapher in Rita Blanca once more.

When I came out I happened to look over at the jail. Ted Bunsen was sitting on the edge of the gallows, swinging his legs and smoking a thin cigar. The man had proposed to me six times—I figured the least I could do was inquire about his toothache.

"Toothache's gone," Ted mumbled. "Doc Siblee pulled the tooth. Now I've got a hole in my jaw big enough to stick a stob in."

"Gargle some warm salt water," I advised. "That usually helps, if you give it time."

"Doc says rye whiskey might provide the best cure," Ted said—it was not a reply that sat easy with me. It would be just like Teddy to get drunk and fall off his own gallows. He didn't strike me as lucky, which meant that he might break his neck in the fall. That might result in quick promotion for Jackson, but I didn't dislike Ted's ticklish kissing enough to really want him to break his neck.

I decided my intervention was doing Ted more harm than good, so I went on home in the deepening dusk. The back porch still held the smell of rum and pipe tobacco, but of the landlady and the hide hunter there was nothing to be seen.

# 12

I HAD BARELY tucked into a plate of flapjacks, sweetened with black-strap molasses, when my brother, Jackson, popped in the door and gave me an irritated look.

"You're late for work!" he informed me. "You've got people lined up halfway to Dodge City, wanting to send off telegrams."

"The Skivvy Kid is even in line," Jackson added, as if he were announcing the arrival of Napoleon or somebody else important enough to make me hurry my breakfast.

"I would have thought the Skivvy Kid would just shoot a line of people, if he found one in front of him," I commented, though all I really knew about the Skivvy Kid was that he wore his long johns winter and summer, and was said to be a fine marksman.

I popped up to my room and hit a lick or two with the comb and the brush—when I looked out the window I saw that there was a big line of people waiting at the telegraph office. From a distance the folks seemed to be in a pretty good humor, idling and gossiping as human beings will when opportunity offers. I borrowed one of Mrs. Karoo's sunbonnets and was quickly out the door.

A cheer went up when folks figured out that I was no fluke—now the women could send off all the wires they wanted to the mail-order stores. The first thing I noticed was that the bull snakes had moved back in.

"Move back a step, miss," I said to the first woman in line. "Let me just evacuate the snake population and I'll get to you as fast as I can."

The bull snakes didn't take kindly to being evicted from their home of recent weeks. They hissed at me in that aggressive way they have, which seemed to irritate a lanky cowboy to such an extent that he picked one of the snakes up by the tail, swung him around a few times, and threw him about halfway to Aurel Imlah's hide yard. The other snake prudently found himself a hole and crawled in it.

"I could probably educate those snakes, if I can have a day or two," I informed the cowboy, who was no more impressed with me than he had been by the bull snakes.

"I got a herd arriving in Dodge tomorrow," he informed me. "I need to be sure the railroad's ready for them."

If you're interested in finding out quick how impatient the human race is, just apprentice yourself to a telegraph operator sometime. The old lady who had been first in line wanted to order pincushions and paperweights and she wanted them ordered from a store in Cincinnati. The cowboy who was hard on bull snakes wanted seventeen cattle cars waiting in Dodge City for noon departure to Kansas City. Preacher Milton was in dire need of extra hymnbooks, the pack rats having chewed up most of the available supply. Leo Oliphant was running low on palatable brown ale—he wanted twenty cases of the best sent out at once. Doc Siblee was out of tongue depressors, and the light twine he used for stitches was nearly all used up.

I really wanted this job, and I hadn't been officially hired yet, so I was as patient as a pet possum, although some requests purely stumped me.

Two stout gray-haired ladies who looked like sisters wanted me to send off a wire to Buffalo Bill—they wanted him to send each of them an autographed picture.

"Get him to send one of him scalping an Indian, if he has one," the bossier of the two sisters requested.

"Now that's a fine thing to ask of a first-time telegrapher on her first day of work," I told them, keeping my tone light and cheery. "I have no way of knowing where Buffalo Bill might be, much less whether he has photographs to spare."

The ladies were unimpressed by my claim of inexperience. They wanted what they had stood in line for, and so far I wasn't providing it. If I ever stood for election in Rita Blanca I had a feeling I might not get their votes.

"Use your wits, young lady," one of them said sharply. "Everybody knows that his wife, Lulu Cody, lives in Rochester, New York. You just send off a wire to Lulu quick. Tell her that we want two pictures, and we want them signed by Buffalo Bill Cody himself."

I was trying to phrase a diplomatic reply to that question when help came from an unexpected source—namely the Skivvy Kid, who happened to be in line right behind the ladies. He wore brown long johns with a cheap gray vest over them. The vest could have used mending. He had a gun stuck in his belt, though not a very big gun. Far from looking like a hardened killer, he looked like a choirboy who had just got separated from his choir.

"It would be a waste of time sending a wire all the way to Rochester," he said. "Mr. Cody's over in Leavenworth at the moment, organizing a buffalo hunt for some rich men."

The two women—by name the McClendon sisters—were loath to credit this information, even though it had come from the famous Skivvy Kid.

"There aren't any rich men in Leavenworth," one of them told him. "We ought to know—our sister Mabel lives there."

"No ma'am, the rich men are coming from Chicago in a special train. If you'll excuse me it's my baby sister's birthday—I'd like to send her a token of esteem."

He coolly stepped around the McClendon sisters—I expected this to bring a challenge, but the Skivvy Kid's information had thrown the sisters into confusion; they abandoned the line for the moment and wandered off to discuss this new development.

The Skivvy Kid had a wide gentle mouth and dreamy eyes—just the sort of eyes I've always been a sucker for. But I was at work and I intended to be as professional as possible. The Kid took a telegraph blank and stared at it for a time, with a sense of strain. I don't think he knew what he wanted to say. Endearments may not have come easy to a man who seemed to live his life in his underwear.

"What's your sister's name?" I asked, in an effort to be helpful.

"Her name's Jesse but we call her Little Peach," he said, the sign of hard effort in his face.

I took the pen and wrote a simple message: "Dear Little Peach stop I bet you're so grown up I wouldn't recognize you stop you'll get a bear hug next time we meet stop love from—"

Then I realized I didn't know his real name.

"Oh," he said, seeing my dilemma. "I'm Andrew . . . just put Andy."

"Let's do a little better than that, since it's her birthday," I suggested.

The Skivvy Kid looked blank. The young fellow was genial, but he wasn't exactly full of talk.

"Love and kisses Andy," I wrote on the telegraph form, and I showed it to him.

"Will that do?" I asked.

"That'll do," he said.

# 13

BEFORE I LET the Skivvy Kid, whose real name was Andy Jessup, escape my office I invited him to take supper with me and my brother, Jackson, at Mrs. Karoo's boardinghouse. He didn't argue the matter—usually, as I came to know, the Skivvy Kid was all agreement.

"I rode a far piece to get to this telegraph office in time to wire my baby sister on her birthday," he told me. "I'm tired. I believe I'll crawl under a wagon somewhere and have myself a snooze."

"All right, but come running when you hear the dinner bell," I warned him. "Vittles don't last long at Mrs. Karoo's."

I saw no need to mention this invitation to either Jackson or Teddy, both of whom were helping the blacksmith cool off horseshoes by dunking them in a bucket of water. I suppose the blacksmith foresaw a big demand, because he was making plenty of horseshoes.

About two o'clock in the afternoon the little ladies who wanted to send off for pincushions or the like began to thin out, making way for the professions of the town—it was the professionals who had suffered most from Zeke Ryan's defection.

Aurel Imlah got there first, with a list of needs that was organized to the penny. He needed bullet molds and skinning knives and a grindstone you would turn with a pedal, in case all his knives needed sharpening at once. He also wanted plenty of gunpowder and some lead ingots. The last thing on his list was flea powder—fifty pounds of flea powder. I suppose there were fleas by the millions in those hides.

"I've had a talk with a few of the deacons," he informed me. "They all think we're lucky to have you. The pay would be twenty-five dollars a month, with lodging thrown in."

"No, that's way low," I told him bluntly. "Look at my log—I've sent sixty-eight telegrams since I opened up this morning. Fifty dollars a month would be more like it—and forget about the lodging. I prefer to pay for my own lodging. I'm not rich but neither am I destitute and I won't be stampeded into accepting a low offer."

Aurel Imlah's jaw dropped. He looked plenty startled by my bold demand.

"Stampeded? Why, Miss Courtright," he said, and then he stopped. His face, what I could see of it above his beard, turned red briefly; but he soon regained his poise.

"I expect I can talk them into the fifty," he said. "But I'm curious. Why wouldn't you want the town to pay your rent?"

"I'm a newcomer to Rita Blanca," I told him. "I don't know who I can trust and who I can't. I'd rather keep control of the door key until I've figured it out."

He didn't say anything more, but he didn't leave, either.

"Do you mind if I call you Aurel?" I asked him. "I grew up in a formal family—well, you know that. But I'm not very formal myself. You're the one person I feel I can trust in this dusty town. I would value your friendship, and I hope you'll value mine."

He looked at me long and hard, as he had that day when he informed me of Georgie Custer's end. That was the day when he told me I was smart.

"Aurel it is," he said, and he chuckled. "Does that mean I can call you Nellie?"

"I'd prefer that," I told him. "After all, Nellie's my name."

# 14

Supper started out to be a fine occasion. Mrs. Karoo had persuaded Aurel to fight the Poles off a nice mess of buffalo liver, which turned out to be as good as advertised. Josh, the old mail runner, taught us how to season it with just a drop of bile from the creature's spleen. Andy Jessup had allowed me to mend his vest—he even borrowed some trousers, so as not to appear a fool in Mrs. Karoo's eyes. We were a jolly company, stuffing ourselves with liver and sauerkraut and fresh snap peas until two fools wandered in and interrupted our fun.

The fools were Teddy Bunsen and Jackson Courtright, who were rude and late. Both of them hung their hats on the hat rack and slipped into their seats, mumbling apologies to Mrs. Karoo for their tardiness. Then they happened to look up at the same moment and it came to their attention that Andy Jessup, the famous Skivvy Kid, was right there at the table, helping himself to a second helping of buffalo liver. Ted Bunsen made a fool of himself first and worst. He sprang up as if jabbed with a needle and the next thing we all knew he was pointing a six-shooter at Andy, who was just salting his dish.

"Hands up, you're under arrest—go put the handcuffs on him, Deputy," Teddy said.

"Now, Sheriff, firearms don't belong at the table," Aurel Imlah said. "Mr. Jessup is our guest. If I'm not mistaken you've scared Preacher Milton so bad that he's fainted."

The preacher did seem to have passed into a dead faint. He slid out of his chair and sprawled on the floor.

I saw my brother stand up and start to do as ordered, but before he could clear his chair I pointed a firm sisterly finger at him.

"You sit down and mind your own business, Jackson," I told him.

"It's bad table manners to handcuff a person who is merely trying to eat a meal."

"But, Sis, I'm a deputy now," Jackson said. "Arresting hostile outlaws is my business."

"Right! It's your business and you've been long enough about it!" Teddy said, in his most grating voice.

"But I'm not hostile and I'm not an outlaw, either," Andy Jessup protested.

Despite my warning, Jackson walked around the table and stood right behind us—naturally I had put Andy next to myself. I was about ready to stand up and whack Jackson, but Andy just smiled, as if to say leave us boys be.

In fact it proved to be an embarrassing moment for my little brother, because the pair of handcuffs he took off his belt would not open. Both were locked, but not around any outlaw's wrist.

"Uh-oh, Sheriff," Jackson said. His face turned as red as a flannel sock.

"Uh-oh, what?" Ted asked, still using his ugly lawman's tone.

"I guess I picked up a pair of handcuffs that we ain't got a key to," Jackson admitted, his face still very red.

"If that's the case you've made a serious mistake, Deputy," Ted said. "Come back over here and take mine."

Then a thought struck him as he reached for his handcuffs—the thought was that he'd left his handcuffs in the jail.

A long silence followed. Jackson couldn't open his handcuffs and the sheriff had none to offer.

"Miss Courtright, would you have a hairpin?" Andy asked.

Jackson got even more red in the face.

"How dare you ask my sister a question like that, you scoundrel!" Jackson hollered.

I handed Andy a hairpin and he turned to Jackson and quickly opened the handcuffs—it took about as much time as it takes you to blink. Then he handed me back my hairpin and asked if someone would please pass the okra.

"Sheriff, if you're really planning to arrest Mr. Jessup, then do it, so the rest of us can resume our meal," Aurel said.

"I second the motion," Doc Siblee said. "Nobody wants to eat a hearty meal like this with a hog leg pointed at them."

"But he's the Skivvy Kid," Teddy said. "And the Skivvy Kid is a well-known outlaw. Some of you ought to be helping me arrest him, but I'd guess you'd all rather feed your faces than see justice done."

Jackson, I believe, realized that the plan to arrest Andy was a lost cause. My little brother was a good deal more sensitive to public sentiment than Teddy Bunsen.

"The Skivvy Kid's just a nickname my grandmother gave me because of my resistance to woolen garments," Andy mentioned. "I'd like to meet the gent who accused me of being an outlaw—I might introduce him to the sport of fisticuffs."

Though not really convinced, Teddy Bunsen at least uncocked his gun.

"Mighty good food, Mrs. Karoo," Hungry Billy said—he wiped his mouth nervously and bolted. As he was leaving I remembered that he had been the first to list the Skivvy Kid among the famous outlaws of the region.

"But, Billy, you haven't had your pie," Mrs. Karoo protested.

"Two funerals tomorrow, I need to practice my hymns," Hungry Billy said, and then he was gone.

Andy Jessup seemed to be an easygoing fellow. I doubt he would have pummeled Hungry Billy much—at the moment he seemed more interested in mixing his okra in with his snap peas.

"It was that train wreck over by Abilene that got people to thinking I was an outlaw," Andy admitted. "A bunch of horses got killed. I was just trailing some of the survivors back to town and some fool decided I'd stolen them."

My little brother, Jackson, was a fair judge of people. I think he soon figured out for himself that Andy was no outlaw. He went back to his seat and busied himself with his vittles. I was beginning to work up a little indignation myself—here I was flirting for dear life with Andy Jessup and the poor boy was having all he could do to stay awake. Probably he was just worn out from having ridden all that way to get the telegram off to his baby sister. Still, no woman likes to waste her flirting, whatever the gent's excuse.

When Andy took himself off to sleep under the wagon I turned my attention to Teddy Bunsen, who had behaved all wrong, upbraiding my brother over the matter of the handcuffs and generally making an ass of himself.

Teddy looked at me as if I was the worst nuisance in the land. He went over to Preacher Milton and tried to bring him out of his faint. The preacher had a big chunk of corn bread clutched in his fist and just as big a chunk lodged in his throat. The minute Teddy turned him over we saw that Preacher Milton hadn't fainted—Preacher Milton was dead as doom.

# 15

ONE THING I noticed on my hard journey west is that death is apt to come in clusters. The day before we went to Rita Blanca, Father suicided himself. Then, the day after we arrived, in the midst of a nice dinner, Preacher Milton choked on a piece of corn bread.

The next death, and in some ways the worst for me, came over the telegraph. The morning after Preacher Milton choked I was just easing into the telegraph office, and just easing out the one remaining bull snake, when a message began to come in. I took it down half asleep until I came to the name Hickok, and then I got the stark news: James Butler Hickok, better known as Wild Bill, was dead of a gunshot wound to the head incurred in the town of Deadwood, South Dakota, where he had gone to gamble.

"Oh Billy!" I said, and then I shrieked so loud that it woke up all the dogs in town, who started howling. Andy Jessup, who had walked over to the Cimarron for an early morning dip, said to me later that the chill of that shriek would be in his memory until the day he died. Teddy Bunsen and my brother, Jackson, came running out of the jail with no shirts on, all because of my grief at the death of Billy Hickok.

I don't know how many times I shrieked, but I do know that by the time I stopped pretty much everyone in Rita Blanca was involved in trying to quiet me down. Aurel Imlah came running from his hide yard, the blacksmith from his forge, and Beau Wheless from his general store.

Jackson later asked me why I took it so hard—but then he hadn't really known Billy. When Bill came to visit us at our hotel in St. Louis he came to see me, not Jackson. Once on our riverboat trip he had even held my hand for a while, after a dance; I suppose I was in love with him by the time he let it go. He went no farther that night, but the shy way he looked at me convinced me he might wish to go farther, someday. And he had promised to come visit us soon in No Man's Land. Most people didn't realize how shortsighted Billy was. He could hardly see across a card table, another thing that touched me. In my lonely times on the Black Mesa Ranch I managed to keep Billy's memory fresh, and I continued to hope that one day he would show up and hold my hand again, and this time, perhaps even on purpose. Our courtship, if that's what it had been, was not lengthy, but in frontier times, with life so chancy, young people had to jump quick if they hoped to have sweethearts, much less wives and husbands.

And now Bill was dead! No wonder I shrieked to high heaven when I heard the news.

When I had calmed a little Jackson tried to persuade me to take the day off from the telegraph office but I wouldn't hear of it.

"Hike on back to the jail and mind your own business," I told him. I had just been the telegraph lady of Rita Blanca for one day—how would it look to the citizens of the town if I deserted my post just because an old sweetheart had got himself killed in South Dakota?

If my brother had looked about him and given it a moment's thought, he would have realized that there were very few frail reeds in Rita Blanca. The frail reeds were pushing up grass burrs in the cemetery—itself just a vague stretch of acreage a hundred yards or so back of the general store. There Beau Wheless and his boy planted the poor souls who just hadn't been strong enough for the place they had been brought to.

The survivors, long denied the chance to get on the telegraph and order things they didn't need because Zeke Ryan had run off with an Indian maiden, were hardly likely to sit home and knit just because I was upset about a dead boyfriend, even if the boyfriend was Wild Bill Hickok.

Within an hour a line had formed again, headed by the redoubtable McClendon sisters, who had pestered me so about autographed pictures of Buffalo Bill. This time they had brought their poultry as reinforcements, two hens with puffed-out breasts just like the sisters. A brown dog trotted over and looked as if he might go for the hens, but they clucked a blue streak and managed to face him down.

What the McClendon sisters wanted was the same thing they had wanted the day before.

"Buffalo Bill is the most famous man in the West," Bertha McClendon reminded me. "If you can't even find the most famous man in the West, then what good are you?" she asked.

"I could send a telegram in Latin—that ought to count for something," I replied.

That was nearly a lie. The Latin I knew was *"O patria, o mores,"* and I wasn't entirely sure that even that little tag was correct; but if I intended to make a go of being the telegraph lady of Rita Blanca, it wouldn't do to let the McClendon sisters wear me down.

At this moment in time, which is to say early August of 1876, all I knew about Buffalo Bill Cody was that he was a skilled killer of buffalo—I believe he supplied meat for the Kansas Pacific Railway, or some railroad at least. I knew some dime novels had been put out with him as the hero, but Father preferred for us Courtrights to read good literature rather than trashy stuff. Of course, I'd seen the dime novels—they were in every railroad station in the land—and if Cody was the man on the cover, then he was a very handsome man, but I would not have been willing to bet that the real Bill Cody looked even half that good. Too many of the swaggering gents who are supposed to be handsome turn out to be spotty and bowlegged upon actual inspection.

Be that as it may, the McClendon sisters were in no mood to give up, so I took Andy Jessup's tip and suggested we float a telegram or two up to Leavenworth. Maybe some autographed pictures would come back someday.

"We need to know his play schedule too," the older sister said.

"Play schedule of what?"

"Why, Mr. Cody's next performance," the younger sister said. "Surely you know that Mr. Cody is a star of the stage, when he's not hunting."

I remembered that I had vaguely heard that Buffalo Bill was trying to be an actor—actually it was Bill Hickok who told me that: he said some fool had got the two of them to be in a play together in Chicago or somewhere. It was called *The Prairie Scout.* Bill Hickok claimed that he had never uttered a single word while onstage, and Cody had uttered very few, due to stage fright. It sounded like a silly business to me. Billy said they were so short on props that they even used red flannel socks for scalps.

But I was determined not to lose my patience with the McClendon sisters, so I promised to include a request for tickets to his next performance.

"I fear it will be a far piece away," I told them. "If there's a stage anywhere around here it has escaped my notice."

"Of course it ain't around here—it'll be in Rochester, New York, in the early fall," Bertha McClendon said. "We should know, our baby sister lives there."

One of the hens had the temerity to jump up on my desk, but I promptly grabbed her and pitched her out the window—this resulted in a spate of intemperate clucking, but little did I care. Hens always think they own the world, but I am quick to show them that they are not welcome on my desk.

About two weeks later, on a sultry afternoon, I got drowsy in my office and slipped into a nap. It seemed someone was playing "Lorena" on a fiddle—that song always makes me sad. Then there stood Billy Hickok, in my dream: he was holding me at arm's length, and he was wearing specs. Usually Billy looked a little puzzled—I put it down to his bad eyesight. But this time he didn't look puzzled. "You're even prettier than I thought," he said. "Now that I can really see you."

But then someone rapped on the window of my office, which ended my best dream about Bill.

# 16

MRS. KAROO, KNOWING that I did not like to leave my post for lunch, showed up a little past noon with two biscuits, a boiled egg, and several slices of her delicious cucumbers. Despite my sad news I had managed to send off twenty-seven telegrams that morning—I was glad to pull my Closed sign down for ten minutes and eat her delicious snack.

The sun was blistering by then. Just as I was finishing, who should show up but Ted Bunsen, my brother, Jackson, and a third man—a skinny fellow who looked distinctly subdued. He had one arm in a sling. Like everybody else in Rita Blanca the trio ignored my Closed sign and got right down to business.

"How well do you know old George Murray?" Teddy asked.

"He and Father were friends—they fought in the war together," I said. "He dropped by Black Mesa from time to time."

"Didn't he try to marry Aunt Sally?" Jackson asked.

"That's right—she wouldn't have him," I replied. "Aunt Sally liked to travel. She married Uncle Bob, who bought her a big boat. I think she mainly used the boat on the Great Lakes. I don't think she had anything in particular against George Murray—it was just one of those things."

"I've got something particular against the goddamn old fool," the skinny fellow said. "He shot me—that's what I have against him, the old bastard."

"Here now, none of your profane cussing," Teddy said, striking the fellow a sudden hard blow to the jaw. "The law here will not tolerate profane cussing when ladies are in hearing," he added.

The blow to the jaw evidently did not impress the victim, whose name was Palmer. He glared like a bear might glare, and with his good arm, which happened to be the right, dealt Teddy Bunsen a blow to the solar plexus that deprived him of the capacity to breathe in air for a while.

"Pound him on the back—be a good deputy," I told Jackson, but the sight of his boss getting whopped in the solar plexus by a fellow with one arm in a sling upset my brother so much that he chose to disregard my advice.

Mrs. Karoo came hurrying along—she managed to get Teddy to stand up straight, after which he was soon able to breathe again.

Mr. Palmer, evidently disgusted with the level of law enforcement in Rita Blanca, tipped his hat to me and Mrs. Karoo and stalked off to imbibe some liquor in one of Leo Oliphant's saloons.

"Want me to shoot him, Sheriff?" Jackson asked. He had his hand on the handle of his pistol but did not actually draw it. It was only Jackson's third day as a deputy, after all—it was clear that he was not yet solid on the finer points of the law.

Though he was now able to breathe a little bit, Ted Bunsen had still not recovered the full use of his voice. He waved vaguely at Jackson—Jackson took it as a sign to draw his pistol, but he didn't shoot.

"Hold off, Jackson," I instructed. "If you're going to be shooting everybody who cusses in front of ladies, Rita Blanca is likely to lose population quick."

"But it's against the law to hit a sheriff—I'm pretty sure of that," Jackson protested.

"Put up the pistol," Teddy managed to croak. "You can't shoot Ed Palmer because he's my brother-in-law."

"I thought your sister lived in Omaha, Teddy," I said. "What's her husband doing way down here? If I ever have a husband, I intend to keep him on a shorter leash than that."

I raised that point in the belief that it never hurts to enunciate firm principles. Though there might be scant likelihood that Ted and I would ever be married, if such should turn out to be the case I wanted him to know that I would not be one to tolerate long absences.

"Ed Palmer wants to be a rancher," Ted explained. "Old George Murray owns a passel of land south of Rabbit Gulch. George is eighty-five and claims to be thinking of retiring, so he sold Ed one hundred thousand acres, and that should have been that."

"What went wrong?"

"Palmer paid the money and that damned old George changed his mind," Teddy told us.

"He now claims he has no interest in retiring," Teddy added. "Every time Ed rides out to claim his property George shoots at him. Mostly he misses, but yesterday morning Ed got too close and the old fool winged him."

"Mr. Palmer doesn't look much like a cowpuncher to me," I said. "What line was he in in Omaha?"

"Dry goods," Teddy admitted.

"This doesn't make sense," I said. "Why would a dry goods salesman think he could make a go of a ranch in No Man's Land?"

But then I remembered Father and all those brochures he read extolling the beauties of the West. If an educated man such as Perceval Staunton Courtright could get sucked in by a bunch of slick brochures, then there was no reason why a haberdasher from Nebraska would behave any more sensibly.

People must love the notion of ranches, particularly people from the East who have no real idea how vexatious and uncomfortable ranch life can actually be.

"I see Mr. Palmer has a problem," I told Teddy. "What do you want me to do—telegraph the army?"

Teddy was silent for a good space of time. He liked to gather his thoughts in his own good time.

"When old George was a little friendlier he expressed a great fondness for you," he said finally. "He told me once that if he were a few years younger he'd marry you. What do you think of that?"

What I remembered was that on one or two of his visits Mr. Murray had cast me looks which were not exactly proper. Once when I'd been washing my hands in a pan of water he had looked at my bare arms in a way that took leave of propriety, in my opinion. I felt a kind of heat coming off him, so I rolled down my sleeves and walked away.

"I didn't much like Mr. Murray, but that's water under the bridge," I told Ted. "Even if the old creature shoots your brother-in-law and five or six other people, I'm not likely to marry him."

"No, but since he likes you I thought we might ride out and visit the man," Ted said. "I'd like to avoid further bloodshed if I can. If you talked to old George maybe he'd ease up on Ed Palmer and let him have the hundred thousand acres."

The suggestion was reasonable enough, but right away, I sensed a plot on Teddy's part to get me alone. Sheriffs don't normally ask telegraph ladies to help them arrest dangerous criminals.

"Ted, I'm the telegraph lady," I reminded him. "I can't be leaving my post just because George Murray is a little unruly."

"The telegraph office ain't open on Sunday," Teddy reminded me. "If you're willing I'll rent a buggy and we can ride out Sunday and visit your father's old friend."

It was plain at that point what Teddy's game was. Protecting Ed Palmer was just an excuse. What he wanted was a good stretch of time with me alone. Obviously he had kissing in mind, and possibly matrimony as well.

"How long's the buggy ride?" I asked. After all, my Sundays were mainly dull. I suppose I could have stayed home and hung curtains. But fighting off Teddy might be more interesting.

"It's about twenty miles out to Rabbit Gulch," Teddy admitted.

"I suppose I ought to assist the law anyway I can," I told him. This caused Ted to brighten considerably.

Of course the dull creature that my upbringing had trained me to be would have insisted on taking a chaperone along on this buggy ride. But the fact is I never held with chaperones. The whole point of courtship, as I enjoyed it, was to figure out ways to be alone with whatever fellow was courting you at the time.

I said nothing about a chaperone. Teddy sure didn't mention one, so we made our date for Sunday.

# 17

IN FACT, GIVEN the choice, I would rather have gone on a Sunday buggy ride with Andy Jessup than with Ten Bunsen—but I was given no choice. Andy had a commission to pick up a string of horses down in southern Kansas somewhere and deliver them to Buffalo Bill Cody to be used in his big buffalo hunt with the dudes from Chicago.

"I suppose that sheriff means to marry you," Andy said, as he was saddling up to leave. We were moping around in the stables and had even exchanged a shy peck or two.

"His courtship rarely pleases me—I suppose I'll end up a spinster," I said. "I'm just too hard to please."

Andy didn't contest the opinion. He gave me another peck and he was gone. His abrupt departure, just as I was beginning to fall under the spell of his dreamy eyes, put me a little out of sorts with this fellow Buffalo Bill. Not only was he the idol of the bossy McClendon sisters, his need to make money off Chicago dudes had caused Andy Jessup to run off and leave me just when I was beginning to want to kiss him.

Just about the time I was closing the telegraph office on Saturday afternoon, old Josh the mail rider came racing into Rita Blanca on a horse so badly winded that we all expected it to die—but the horse turned out to be a tough little mustang that defied our expectations. When Josh yanked the saddle off, the little pony rolled in the dirt a few times, blew out his breath, and was soon eating oats in the livery stable.

In fact, old Josh came closer to dying than his mount. He was white as a sheet and could hardly summon words out of his mouth.

"Yazee gang!" he managed finally. "Yazee gang—killed George Murray and dern near caught me."

He had no sooner said it than every man in hearing distance raced off to grab up armaments. My brother was quickest. He had the ten-gauge of Father's, and his new pistol as well. Ted Bunsen strapped on two pistols and emerged from the jail carrying a repeating rifle. Drunks poured out of the saloon, most of them armed to the teeth; those who were weakly equipped raced into the general store and bought what weapons they could afford. Aurel Imlah was the last to arrive but he made up for it by carrying two buffalo guns.

As I understood it, the Yazee gang consisted of six wild brothers of that name. They tore through Arkansas and Kansas and wherever else they felt like going, burning houses and killing men, women, and children without compunction. Bert Yazee, the oldest brother, reveled in busting people's skulls with a big war club he had taken off a Ponca Indian. It was said that Bert Yazee gave no more thought to busting skulls than he would have to busting an egg.

Of course, after the war, several of these wild gangs looted and burned in Kansas and Missouri. One of Father's reasons for settling in No Man's Land was that there was nothing out there for such a gang to loot.

My first thought on this occasion was to worry about dreamy Andy Jessup—what if they had ambushed Andy? But fortunately, Andy had ridden off to the east and Rabbit Gulch was to the west.

But what about us? Most of these drunks were not fighting men.

Matters weren't helped by details old Josh added once he caught his breath.

"They cut old George's ears off and nailed them to the front door," Josh informed us. "I don't know what became of his eyeballs," he added casually.

"Uh-oh," Ed Palmer said. "Uh-oh."

From the greenish look on his face I judged that dry goods in Omaha were looking better and better to Mr. Palmer.

"Josh, I think you ought to spare us any more details," Teddy suggested. "There's a lady here, remember?"

In fact, there were several ladies there by this time. The McClendon sisters were there, as well as their hens, and the blacksmith's wife, a big, stout woman who armed herself with a meat cleaver.

"Do you reckon they'll come down on us, Josh?" Ted asked.

"Did you bury George Murray?" he asked the old rider.

"Bury George? . . . With the Yazees in the neighborhood?" Josh said. "Are you crazy? Once I seen what they did to George I was in no mood to dig a grave. I ran for my life but even so they spotted me and gave me a hard chase."

Suddenly Mrs. Karoo began to ring her dinner bell—she rang it for dear life.

We could all see her—she was pointing to the southwest, where a fast-moving dust cloud seemed to be moving our way.

"Uh-oh," Ed Palmer repeated, to the irritation of his brother-in-law Ted Bunsen.

"If you don't stop saying 'Uh-oh,' by God I'll shoot you," Teddy said.

"I'm your brother-in-law," Ed Palmer reminded him, but Ted did not rescind the threat.

Aurel Imlah wore a little spyglass on a leather cord around his neck. He used it to spot distant buffalo, I suppose. He trained his spyglass and watched the dust cloud closely, while the rest of us stood around on one foot and then the other, wondering what he was seeing, and how it might feel to be massacred.

"Bert Yazee's still riding that big roan horse," Aurel announced casually, "but on the whole those scoundrels are poorly mounted."

"Think they'll charge us, Aurel?" Beau Wheless asked.

"Eventually, I expect . . . but not today," Aural concluded. "They want to scare us first—get us jittery."

"Hell, I'm jittery already," the blacksmith said—and he was the largest man in town.

Aurel walked off back to his hide yard. Mrs. Karoo stood by her bell, but she was no longer ringing it. Several of the drunks had begun to drift back in the direction of the saloons. Jackson Courtright had cocked his new pistol, a point of technique that drew comment from the sheriff.

"Don't be lolling around with that pistol cocked, Deputy," Ted told Jackson. "It might go off and kill a chicken, or something."

Then Ted turned to me.

"I guess tomorrow might not be the best day for our buggy ride," he told me, with a disappointed look.

"Nope," I agreed.

I felt a little sorry for Ted—he sure did look disappointed.

# 18

THE REGULARS AT Mrs. Karoo's supper table lingered a little longer than usual on this particular Saturday night. Perhaps it was because she had made a cinnamon custard for dessert—and fortunately she had made lots of it, for everyone took a second helping.

There was not much talk. We all had the Yazee gang on our minds. Doc Siblee remarked that the preacher had picked a bad time to choke on the corn bread.

"He could have prayed for us," he pointed out.

"There's only six of them," Aurel reminded us. "A whole town ought to be able to fight off six killers."

"A doubtful thing is the quality of our marksmanship," Teddy admitted.

"If the Yazees make a run at the town it'll be mostly close-range shooting, I would hope," Aurel pointed out.

Then he lit his pipe and Mrs. Karoo lit hers. She got out the rum and everyone except my brother, Jackson, indulged in a snort. A snort happened to be enough to make Hungry Billy drunk—he soon wobbled off into the night. Doc Siblee went with him and the rest of us moved out onto the porch. The evening star was especially bright that night, as bright as I've ever seen it. Far in the western distance we heard a deep lowing, a sound that seemed to interest Aurel Imlah a lot more than the Yazee scare.

"Buffalo," he said. "It could just be two, but I'd like to hope it's a whole bunch."

"Be handy to have you here if the Yazees attack," Teddy said.

Aurel enjoyed a puff or two before he answered. I think he liked the notion that he was supposed to stay and protect the town, which is more or less what Teddy was suggesting.

"That sorry Bert Yazee is no early riser," Aurel remarked—it was his only remark. Pretty soon he left and, I suspect, went to alert his skinners that there might be buffalo to be skinned on the morrow.

When Jackson and Teddy paid Mrs. Karoo the usual compliments, I walked partway back to the jail with them.

"Are you scared, Nellie?" Jackson asked.

"I don't know what I am," I told him honestly, for I was neither terrified nor exactly calm. The dangers of violent death just seemed to be part of life, in the West. Even in Virginia plenty of people got murdered right in their homes. A few years back there had been a madman around Waynesboro who went around cutting people's heads off with a scythe. Naturally we were all terrified and cut down on our picnics until a farm woman who knew how to use a shotgun shot the madman dead.

Since it was such a pretty night I thought Ted Bunsen might want to indulge in a little courting—after all I didn't walk down to the jail every night—but he had his mind on the Yazee gang and failed to notice that a small opportunity had been lost.

"We best clean all the guns," he said to my brother, which I guess they did, leaving me standing in the street flat-footed. I didn't want much from Teddy, but I did want something—if not from him, then from somebody, or maybe just from life itself.

Mrs. Karoo looked relieved when I stepped back into the boarding-house, which surprised me. I hadn't been gone that long or that far.

"In Indian times you might have been snatched between here and the jail," she explained. "I guess I still get nervous."

"If anybody had tried to snatch me, you bet I would have raised a ruckus."

"Not if you had been whacked on the head with a tomahawk first," she said. "You would have been unconscious—and then you would have just been gone."

It was a chilly thought, I had to admit.

"I was east of here, with the Choctaws then," she said. "They were settled Indians. But Aurel was here when the Comanches ruled No Man's Land. He's the one to tell you about the Indian times."

"And he thought the Comanches were worse than this Yazee gang?"

"Oh yes," she said with certainty. "The Comanches were worse."

# 19

THE SUN CAME UP and no Yazees came with it—we all had a normal breakfast.

Watching Aurel Imlah and Mrs. Karoo with their pipes convinced me I wanted to learn to smoke one—the tobacco had such a pleasing smell. When I mentioned as much to Mrs. Karoo she offered to come with me to Beau Wheless's store to help me pick out my first pipe.

"Something ladylike, of course," she said. "Mr. Wheless has a good selection. I'm about ready for a new pipe myself—we can take a look."

Several of my Virginia aunts smoked pipes, though my mother didn't. She would not have approved of my pipe smoking but I was a grown woman now and I could choose my own vices, I guess.

Beau Wheless, ever the merchant, soon had fifteen or sixteen pipes out of his big pipe case, all of them spread on a counter while he explained the virtues of each one. I had not expected there to be such variety and was trying this one and that one, trying to see which one looked best with my complexion, when Beau Wheless suddenly looked up and got quiet.

At first I didn't know why—nor did Mrs. Karoo, who had already picked out her new pipe and was trying on a bonnet. But she looked up too. The blacksmith was in the store, buying himself a new sledgehammer. He looked up, puzzled. Then the old lady who was counting change suddenly stopped counting.

For no reason that I could immediately pinpoint, everyone in the store suddenly got quiet.

Hungry Billy Wheless, who had been lounging on the porch, doing as little as possible, suddenly rushed in, white as a sheet.

"It's them, Pa!" he said—then we all began to hear the distant rumble of hooves and some faint yelling.

I've come to think that in times of crisis human beings don't have it in them to be rational.

The Yazee gang was riding down upon us, six abreast. We all ran outside and confirmed that fact. The sensible thing, then, would have been to run and hide—but did we? Not at all. Instead we ran out into the street, in order to get an early look at our own doom. I suppose if it had been a tornado bearing down on us, or a prairie fire or a tidal wave, we'd have behaved just as foolishly—like chickens with their heads cut off, or something.

There it is: out we all ran, offering our foolish selves to the killers, quite unaware, of course, that we were about to witness one of the most talked about gunfights ever to occur in the American West, or anywhere.

The Yazee gang came trotting toward us, coming steadily on but not at a dead run or anything. They all had rifles except Bert Yazee, who had his big club. Being six abreast, they pretty much filled the street. Then, as we all watched, Bert Yazee pulled up, and so did his brothers. Bert lifted that big skull-smashing club over his head and let out a high yell, after which the Yazees came racing straight toward us, this time at a dead run. They were coming to massacre us all.

My first thought as a sister was to race over to the jail and protect my little brother—how I expected to accomplish that I had no idea. But I started running and got nearly to the middle of the street, which had come to look as wide as an ocean, when I realized I wasn't going to make it: the Yazees were coming at me too fast.

Ted Bunsen came running out of the jail with his rifle raised, but before he could shoot, one of the Yazees shot him and sent him sprawling, whether dead or alive I didn't know.

"Nellie! Come back!" Beau Wheless yelled, but by then it was too late to turn back. There I was, facing six wild killers, with no weapon of any kind.

I'm dead, I thought—I'm dead!

And at that moment I didn't really seem to mind all that much. I felt rather distant from it all, as if I were already gone.

Then Jackson, my brother, came stumbling out of the jail, looking as if he had just awakened. His hair stood up, his shirttail was out, and he was barefoot. His aim, I believe, was to rescue me, but for that it was too late. But Jackson was a swift runner and managed to get to my side when the Yazees were still maybe forty yards away. He had his holster and his new pistol was in it but so far it had not occurred to him to draw the weapon.

"Jackson, draw your gun!" I yelled. "Draw your gun or we're dead!"

The only reason we weren't already dead, I'm convinced now, was because Bert Yazee wanted to club one or both of us with his big club and slowed the advance just a little. I could see Ted Bunsen struggling to sit up but he was not going to be able to be any help—now the Yazee gang was closing with us fast!

When Jackson realized he had his pistol, he did draw it, but my Lord! He was slow as molasses. Getting his pistol out of his holster seemed to take a week, and then he nearly dropped the pistol, which, so far as I knew, he had never fired.

"Jackson! Shoot!" I yelled. Jackson frowned for a second, as if annoyed by my bossiness, and then he finally cocked the pistol. By this time the Yazees were on us—I saw Bert Yazee with his killer's grin raise that big Ponca war club, meaning to club Jackson first.

But before the club fell Jackson raised the pistol and shot Bert Yazee dead as dead.

Then Jackson swung his pistol in a short arc and fired five more times. Each shot rendered a Yazee fully as dead as Bert. The last killer fell under his horse's feet and got thoroughly trampled as well.

On the faces of the dead men were looks of profound surprise.

Jackson looked at his pistol as if he had never seen such a thing as a revolver before.

"It's a good thing there wasn't seven of those killers," he said mildly. "I used up every one of my bullets."

Ted Bunsen got to his feet and managed to hobble over—he had only been hit in the shoulder. He stared down at the six dead men, looking puzzled, as his eyes were showing him something he couldn't quite believe.

Ted didn't say a word, nor did most of the townspeople, at first. Rita Blanca was quiet, except for one of the Yazees' horses, which had wandered off to a water trough and was sucking in water, loudly.

We weren't dead—none of us—and yet death had come so close

that it took a while for us to accept that we were still alive. A stillness settled over us. Even Beau Wheless was silenced for a time. How could it be that we were really spared? How could it be that in no more than a few seconds my little brother had wiped out the deadliest gang in the West? Nobody knew about shock in those days—we were all in it, but we didn't have the word.

The person least affected was Jackson Courtright himself.

"Jackson, you're a hero," I told him. My voice sounded like the voice of someone else, not me. It was the voice of someone who had been as good as dead, and yet was still alive.

"You're not just a hero, you're a big hero!" I told him. "You wiped out the whole Yazee gang! That makes you the biggest hero in the whole West!"

Jackson was just a youth, seventeen years old, and he had done the only thing there was to do, other than die. He hadn't died, and he still looked sleepy. In fact he yawned while I was telling him what a big hero he was.

"I guess shooting a pistol is a lot easier than I thought it would be," Jackson said. "When I finally got it out of my holster it was like it just became part of my arm."

He was standing now three feet from the corpse of Bert Yazee, the most feared killer in that part of the world, but Jackson didn't look at Bert or any of the other dead Yazees. Dealing sudden death to six humans—even if they had been merciless killers—might give most of us qualms, or queasy stomachs, or twinges of conscience, or something, but it had no affect on my brother that I could tell. If he'd had a plate of flapjacks in front of him I expect he would have eaten them without sparing a thought for the Yazees.

There may just be something in the Courtright character—something a little cold-blooded. We're not ones to weep for a man—at least not long.

There's just a distance in us—Virginia gentlefolk that we may be.

"I need to get my boots on," Jackson said. "I'm apt to get bit by a stinging lizard, or else step on a grass burr. I hate those mean little stinging lizards!"

Then, with the whole town watching, Jackson strolled back into the jail and finished his nap.

# BOOK II

---

# Telegraph Days

# 1

THE FIRST PERSON to recover from the shock of the big fight that wiped out the Yazee gang was Beau Wheless—for maybe ten minutes Beau was as stunned as the rest of us, but then his business instincts kicked in and kicked hard. A capacity for rapid response to commercial possibility probably explains why Beau Wheless was the richest man in Rita Blanca.

"Come on, Billy, help me line up these Yazees," he said to his son. "Let's pile up their guns and valuables—and search close. I think we've got the makings of a fine little museum here."

I thought the man must be daft.

"Museum of what—dirty clothes?" I asked.

But Beau was energetic, not to mention smooth. His eyes were already looking far ahead in time and seeing the endless march of dollar signs, visible at the moment only to himself.

"Let's call it the Museum of the American Outlaw . . . what better place to have it than right here in Rita Blanca?" he said.

It takes a true businessman to look at six bloody, bedraggled, filthy corpses, their eyes open to the heaven they wouldn't be going to, and see a museum.

"Would you charge admission?" I asked—my glimpse into how the mercantile mind worked made me think there might be something to this fellow Beau Wheless after all.

"Free admission to reporters and a dime to strangers and idle passersby," Beau said. "Maybe we'll raise it to a quarter later on."

"Okay, where will this museum be?" I asked.

"In the window of my store, to start with—until we get a nice room ready for it," Beau said.

"And where are all these reporters you said could get in free?" I asked.

Just then Hungry Billy gave a cry, dropped to his knees, and puked. He had just pulled a sack full of objects I couldn't identify out of Bert Yazee's saddlebags.

"Ears," Ted Bunsen declared, when he went to take a look. "Billy's found a big bag of ears."

"They'll be perfect for Beau's museum," I said, rather tartly.

In fact Ted Bunsen looked peaked. Being shot in the shoulder was clearly a source of discomfort.

"I'm taking you to Doc Siblee," I told him. "You could have a broken collarbone."

For once Teddy didn't argue with me. I think he was feeling pretty low. For one thing he was shot, and for another, he had not played a very effective role in the defense of the community that was paying his wages, such as they were.

My little brother, who had never fired a pistol before, had become a great hero, while Teddy had been able to be no help. In the heat of battle he probably didn't think about that angle, but the battle had cooled and there it was.

Stiff as I usually was with Teddy, I didn't enjoy seeing him so disappointed with himself.

"Now, Theodore," I told him, "I want you to cheer up. This is No Man's Land. There'll be plenty more outlaws for you to slaughter, I'm sure."

"Doubtful," Teddy said, though he smiled when I gave his hand a good warm squeeze.

The Doc was not long in discovering that I had been right in my diagnosis. Sheriff Ted Bunsen had a broken collarbone.

# 2

IT WAS IMPORTANT that I took the trouble to walk Ted to the Doc's. Otherwise he might well have balked, as men are prone to do when anything medical is suggested to them.

But I was not through with Beau Wheless and his plans for an Outlaw Museum. By this time Hungry Billy and the helpful blacksmith had drug the dead outlaws to the undertaker's shed, where they were rapidly being squirted full of embalming fluid.

"We can't allow them to get rank before the reporters get here," Beau informed me. "Have you sent off any telegrams yet?"

"No, but I'll inform the paper up in Dodge," I said. "It'll be a relief to travelers to know they don't have to worry about the Yazees anymore."

"Do it!" Beau said. "Then we can expect a crowd of reporters to come down on us in about three days."

"Three days?" I asked. "We're a long way from anywhere, Beau—or haven't you noticed?"

"Nobody can cover distance like newspapermen on the scent of a story," he said. "Half the forts in Kansas are full of reporters who are just waiting for some general to corner some Indian that the U.S. Army can blame Custer on."

"But Custer wasn't killed in Kansas," I pointed out. "He was killed in Montana."

"All that means is that the reporters will be drinking too much whiskey and losing money at cards—our story will be the biggest thing on the horizon, as soon as you send that wire."

The casual way Beau said "our story" irritated me for a moment. Strictly speaking, it seemed to me, the story involved only my brother,

Jackson, and the now-defunct Yazee gang. And yet Jackson was over in the jail, taking a nap—he had no inkling yet that there even was a story, one that would render him famous for the rest of his days. The Yazees would be famous too, although their fame would have to be posthumous.

Beau Wheless already had his big camera out—he meant to photograph the dead Yazees as soon as the embalming was done.

"Here's a notion for you, Nellie, once you get that wire off," Beau said. "You need to write up a booklet about all this—there's a printer in Dodge who could print it off for you," he told me, with a gleam in his eye.

"You've seen outlaw books," he went on. "They needn't be longer than dime novels. I'll pay for the printing and we'll split the profits down the middle—if you'll hurry and write it up, maybe we can get it on sale before the hordes arrive."

I had a hard time imagining hordes in Rita Blanca, but Beau Wheless was an experienced man and I was just a young woman. The only thing I didn't like about Beau Wheless was his Adam's apple, which was large; it jerked around unattractively when he talked.

"I've never written a booklet before, but I suppose I can put my mind to it," I said. "But let me remind you that I'm not destitute. I can pay to have my own booklet printed, and then I wouldn't have to share the profits with anyone. Of course, if you chose to sell the booklet in your store you'd be welcome to a fair commission."

Beau looked a little pained.

"But it was my idea," he said.

"And it was my brother who kept you from being slaughtered," I reminded him.

"Go write it, then," Beau said. I suspect he saw his defeat as temporary.

"Avoid long sentences if you can," he advised. "People who read outlaw books don't care to have long sentences wrapped around their throats."

Then he and Hungry Billy and the blacksmith propped the dead Yazees up on some boards they had knocked together.

All afternoon, as I was in my office scribbling out the story of the big shoot-out in Rita Blanca, I could see Beau Wheless popping in and out of his little photographer's tent, taking picture after picture of the once dreaded Yazee gang.

# 3

SCRIBBLING OUT STORIES and sketches has always come easy for me. From girlhood I had written little stories, more or less in the manner of Mrs. Edgeworth's or Mrs. Ewing's. Mrs. Browning was, for the time being, still more than I could aspire to. I kept my sketches in a box, which I forgot to bring with me when we headed west. I let my big sister Millicent read a few of my sketches and she thought I ought to be sending them off to magazines—but then Milly died and I let that project drop.

The story of the Yazee battle was a good deal different from what I was used to writing. It wasn't based on vapors in my head or flutterings in my bosom. There had been a real gunfight that happened on a real street in a real town. Many of the townspeople had observed it: Doc Siblee, Ted Bunsen, Hungry Billy, the blacksmith, and plenty of others. Later quite a few of these spectators complained that they deserved more attention than they got, but I was the one writing up the event and I did my best. The fact that there were hurt feelings on the part of a few soreheads for the next fifty years was merely one of the many aspects of life that were out of my control.

Of course, right up I had to back my narrative up a few pages and explain who the Yazee brothers were, and why they needed killing. I had to get in Bert Yazee's penchant for using a war club and all that.

Also, I had to explain exactly where Rita Blanca was, no easy task. Since Rita Blanca wasn't part of a regular state I finally resorted to Father's pocket atlas and just put in the latitude and longitude as best I could work them out.

Once those ticklish matters were out of the way I sailed right into the big charge of the Yazees. I didn't hesitate to put myself into the story—after all, I had been in the story. I was already out in the street, facing the six horsemen, before Ted Bunsen came out and got shot in the collarbone. I had had to yell at Jackson, when once he appeared, just to get the boy awake enough to deal with our peril. If I hadn't insisted that he draw his pistol and shoot, Jackson might have stood there with sleep in his eyes while the two of us were ridden down.

Of course, I didn't stint when it came to giving full credit to my brother for his exceptional shooting. Doc Siblee later told me confidentially that every member of the gang had been shot dead in the heart.

"I wouldn't have believed it if I hadn't seen it," the Doc said. "Few gunshot wounds are instantly fatal—but those six were instantly fatal, and you can quote me on that."

I did quote him on that, only to have various experts from various countries weigh in on the matter, most of them contradicting our good doctor and claiming that nothing of the sort could have happened.

All afternoon, while Beau and Hungry Billy took pictures, I stayed in the office and let my pen race. Oh, how it raced! Before it stopped racing I had more than fifty pages ready for the printer, who, inconveniently, did business some one hundred and fifty miles from where I sat.

When I showed my manuscript to Beau he was quick to approve.

"You're a fine hand with the pen, Nellie," Beau allowed. "What title are you going to fit onto this tale?"

In my haste to get the facts down I had given no thought to a title, but I knew I had better come up with something quick or Beau would think of one and use it to claim fifty percent of the profits.

"*Banditti of No Man's Land,* how's that?" I asked him.

"Too short," he ruled at once. "You need a little more than that."

I suppose that was fair. A little more weight in the title might not hurt. I went over to the counter in Beau's store and came up with this lengthy effort:

*The Banditti of No Man's Land. A True and Authentic Account of the Destruction of the Yazee Gang, Terrors of the Prairie. Eyewitness Account of the Heroic Stand Made by Deputy Jackson Courtright. Six Outlaws Shot Dead in the Heart. Miraculous Marksmanship, Claims Local Doctor.*

Beau thought that that title was adequate—the one problem that remained was how to get it to the printer in Dodge City.

"The fastest way's horseback," Ted Bunsen advised. He was looking wan and moving slow.

"I'll take it, Sis—I know how to get to Dodge," Jackson volunteered.

"*We'll* take it!" I corrected. "I'm not sending my booklet off with anyone as absentminded as you. You might forget what it was and start a fire with it, or something. I can't risk it."

"If you were planning to start off on that mule you'll never get there," Aurel Imlah commented, referring to Percy, of whom he had a poor opinion.

"Joe Schwartz took over those Yazee horses," Ted pointed out. "I doubt he would mind loaning you a couple of nags for a few days."

"If he should balk I'll counsel him," Aurel said, but Joe never even came close to balking, though I believe it shocked him a little when I sashayed in wearing trousers. The pants had been Father's. I was not about to set off on a trip through wild country trying to balance myself on a sidesaddle.

"Nellie's always been a tomboy," Jackson said to Joe.

Later I reminded my brother privately that I was no kind of boy, tom or otherwise, and I expected him to remember that fact.

I chose Bert Yazee's big roan horse and appropriated his saddle as well.

Jackson Courtright had always been prone to gentlemanly indecision. The way to get him into action was not to give him any choice. The Yazee gang hadn't given him any choice, but even then, he waited until the last second to pull his gun and shoot.

Faced with a pen full of horses to choose from, Jackson's indecision flared up again. He rode all five of the remaining Yazee horses, trying to make up his mind. He liked some things about a bay, and some things about a sorrel, and some things about a black, but he could not decide. The one horse he hadn't tried was a small, squatty mustang. I am not noted for my patience—forty-five minutes of watching Jackson switch from one nag to another had me grinding my teeth.

"Jackson, make up your mind," I said. "It's a far piece up to Dodge."

Still, the young fool hesitated. It had begun to dawn on him that he was now a local hero—he got that stubborn look men get when they get tired of having a woman boss them around.

I had seen that look on Jackson before—Father looked exactly the same way when anyone, male or female, tried to tug him to the point of decision.

"All right—you can stand there till you petrify," I told him. "I'm going to Dodge City and I'm leaving now—you'll have to settle on a mount and catch up as best you can."

I guess I was now considered a solid citizen of Rita Blanca, because half the population turned out to see me off. Mrs. Karoo had prepared a little hamper, which we strapped in my saddlebags; even the Mc-Clendon sisters seemed to have softened a little.

"You hurry back, Miss Courtright," Melba McClendon said. "We can't afford to be without our telegraph lady too long."

"Can't afford it—we need to keep up on the whereabouts of Buffalo Bill Cody," Bertha McClendon assured me.

Both hens cackled, as if seconding the motion.

As I was about to ride off Aurel Imlah made a motion with his head, as if he wanted a private word with me, so I trotted over. Aurel was still smoking his long-stemmed white pipe.

"Miss Courtright . . . ," he began, but I stopped him.

"Please remember to call me Nellie, Aurel," I told him. "I do get so tired of gentlemen being formal."

Aurel Imlah smiled. I don't think he liked being formal either.

"There's a bunch of brothers up in Dodge City," he cautioned. "Their name is Earp. One of them's the marshal. His name is Wyatt. I don't know exactly how many Earps there are, but there may be at least five. I'd avoid them, if I were you—especially Wyatt."

"I was in Dodge City once and didn't like it," I told him. "I'll be happy to avoid them if I can."

"That's the best plan, I suspect," he said.

"What's bad about the Earps?" I asked. He had got my curiosity aroused.

"They're coarse—particularly Wyatt," he said. "Damn coarse."

"Coarse, is he?" I said. "Coarse."

Aurel Imlah nodded and I rode out of town.

# 4

THE TRAIL TO Dodge City was not hard to follow—thousands and thousands of horsemen, both red and white, had loped or trotted across it; there had been hundreds of wagons too, bound west for Santa Fe or east to St. Louis. The thick, restless prairie grass might have covered up the tracks of the many horsemen, but the wagon wheels cut deeper, and there were enough ruts to keep even a greenhorn more or less on track.

I was hardly out of sight of Rita Blanca when Jackson caught up with me. He had chosen the little mustang after all—a good choice, in my opinion, despite the little gelding's squatty appearance.

"I favor short horses," Jackson said. "That way, if you get thrown off, you don't have far to fall."

I noticed that Jackson not only had his new pistol, he also seemed to hold nearly a whole box of shells. He also had a big knife stuck in a scabbard that went halfway down his leg. My little brother, the hero of the battle of Rita Blanca, had turned up armed to the teeth.

No wonder he had taken so long to choose a mount. He wanted to choose a few other things, while he was at it.

"Who paid for that cartridge belt and that pig sticker?" I asked.

"Charged them," Jackson said. "I'm a deputy now. I make fifteen dollars a month."

Far ahead of us, on the plain, a thunderstorm was rumbling up. Lightning was shooting out from under some high dark clouds.

"I'm surprised you didn't buy a Winchester and maybe a buffalo gun," I told him. "How many months' wages did all this set you back?"

Before Jackson could get around to answering, the thunderstorm broke and spitting rain drenched us both. I could have been no wetter if a bucket of water had been poured over my head. But the little prairie storm soon passed on and the hot sun soon had us steaming again.

A beautiful double rainbow was the nicest consequence of the shower.

"I have to use weapons," Jackson told me, without directly addressing the cost of the knife and his new equipment.

"There could be other outlaws," he reminded me. "Irish Roy could be there somewhere. It's best to be equipped."

"It's best not to be getting a big head, Jackson Courtright," I told him. "Irish Roy or some other outlaw may turn out to be a better shot than you."

That got my brother's back up, as I knew it would.

"I doubt there's an outlaw in this part of the country that can shoot better than I do," he said.

Well, he was young—young men are prone to vanity.

"Pride goeth before a fall," I reminded him, though I was not really expecting pride to fall as quickly as it did.

"It's going to be supper time pretty soon," he said. "What are we supposed to eat?"

Before I could even mention the hamper from Mrs. Karoo we rode over a ridge and saw five or six big jackrabbits nibbling on a nice patch of grass. They were not more than twenty feet away, and so casual that they didn't shy from the horses.

"We have a hen from Mrs. Karoo, but we might as well save it, since there's a fat bunch of rabbits," I said. "Shoot us a couple and we'll have rabbit for dinner, Deputy."

"Fair enough," Jackson said. There was a good-sized rabbit right in front of him. Jackson took out his new pistol, took rapid aim, and fired.

I don't know where that bullet went but it didn't go near the jackrabbit, who seemed quite undisturbed by the fact that he had just been shot at.

"Damn it!" Jackson said. My brother did not usually swear.

He leaned forward and fired twice, with the same result.

"Goddamn him, he's twitchy!" Jackson exclaimed. His face had begun to get red, as it always does when he's thwarted.

Jackson had two more shells in his pistol. He fired them both. The big jackrabbit hopped away a few feet and went back to nibbling grass.

Sheriff's Deputy Jackson Courtright had an empty gun, and no fat rabbit to show for it.

"Well, it's a good thing we've got that hen," I said.

# 5

IF THERE WERE contests for who could sulk the longest, Jackson Courtright would take the world championship. Of course, he came by this trait naturally—Father once sulked for a whole summer, so long that none of us could even remember what he was sulking about.

After missing the big jackrabbit six times running with his new pistol my brother, Jackson, pulled a towering sulk. He refused to taste a bit of Mrs. Karoo's hen, or her corn bread, or her tasty carrots, or the nice piece of mince pie she had wrapped up for us.

I ignored his sulk as best I could and had a healthy sampling of hen, corn bread, carrots, and pie.

When Jackson Courtright finished off the Yazee gang and went back into the jail to complete his nap, I don't think he gave any particular thought to what he had just done. I was the one who proclaimed him a hero, but I was merely his big sister, so he didn't pay much attention to me, either—at least not right away.

But when he woke up from his nap and everyone in Rita Blanca began to bow and scrape, it didn't take long for the praise to puff him up. Jackson had never been exactly modest, but he was a lot less modest now than he had been before the fight.

"There was something wrong with that jackrabbit," he announced, while I was eating. "That wasn't a normal jackrabbit."

"It looked normal to me—don't go blaming the rabbit because you couldn't hit it," I said.

"If it's around tomorrow I guess we'll see who can hit it," he told me.

"We've got bacon, thanks to Mrs. Karoo," I reminded him. "And Dodge City's still a far piece. We need to be off at first light."

"Leave whenever you please," Jackson told me. "I'll catch up with you as soon as I kill that rabbit.

"Mind your own business," he added, for emphasis.

We were, at the time, on one of the flattest plains in Kansas, a state noted for its flat plains.

"What if you get lost?" I inquired.

"You're a girl," he said. "I expect you'll be the one to get lost."

Actually it had occurred to me that despite all the tracks, we both might get lost. I had brought Father's old compass to answer that risk.

"All right, Jackson," I told him. "I see no point in arguing with a brick."

"A rabbit that fat will make a mighty good eating," Jackson said, and that brought an end to conversation for the night.

# 6

I WOKE WITH the dawn—a mighty big dawn on that great grassy plain. Being a believer in a hearty breakfast I made coffee and fried up a sizable portion of Mrs. Karoo's bacon. There was also a cold spud or two.

Jackson was still sulking. He accepted some coffee but turned up his nose at the bacon.

"I intend to kill what I eat," he said. I noticed that he had reloaded his pistol.

"How many bullets does that cartridge belt hold?" I inquired.

"Fifty," Jackson said.

"The fact that you earn fifteen dollars a month doesn't make you rich," I reminded him.

"Go to hell," Jackson said.

Most sisters have heard such sentiments from their brothers at one time or another. I paid it no mind. In fact I was looking forward to being an author. I could hardly wait to see my scribblings in print. If my brother chose to be mulish, that was his lookout.

I had hardly traveled a mile before I heard the crack of Jackson's pistol. Evidently he had closed with the jackrabbits. He shot five or six more times and then I ceased to hear the gunshots. Of course, I liked teasing my brother—what sister wouldn't?—but I did fully expect him to show up with a few jackrabbits, eventually. They aren't large targets, but then the human heart isn't a large target either, and Jackson had punctured six of them.

But I rode all day, under the burning sun, alone. If Irish Roy or any outlaw had popped out of a gully he would have had me. My only weapon was a small hatchet, useful for cutting firewood. I had supposed I would have the protection of the well-known Deputy Jackson Courtright, savior of Rita Blanca—but at the moment, the deputy was missing.

It was five in the afternoon when I spotted a dot on the horizon. In that part of Kansas dots stay on the horizon for a long time; it was almost an hour later when the dot turned into my brother. He caught up with me but made no greeting. There were no dead jackrabbits hanging from his saddle strings, but his ammunition belt, which had been full, was now half full at best.

There's a time to tease and a time to hold off teasing, and I had the feeling that this was a time to hold off. The hero of Rita Blanca was clearly not shooting his best.

"I'm glad you made it back," I told him. "I don't like camping alone."

"You could have sent the dern book with me," Jackson said. "That way you wouldn't have had to camp at all."

"It's my book, Jackson—I guess I have the right to supervise the printing."

"Beau Wheless thought that book up," Jackson said, in a tone that I didn't really appreciate. I felt like slapping him, to tell the truth, but before matters went that far I spotted a yearling steer grazing about one hundred yards away. The steer appeared to be slightly crippled. Spotting a lone steer was nothing unusual in that part of the country— cripples were often dropping out of the herds. Normally the cowboys would butcher such an animal, but this one had escaped, which was lucky for us. My thoughts quickly turned to beefsteak.

"I was wondering what we were going to do for supper," I said. "We're down to two spuds and a few carrots. Shoot that lost yearling and we'll feast."

Jackson immediately perked up at the opportunity. He was mainly a sunny boy, rarely capable of long sulks, as Father had been.

The yearling was a little skittish—it didn't allow Jackson to get right up on him, but Jackson eased along until he got to within about thirty feet. Then he leveled his pistol and fired.

The steer didn't flinch, as he would have if hit. He didn't like the sound of the gunfire, though, and went loping off, dragging one foot. Jackson fired a couple more times, but the yearling took no notice.

Jackson put spurs to his horse, caught up with the yearling, and fired three more times, but the yearling just kept going.

I expected Jackson to reload and keep trying. He pulled up his mustang and just sat there, empty pistol in hand. He looked confused. Then he put the empty pistol back in his holster and sat there some more.

I suppose it was then that I realized my brother had a big problem. He had economically killed the whole Yazee gang—six shots, six men—but now he couldn't hit a crippled steer from thirty feet away.

From then until the sun went down neither of us could think of much to say.

# 7

ABOUT THE ONLY difference between Rita Blanca and Dodge City was that Dodge City had a railroad. Both communities consisted of one long street with hovels and cheap frame houses on either side. Wagons came and went, and of course there were plenty of cowboys around, but I felt so glum about the situation with Jackson that I was not disposed even to find a good-looking cowboy to flirt with.

I was glum, but Jackson was in a deep funk. Somehow he had gone from being the best pistol shot in No Man's Land to being just an awkward seventeen-year-old who couldn't hit anything, from any distance. I was afraid he might shoot his own horse between the ears while aiming at a jackrabbit or a yearling. At least I hoped he wouldn't shoot his own horse, but it was a possibility that could not be entirely ruled out. And here we were approaching a town that was noted for its gunfighters—Billy Hickok, for example, or this fellow Earp, whom Aurel Imlah accused of being coarse.

When we finally came in sight of the ugly straggle of shacks and saloons that constituted Dodge City, Kansas, I thought it best to pull up for a moment and assess the situation.

"What am I going to do, Sis?" Jackson asked, his young brow as deeply furrowed as I had ever seen it.

"I can't hit the side of a barn," he added, glumly.

"We don't need to worry about you hitting the side of a barn," I told him.

"It's moving targets like this Marshal Earp that we have to worry about."

"But I hit the Yazees, every damn one of them," Jackson reminded me.

"The stakes were high on that occasion—I expect you got inspired." Jackson approved that comment.

"That's it! I got inspired," he said.

"Poets can get inspired—I suppose pistoleros can too," I added.

"The problem is, I ain't inspired anymore, which means I can't hit the side of a barn," he concluded.

"It does appear so," I admitted. "But there's no need to hit anything, right now. We came to Dodge City to get a book printed, not to engage in shoot-outs."

"I don't want to get in a shoot-out," Jackson admitted. "But this is supposed to be a mean old town. What if someone insults me—or you? Do you reckon I could get inspired enough to kill him?"

"From what I've read of poets, inspiration is pretty fickle," I told him. "What I think is that you ought to stop being a deputy until we finish our business here and head back home."

"Stop being a deputy?" Jackson asked—he immediately got red in the face. It was clear that the notion did not appeal to him.

"All right," I said, seeing that there was no point in pushing that suggestion. "You can stay a deputy, but do me one practical favor: put away that fancy knife and that fancy gun belt.

"And it wouldn't hurt to put the pistol and the holster in your saddlebags with them."

Once again, my suggestion didn't please.

"I'm a lawman—I like carrying a gun," Jackson said.

"I know you do," I told him. "And no reason you shouldn't. When we get home I'll buy you plenty of ammunition and you can practice until you're as good as anyone. But right now you aren't expert, except maybe in life-or-death situations, which is the very kind of situation we ought to avoid."

"I ain't taking off my pistol, Dodge City or no Dodge City," my brother said, exhibiting the well-known Courtright stubbornness.

"What about the knife and gun belt?" I persisted.

Jackson stuck out his jaw, as if he was determined to balk, but I just sat and let him think about it and finally he relaxed the famous Courtright jaw.

"I guess I wouldn't object to hiding my knife and gun belt—I've shot up most of the shells in the gun belt anyway."

Half a loaf is better than none—it's not a rule I could live by, but if it got us in and out of Dodge City alive, then who was I to argue?

# 8

IT WAS SOON evident that the citizens of Dodge City were not over-burdened with manners. Most of them didn't have anything better to do than stare at strangers; nor did they have any suspicion that staring at strangers was rude. Jackson and I trotted down the middle of the one wide street, and many an ugly head turned to look us over. Fortunately I can summon the well-known Courtright hauteur, available as needed, and I easily froze out such citizens as were unlucky enough to meet my eye.

Four men in black hats and dusty black coats were lounging in front of what seemed to the busiest of the numerous saloons. The men looked like brothers, but then again they could have just been partners in crime.

We didn't stop to inquire.

Even though I had given the men the merest glance I could feel their eyes following us as we passed on down the street. I told Jackson not to look at them, and he didn't, but I still had the feeling that the Earp brothers, for that was who the men were, felt it was their right to watch our every move.

It made me want to go back and slap their faces, which is what I would have done in Virginia if four ill-mannered ruffians had stared at me so insolently. But I wasn't in Virginia—I was an author on the look-out for a printer and couldn't afford to be sidetracked because a quartet of uncouth men had nothing better to do than stare at me.

Fortunately the printer's office, which also happened to be the newspaper office, was in plain sight toward the north end of the one long street.

An old bald man with big freckles on his head seemed to be in charge. The print shop was uncommonly untidy and the old printer himself could be fairly described as a kind of human inkblot; but he was friendly to a fault—probably glad to see visitors walk in who behaved decently and could actually read. The printer's name was Tesselinck—I believe he may have been a Dutchman or something. Now and then he would forget himself and suck on his own pen—all in all not an attractive habit, but we were in Dodge City, where mere friendliness counted for more than it might have in other places.

I plunked my scribbled-up manuscript down on his counter and got right to the point.

"This is a write-up about the big shoot-out with the Yazee gang down in Rita Blanca," I said. "I sent a telegram about it. I'd like to get it printed up as soon as possible—my brother and I are anxious to head back."

"Are you the telegraph lady down in Rita Blanca?" he asked.

"Yes sir, that's me."

"Not many females are trained telegraphers," he commended.

"Sir, I have no interest in statistics," I told him. "Will you print my booklet or won't you?"

"I see you're crispy," he said pleasantly. "I'm a printer, that's my calling. I will print your book but I have to admit that my eyesight's feeble. I might need some help with the handwriting."

"I'll help you," I promised. "How long do you expect this will take?"

Mr. Tesselinck rifled through the pages, getting several of them smudged with ink.

"I'm hoping to get two hundred copies," I explained, at which the inky old printer made a gesture of hopelessness.

"I don't have that much paper," he said. "I might manage fifty right now, and I'll do the rest when my big paper order comes in."

"I suppose fifty's a start," I said.

"How about a cover?" he asked. "It'd sell better with some kind of picture on the cover."

Jackson, who had a fair hand for sketching, was looking bored.

"My brother can draw a cover," I told the printer. "Could you loan him a pen and some paper?"

In a minute Jackson was equipped with some big pencils and a good scratch pad.

I supposed Jackson would consult me about the content of the picture, but he didn't. When he had done about a third of the cover I asked to see it, a favor he allowed reluctantly.

The picture showed Jackson himself, or his equivalent, in a black coat and a black hat, neither of which he possessed, shooting at six startled outlaws, whose horses were rearing and plunging about. One outlaw lay dead in the street and another was in the process of toppling off his horse. The detail of the horses was particularly fine—Jackson Courtright was certainly no slouch when it came to drawing horses in motion.

In the drawing Jackson had on boots, when in fact he had been barefooted; but the change that annoyed me most was that he had simply left me out.

"Jackson, where am I?" I asked. "I was five feet from you when you shot the Yazees—I'm the one who yelled at you to draw, remember? Why'd you leave me out?"

Jackson looked annoyed at being questioned. Why should anyone, particularly his sister, question him? After all, he was the regnant male.

"You're a girl," he said smugly. "I saw no reason to put you in."

Quick as a striking snake I slapped his face.

He turned beet red, threw down the sketch, and stomped out the door. It was hardly the first time the little coward had fled my temper. We were brother and sister, after all.

Mr. Tesselinck went right on numbly setting type. His eyesight seemed to have improved.

"Do you have anything against girls?" I asked. I was pretty mad.

"Not a thing, Miss Courtright," he said. "In fact, I married one."

# 9

JACKSON CAME BACK and sulked awhile but I bluntly tackled him on the matter at hand.

"Haven't you ever heard of damsels in distress?" I asked him. "Plenty of dime novels have damsels in distress on the cover."

"Who says you were in distress?" he asked. "You seemed cool as a cucumber to me."

But he finally agreed to sketch me in, and even drew me in profile, which is what I preferred. And when my little outlaw book was printed, I was on the cover for the first few editions. But the book kept being printed and reprinted until more than a million copies were in circulation, in the process of which I slowly slipped off the cover, seldom to reappear, which proves nothing at all except that the world belongs to men.

Meanwhile, back at Mr. Tesselinck's inky print shop in Dodge City, Kansas, the typesetting went on until the sun went down, at which point Jackson and I had to face the prospect of spending the night in this ugly, dirty town.

When we asked Mr. T., as we had begun to refer to him, whether there was a boardinghouse in town he shook his head. "There's a boardinghouse, all right," he said. "Marshal Earp's sister-in-law runs it—I fear it's largely a house of ill repute."

Jackson perked up at that news. Having failed so far to locate any decent kissing, I expect he would have made do with some of the indecent sort, but I was determined not to let him slip off down the road of bad habits on our trip.

Mr. T., though inky, had neighborly instincts. Once he realized that we were stuck in Dodge, he immediately invited us to spend the night at his house, which was just behind the shop. He had a wife named Maudie, and was confident enough as a husband to be sure Maudie would have us.

He was right. Maudie Tesselinck was pretty, jolly, chubby, and as full of mischief as a parrot. Her house wasn't neat but it was cheery. Maudie had a big salt-cured ham hanging in her kitchen. Ham and red gravy formed the basis of our dinner.

"It's a trial, having to live with an old man who sucks up ink," Maudie informed us cheerfully. "Besides that, his head's just getting to be one big freckle."

Then she cackled merrily at her own domestic plight, and gave us some muffins with molasses.

"I've heard there's a large criminal element in Dodge City?" I asked. "Is that true?"

"There's five Earps—there's your criminal element," Mr. Tesselinck told us firmly. We had discovered that his first name was Joel but we weren't sure we were welcome to address him informally yet.

"Pond scum!" Maudie said emphatically, referring to the Earps. "Dog dung—that's all they are."

"I think we saw the Earps this morning, as we were riding in," I mentioned.

"If you passed the Tascosa Saloon you saw them," Maudie said. "They're always there, looking for a sucker or a weakling to pounce on."

Joel Tesselinck played the harmonica, and we all sang to our hearts' content.

Jackson had a fine baritone voice, and I once thought of being an opera singer myself. Maudie brought out some castanets, and we all fell to dancing—now and then Maudie would even throw in a Swiss yodel. If there had been any neighbors I'm sure we would have kept them awake—I suspect it was mostly the coyotes who listened to our concert. A few of the coyotes even made free to join in.

When it came time for bed Maudie made me a pallet on a little porch where she did her churning. Jackson was assigned a settee, which was too short for him and gave him a crick so bad that he spent most of the next day trying to get his head realigned with his neck. Joel Tesselinck boasted such a mighty snore that it kept us both awake.

How Maudie slept with a snore like that was a mystery—I suppose wives just somehow get used to husbands. Next morning she was as lively as ever. She kept four or five tame geese and gave us each a goose egg for breakfast, a dish that filled me up from toe to crown.

When we were leaving, Maudie gave me such a hug that I knew I had found a new friend.

"Just ride on past the Earps and button your lip," she said as I was getting ready to visit the print shop and pack my booklets.

It sounded like good advice to me—the Earps' grimy appearance had put me off them anyway. One of Maudie's geese followed me all the way to the print shop but I have little patience with geese and ignored this one as best I could.

# 10

WITH MY HELP Joel Tesselinck soon finished printing up my booklet, while Jackson applied himself to gluing on the covers. Joel ran out of paper one shy of fifty—forty-nine copies is all we had to take home with us.

"That order of paper could come any day," Joel assured us. "You're welcome to stay around and wait, if you like. Maudie enjoys your company."

"I wish we could stay," I said, "but I'm the telegraph lady of Rita Blanca and I have to get back to my duties. Forty-nine copies is better than none."

Little did I suspect, at the time, what a rarity had been created that day in Dodge City. Long after No Man's Land became a part of the state of Oklahoma, when there were only a few old-timers left who could remember seeing the West as it had been and maybe made the acquaintance of such famous figures as Custer and Cody, Hickok and the Earps, people began to make collections of books about the Western life that was now long gone. The bright star of outlaw books was that first little forty-nine-copy edition of my *Banditti* write-up.

Joel Tesselinck was true to his word. He soon got in his paper and printed off the other one hundred and fifty one copies, which he promptly dispatched to Rita Blanca by old Josh, the mail runner.

But the paper for the new batch was of a different weight from the paper of the first batch, so the great prize for collectors was that first little forty-nine-copy run. I was told that a collector in Kansas City paid five thousand dollars for a copy of that first little print-up—though that may be an exaggeration.

After all, some of the finest homes in the West could be bought for a lot less than five thousand dollars. But there are hundreds of fine homes in the West, and only the forty-nine copies of my book—so if rarity is the standard, I guess my *Banditti* booklet deserves the prize.

All that, however, is well ahead of my story.

We wrapped the forty-nine booklets in two neat packages, tied with string. When it came time to go Jackson was aching to put his fancy gun belt back on, but I persuaded him to hold off until we were out of town. Instead of going back down the main street, past the saloons and their riffraff, we cut back behind the saloons and would have passed out of Dodge City without incident had it not been for the inconvenient fact that the Earp brothers were also out behind the saloons, in the process of shoeing their horses. Three of the Earps were in their undershirts, working at their sweaty task, while the fourth brother, who turned out to be Wyatt, seemed content to supervise. He still wore the same grimy coat and dusty hat.

"Uh-oh, there they are," Jackson said, when he saw the four Earps.

"I'll do the talking, if there is talking," I informed him.

The three Earps who were working away at their horseshoeing glanced at us without much interest, but the indolent Wyatt, who sported a mustache that looked nearly as scratchy as Ted Bunsen's, strolled out to intercept us.

"Hold up there, young lady," he said. "What's a pretty pullet like you doing in my town?"

"I had some printing business to attend to, if you must know," I told him. "What makes you think it's your town?"

"Because I'm Wyatt Earp," he said, "I'm the marshal here in Dodge."

"That makes you an employee, not an owner," I pointed out. "The town can buy you or the town can fry you."

I looked him in the eye, dispensing a bit of Courtright hauteur along with my glance.

Marshal Earp looked shocked. I doubt anyone had stated his true position quite so bluntly, much less looking at him as if he were merely an insolent worm.

"She's got you there, Wyatt," one of the sweaty brothers called out. "The town can buy you or the town can fry you."

"You shut up, Virg," Wyatt said, without even turning around. He did turn red in the face, though. Though he did not appear to be as old as some of the brothers, I suppose he had appointed himself the boss of the family.

"Where do you think you're going, anyway?" Wyatt asked me. "There's nothing much but prairie in the direction you're pointed."

"That's incorrect, Marshal," I said. "There's the town of Rita Blanca, and we'll be slow in getting back to it if we stand here exchanging pleasantries with you and your brothers half the day."

At that all three of the horseshoeing brothers snickered. It was clear that they were prepared to enjoy seeing their ill-tempered brother taken down a peg. That's usually the way it is with family groups.

Marshal Earp wasn't liking the drift of the conversation, but he didn't seem to know how to regain his advantage—or the advantage he first seemed to assume.

"Who's that boy?" he asked, pointing at Jackson.

Jackson hated to be called a boy. He turned red in the face himself, but I gave him a stern look and he managed to hold his tongue.

"That's my brother," I said. "If you're through jabbering we'd like to be on our way."

"Rita Blanca's a far piece," Wyatt said. "You'll be having to camp."

"If we do, it's our lookout," I replied—this struck the brothers as hilarious, though I had not meant to be funny when I said it. The brothers temporarily left off horseshoeing in order to watch me take their brother Wyatt down a peg.

This was too much for Wyatt, who whirled on his brothers in a fury.

"For two cents I'd cut you all down!" he yelled.

The brother called Virg at once put down his farrier's hammer, dug in his pockets, and came out with two pennies—these he casually pitched in the direction of his brother Wyatt.

"I doubt that comment," he said. "If you shoot us you'll have no one to do the work when your horse comes lame due to having shoes that don't fit."

"And we know you're too tight to hire a professional blacksmith," another brother observed. "Without us you'd soon be stranded," he added.

"I can hammer a shoe on a goddamn horse if I must!" the marshal informed them loudly. "All three of you can go to hell, as far as I'm concerned.

"I'm the marshal of Dodge City," he said, with emphasis, "and you all are just my deputies."

"I'm a deputy," Jackson suddenly piped up.

I could have kicked him—but the kick would have come too late.

Wyatt looked at him in puzzlement, probably thinking that he had misheard.

"I'm a deputy in Rita Blanca—Sheriff Bunsen will vouch for me," Jackson declared.

All four Earps seemed momentarily stunned by Jackson's claim, which they probably considered improbable.

Brother Virg was the first to recover.

"We heard some tale about the Yazee boys being wiped out—it came over the telegraph, I understand," he said. "The rumor is that a young deputy shot all six of them dead.

"So many lies come over the telegraph that we didn't pay much attention to the report," he admitted.

"Excuse me, but I happen to be the telegraph operator in Rita Blanca," I told them. "For your future information, no lies come over my telegraph if I can help it. And the Yazee brothers are entirely dead."

Before the Earps could respond I ripped open one of the packages of my booklet and handed a copy to Marshal Earp. Of course at the time I had no idea it would become so valuable or I wouldn't have wasted one on a yokel such as Marshal Earp.

But I had been warned about the Earps, and I wanted to go. The booklet would explain matters to the Earps, if they were really interested.

Wyatt stared at the booklet a moment, and then walked over and handed it to Virgil.

"You're our best reader, Virg," he said. "See what you think."

We trotted off to the southwest, and no one tried to stop us. Jackson and I were probably a bigger surprise to the Earps than they were to us.

I didn't suppose for a moment, though, that we'd seen the last of the famous marshal of Dodge.

# 11

I SUPPOSE THERE'S nothing like a little female impertinence to attract a certain kind of man. I knew I had made a strong impression on Marshal Wyatt Earp and I fully expected him to show up in my life again someday, looking moony.

What I didn't realize is that I'd made an even stronger impression on his brother Virgil—the Earp who had been assigned to read my little *Banditti* book.

When supper time came Jackson and I were forced to rely once more on the ubiquitous prairie chicken. Maudie Tesselinck had offered us goose eggs, but I found goose eggs too rich to digest. I asked Jackson to get us a couple of prairie chickens, which rather put him on the spot. I knew after the embarrassment of the crippled steer he was not really in the mood to be shooting at birds with a gun, but he had put on his fancy gun belt and his expensive knife and was about to go harass the prairie chickens when he spotted a rider coming our way.

"I guess it's that darn marshal," he said. "I suppose he means to arrest us."

"I doubt it," I told him. "He's probably just got courting on his mind, which is my problem and not yours."

"You think every man you know is out to court you," Jackson grumbled.

It was a fair criticism. I had always been the prettiest Courtright, not to mention the smartest, and I do expect my share of masculine attention.

When I turned to inspect the oncoming rider I soon realized it wasn't Wyatt Earp.

"It's not Wyatt," I said. "It's Virgil, their best reader."

"Hello folks—got any vittles?" Virgil asked when he had loped up.

"We're hoping for hens—prairie hens," I said. "My brother's just about to go gather in a couple.

"Please feel free to dismount," I added, since Virgil Earp was still planted in the saddle.

He did dismount, but slowly, as if he might be stepping into quicksand. By good luck Jackson soon had us three plump hens—he chunked them, which was the surest way.

"It wouldn't be economical to waste shells on a prairie chicken," he said.

Virgil Earp had worked up such an appetite that he consumed his hen while it was only half cooked. He contributed nothing to the conversation but his bird was soon reduced to bones. Virgil had clear blue eyes and a nice mouth.

Even without conversation, I was beginning to suspect that Virgil Earp was sweet.

"Why'd you follow us?" I asked him boldly.

Virgil seemed embarrassed by the question—he shrugged, as if to indicate his confusion, but he could not really rise to the question.

I thought I'd try to help him.

"I bet you liked my book so much you couldn't wait to talk to me about it," I said.

Virgil looked even more embarrassed—in fact he blushed.

"Wyatt, he always makes it out that I'm a fine reader, but it ain't true," Virgil confessed. "I can puzzle out some words but that book of your was such a thicket of print that just looking at it made my head swim."

"That dern book was probably all lies anyway," Jackson said—an unwelcome opinion and one that startled me. I suppose there's no overestimating the venom little brothers store up in regard to their big sisters.

"Jackson, you're the hero of that book," I pointed out. "It's about you saving the town from the Yazee gang. Why would you be telling our guest that it was mostly lies?"

"You have got me into trouble many times by lying," Jackson said, after which he shut up and sulked.

Virgil Earp seemed to take little interest in this family dispute. He had not cared to tell me why he followed us, but the way he kept sneaking looks at us gave me a pretty clear idea of what was on his mind. He seemed to have no interest at all in my book, or Jackson, or the Yazee gang.

"I'm the deputy that killed the whole Yazee gang," Jackson informed him.

All of a sudden my little brother began to want attention—he was eager to make an impression on one of the famous Earp brothers.

"Probably just beginner's luck," Virgil said, referring to Jackson's famous feat.

Jackson looked crushed. Probably Virgil Earp had just casually stated what Jackson had been feeling ever since the shoot-out: that his slaughter of the Yazees was just beginner's luck.

He didn't say another word, but he took his bedding and walked off into the dusk, meaning to make his own camp.

"Your little brother's touchy," Virgil said mildly. "If he really killed all them Yazees, then why wouldn't it be beginner's luck?"

"Let's stick to the point, Mr. Earp," I insisted. "I asked you why you followed us way out here, and so far I've had no answer."

"Why, I want to marry you, why else would I come?" Virgil said. "I'm tired of living with Wyatt and Morgan and Jim. Wyatt's mean and Morgan and Jim are lazy—I do most of the work but I get few compliments."

It was a proposal, if not a very elegant one. Personally I have rarely been put off by proposals, however awkwardly phrased. After all, a proposal is a compliment. Back in Virginia, as a lively young belle, I received at least fifty proposals, many of them as awkward as Virgil Earp's.

"I can see why your troubles with your brothers would be irksome," I told him. "But that's one trouble, and marrying me is another. I'm the telegraph lady of Rita Blanca, which is a heavy responsibility. I fear it leaves me insufficient time for matrimony."

I don't believe it had occurred to Virgil Earp that a woman might actually turn him down. After all, his family had long held a commanding position, if only in Dodge City. The Earps were in the habit of choosing, not of being chosen. The notion of rejection was a notion that seldom entered their heads.

"You mean you won't marry me, you fool?" Virgil said, a look of frank astonishment on his face.

"No sir, I won't," I told him. "I have my job and I also have my fiancé, Sheriff Theodore Bunsen."

Ted Bunsen wasn't exactly my fiancé, but I had no qualms about using him as an excuse.

"Thanks anyway, Mr. Earp—I do appreciate your interest."

"What's a dern sheriff got to do with anything?" Virgil asked. "We Earps don't tolerate sheriffs. If this one won't listen to reason, I'll just kill him."

I saw that the young man was in earnest. To him it was that simple. Killing—plain, simple, immediate—was the frontier way of removing animate obstacles, whether beast or man.

When Virgil Earp had shown up, with his sweet blue eyes and shy little smile, I had beguiled myself with the notion that he was the good Earp, a big cut above his brothers. His blunt and stubborn approach to matrimony caused me to rethink this conclusion.

"You mean I've ridden all the way out here to court you and you won't marry me?" Virgil said, looking agitated.

"Mr. Earp, let me remind you that we've only met this morning," I said.

Virgil Earp just looked blank—in his mind the fact that we had only met that morning had no bearing on the question at hand.

"I am hardly the sort of woman who plights her troth between dawn and sundown," I told him firmly.

Actually, I was exactly that kind of woman, but I was in no mood to admit it to Virgil Earp.

Virgil squeezed his temples, as people do when they're experiencing a headache.

"Damn it, you're just too yappy!" he concluded. "Morg said I should let you be, and Morg was right."

"At least you enjoyed a tasty partridge," I pointed out.

"My brothers will josh me good, when they hear about this!" Virgil said.

Then he got on his horse and rode away.

# 12

"IT'S A PUZZLE to me why fellows keep proposing to you, Nellie," Jackson remarked, as we kept plodding on toward Rita Blanca.

"Why wouldn't they?" I inquired.

"Because you're not very nice," Jackson declared.

"Well, I could be nice, if I was approached properly," I told him. "The problem is that I can't find a gentleman who's polished enough to approach me properly."

"Being picky is a good way to end up an old maid," Jackson pointed out—and then he saw something which made him forget whether I was nice or not.

"Is that a white mule?" he asked, pointing to the south. "You rarely ever see a white mule."

Sure enough it was a white mule making its way across the prairie, with a stout lady on it. Two small brown men, each leading a pack animal, followed the white mule with the stout lady on it. Besides leading a pack mule, one of the small brown men carried a good-sized parasol, which he endeavored, more or less, to keep between the stout lady and the strong prairie sun. Fortunately for the two brown men the white mule was proceeding at a very slow pace.

And if that wasn't enough to think about, a giant gray dog the size of an antelope bounced up and began to bay at us.

"Well, Jackson, it's a small world," I told him.

"What's small about it? This seems like a pretty big prairie to me," Jackson insisted.

"It is a big prairie but the heavy woman with the two sepoys and the white mule and the Irish wolfhound is Hroswitha Jubb—the author of *Jubb's Journey* to here and there," I pointed out.

"Oh my Lord—you mean that bossy writer who married Uncle Teddy?" Jackson asked.

"That's right—we met her in Richmond," I reminded him.

The Irish wolfhound was still baying at us, and the hackles on the back of its neck were standing up.

"Hers are the most popular travel books in the world," I reminded him. "I read *Jubb's Journey to Tashkent* while we were on the boat from St. Louis."

Jackson showed less interest in Ros Jubb or her books than he did in the wolfhound.

"A dog that big could chew off your leg so fast you wouldn't even miss it," he observed.

Ros Jubb turned around to shush the dog and immediately recognized two of her in-laws. She was wearing a pair of large green goggles but immediately took them off when she spotted us. As I expected, as soon as her dog settled down, she got right to the point.

"Hello, Miss Courtright—I'm glad it's you," she said. "I'll be wanting an exclusive interview with Jackson as soon as we make our camp."

No one had ever accused Hroswitha Jubb of being likable—our Uncle Teddy had nearly resorted to poisoning himself in order to escape her, but he finally chose the less painful option of moving to San Francisco.

"As to that, Aunt Ros, you'll have to speak to our representative, who resides in Rita Blanca," I told her.

"What do you mean, your representative, young lady?" Ros bellowed. If she had had a poison dart about her at that moment I suspect she might have thrown it at me.

"His name is Beauregard Wheless—and you can locate him at the general store," I said. "I'm sure he would be happy to arrange an interview, though several reporters are there ahead of you," I told her. I didn't actually know that any reporters were already in Rita Blanca, but it wouldn't hurt to have Ros worry about the prospect a little.

"Since when do young ladies of good families have 'representatives'?" she asked, not at all happy with the information I was providing.

To devil her even more—after all, she was my aunt—I reached in my saddlebags and extracted a copy of my *Banditti* booklet, which I handed to her. I was down to a mere forty-seven copies and we weren't even back to Rita Blanca yet.

"If you're interested in the famous shoot-out, here's my own account, Aunt Ros," I told her. "It is strictly factual. I plan to sell it for twenty-five cents, but since you're my auntie, your copy is free."

My aunt Ros took the booklet and looked at it skeptically—probably she was shocked that a member of her own family would be so bold as to get ahead of her on a writing project.

"You're a severe disappointment to me, Nellie Courtright!" she said in a viperish tone. "I shall have to speak to your parents about you, on my next opportunity."

"I fear you'll have a long wait, Auntie," I told her. "Mother and Father are both dead."

Then she turned her attention to Jackson.

"Did you actually shoot six men, Jackson?"

"Yes, ma'am, I didn't miss a one," Jackson told her.

"And you didn't think it proper to talk to your famous auntie about this shoot-out?" she asked him. "After all, I am a world-famous writer."

Jackson just shrugged. "I didn't know you was anywhere around," he said—truthfully, no doubt.

Aunt Ros put her green goggles back on—they made her look like some species of giant fly. She didn't favor either of us with another word—she just nodded to her sepoys, flicked her white mule with a small mule flicker, and plodded off, followed by her sepoys and her wolfhound.

"I wouldn't mind having a white mule myself," Jackson observed. "When it's a question of prairie traveling, I mostly prefer mules over horses."

"I have no preference," I admitted, "but the nature of the mount is not my worry right now. As soon as it's light tomorrow morning I want you to hurry on to Rita Blanca and see our representative, Beau Wheless, before you talk to a single reporter. You tell Beau to insist on ten dollars an interview—not a penny less, not even to Aunt Ros."

"Ten dollars?" he asked, looking puzzled. "Why would anyone pay ten dollars to talk to me?"

"Because you shot six Yazees and you're a hero," I reminded him.

"Oh," my brother said.

# 13

BY THE TIME I had been back in Rita Blanca thirty minutes I'd sold every single copy of my *Banditti* booklet. Demand was so fierce that I didn't even keep one for myself. Nearly fifty people were lined up at the telegraph office when I trotted up. The crowd practically tore off my saddlebags in their desperate hurry to get their copy of the book. Talk about selling like hotcakes! The forty-seven copies immediately changed hands—I had to get out a big tablet and take down the names of all the disappointed customers who wanted to secure a copy once the new batch arrived.

Now that I've had most of a lifetime to think about the matter I'm convinced that there's no power like outlawry to heat up public curiosity. Folks just can't get enough of outlaws, don't ask me why! Just for firing off the six bullets that killed the six Yazees, my brother, Jackson, became famous for the rest of his life, a fact that Jackson, who was mostly a nice boy, hadn't really come to grips with yet.

I had been right about the reporters too. Several members of that species were waiting with the others at my office: they had hired a stagecoach in Leavenworth and had come racing hell-for-leather over the prairies, while several others, from papers all over the country, had bought or rented horses in order to join the chase. According to Aurel Imlah, nearly twenty reporters were in town—they formed a raucous mob at best.

As soon as would-be booklet buyers stopped writing their names on my tablet I rushed off a quick telegram to Joel Tesselinck, telling him to double the order and dispatch the books by Pony Express or any express. Then I closed my window and skipped over to the jail, where I found my admirer Sheriff Ted Bunsen smoking a cigar and drinking straight whiskey out of a glass.

"Uh-oh," I said. "Are you drinking whiskey while on duty, Theodore?"

"What's it look like?" Teddy countered, in that tone men use when they consider that women are being bossy.

"When I left this place you were dour but reliable," I pointed out. "Now I'm back and you're drinking."

Actually, just looking at Teddy touched me a little. He was so hopeless I could almost find it in me to be in love with him. A helpless, hopeless man is often pretty close to irresistible, or at least that's the case if you're stuck in Rita Blanca, as I was.

"I suppose Jackson's hiding from the reporters, like I told him to," I said.

"Hide from a reporter—it'd be like hiding from a flea!" Teddy said. "Some of them have been here two days, waiting for you to get back so they can pester Deputy Courtright. And all because of beginner's luck."

As I said, the man's melancholy touched me. I took his face in my hands and gave him a little kiss.

"Listen to me, Teddy—this is Rita Blanca's one chance to make some money," I said. "These newspapermen are Yazee crazy—they'll pay good money for interviews with anyone who witnessed the shoot-out. I'm surprised Beau Wheless hasn't already set things up. I suppose he got overwhelmed."

"He didn't get overwhelmed," Ted told me. "He got dead."

"What?"

I was purely stunned. Beau Wheless, the principal merchant of Rita Blanca, dead. I felt trembly for a moment from the shock.

"That mangy old cat that nobody likes bit Beau on the finger," Ted explained. "The wound didn't bleed—in no time Beau got blood poisoning so bad the Doc couldn't save him. We buried him yesterday. Now the whole shebang belongs to Hungry Billy."

It was true that nobody liked the mangy cat, which had hissed at me several times.

"Is that why you're drunk on the job?" I asked Ted. "Because you miss Beau?"

"Oh no," Ted admitted. "I was not that fond of Beau—he always overcharged for brooms and the like."

"Then why are you drunk?" I asked.

"Because we think the Indian's around," Ted admitted. "Josh Tell thinks he glimpsed him."

Aurel Imlah had once mentioned the Indian, when he was visiting Father. He was said to be a giant outlaw who roamed the plains alone. No one could say exactly what crimes he may have committed, if any. Aurel thought he might have glimpsed him once, from a distance, in a snowstorm. No tribe claimed the Indian, evidently. No lawman had ever gotten close to him, and no soldier had ever shot at him.

"I don't know that I believe in this Indian. Sounds like the work of somebody's imagination."

"If you don't believe he's out there, then you're a fool!" Teddy said. "It's from worrying about the Indian that's got me drunk on the job."

"Even if he exists, he's just one Indian," I pointed out. "I doubt one Indian could massacre a whole town."

Teddy didn't answer—he didn't stop drinking, either.

# 14

ONE THING I had figured out in my twenty-two years is that in a crisis situation it's a mistake to stop and think. If Jackson had spent even one second thinking about the rampaging Yazees, he and most of the rest of us in Rita Blanca would now be dead.

So, when I found Ted drunk in his jail cell and the street buzzing with reporters, I didn't hesitate. I grabbed a shotgun from Ted's arsenal, went out into the street, and fired both barrels straight up in the air—too straight, as it happened: number four shot was soon raining down upon us, along with a crow and a pigeon that had accidentally flown into the blast. Fortunately neither of the birds hit a newspaperman in their descent.

At first blush the newsies appeared to be a scraggly lot, the sort of men who smoked their cigars down to stubs and spilled whiskey on their vests.

The shotgun blasts easily got their attention.

"Nothing to be alarmed about, gentlemen," I said. "I'm Marie Antoinette Courtright—call me Nellie for short—and you'll all need to file your stories with me at the telegraph office, which is just up the street and will be open for business in ten minutes."

"That's all very well, Miss, but where's Deputy Courtright?" a wiry little terrier of a fellow asked me. His yellow cravat was far from spotless; his name was Charlie Hepworth—many years later I was to work with Charlie Hepworth again.

"The deputy's attending to some bookkeeping at the moment," I told them. "He happens to be my brother."

"Who cares if he's your brother?" a tall, skinny fellow declared. He had a face as thin as a china plate.

"The deputy will soon be available for interviews—though not free gratis, of course," I informed them.

The announcement was not well received, to say the least.

"What do you mean, not free gratis?" the tall fellow said. "I'm Cunningham Calhoun, of the *New York World,* by the way, and most people are familiar with my byline."

"Not most people in Rita Blanca, sir—our newspapers arrive irregularly, if at all," I reminded him. "We're in No Man's Land, remember."

"No Man's Land—is that where we are, Miss?" a tall, smiling fellow with a few too many teeth crammed into the front of his mouth inquired. I liked the man right off, don't ask me why. He wore a red bowler hat, the first I'd seen.

"I thought we were in Texas," he added. "Our readers welcome news from Texas."

"You're off by a day or two if you're looking for Texas," I told him. I liked him so much I might have eloped with him to Texas, if he'd asked me, but failing that, there was money to be made.

"How much are we supposed to shell out for these interviews?" Charlie Hepworth inquired.

"A mere ten dollars apiece," I told them, deciding on the bold approach.

The newsmen looked a little annoyed, but none of them threatened to leave.

"I hear Hroswitha Jubb's headed this way," the young charmer with the red bowler and the snaggle teeth remarked. "Know anything about that?"

"She's my aunt," I informed them. "We passed her yesterday. Aunt Ros moves at a calm pace but I expect she'll be showing up later in the day."

"We've heard about an Indian—what can you tell us about him, Miss?" Cunningham Calhoun asked.

"I'm a telegrapher, not a bulletin board," I told them. "I'm managing the Yazee story, which so far as I know is the only story. Rumors about an Indian are probably just yarns."

But the young fellow in the red bowler had a mind of his own.

"Oh, I don't know, Miss," he said. "These outlaw stories are a dime a dozen. I'd rather find out about the Indian, if I could do it without getting scalped."

"Now, stop your yapping, Zenas," Charlie Hepworth told him irritably.

"That's right, Zenas," Cunningham Calhoun put in. "We've traveled here in grave discomfort to get the Yazee story, and I mean to get it and, I hope, get it now."

The young fellow named Zenas just laughed and wandered off. He had never bothered to line up anyway. His casual attitude toward the Yazee story irritated me but I suppose if I had been a reporter I'd have been more interested in the Indian, myself. After all, as Zenas suggested, heroes killing outlaws happens in a lot of stories—all the way back to David and Goliath, I suppose. It just so happened that my brother, Jackson, had been the David in this case.

But a giant Indian roaming the prairies, only glimpsed in snowstorms here and there—now that was original, as the young man named Zenas had figured out at once.

Eager as I was for Jackson to show up and start earning ten dollars an interview, the pesky side of me made me kind of turn. To their annoyance I left the sweaty group of whiskey-stained reporters and went right down the street after the reporter with the red hat.

When I caught up with him he was out behind the general store, staring at the wide prairie as if he expected the big Indian to rise up and announce himself in some newsworthy way.

"Excuse me, sir—I didn't get your name," I told him. "I need to put you on my list, assuming you do want to interview my brother."

"I'm Zenas Clark," he said, ignoring my ploy about the list. "I have a question for you."

"What?"

"If we were to get better acquainted would you ever expect me to call you Marie Antoinette?

"A name like that could dampen the flame," he said, with an engaging smile.

I should have slapped him but instead I blushed. I've always found it devilish hard to maintain a solid stance when standing face-to-face with a fellow I might end up kissing.

"You're as rude as a rooster, Mr. Clark," I told him. "What makes you think there might be a flame?"

But that was bravado—just bravado. I was smitten with this fellow Zenas Clark, and he knew it.

"You only need call me Nellie," I conceded.

# 15

THE FACT IS I've never been able to keep my hands off any man with even half an ounce of appeal—my susceptibility, which, I suppose, is what you'd call it, showed up at an early age, which may have been one reason Father chose to haul me out in the middle of a howling wilderness, to a place where there were very few men for me to seduce.

In sedate Virginia my behavior with the young males of my acquaintance was a scandal. I was too wellborn to be called a slut, though if I'd had bolder male cousins I might have deserved the word. At first I had to content myself with a lot of playing doctor, sneaking my little boy cousins into the barn and persuading them to drop their pants so I could inspect their little pricks, offering them, in turn, a leisurely look at my little pink notch.

Of course, I was eager to get beyond doctor-and-nurse games, which, fortunately for me, I was able to accomplish when my tall, lanky cousin Templeton spent a summer with us. Cousin Templeton was three years older than me and rapidly introduced me to the pleasures of copulation. The act, I found, took mastering, but I was getting the go of it pretty well when my pesky cousin Julia spotted us doing it, and promptly told the grown-ups, after which cousin Templeton soon found himself shipped off to West Point, shortly after which our family headed west.

It soon developed that my new admirer, Zenas Clark, was every bit as entertaining when it came to copulation as Cousin Templeton had been. He happened to notice that Joe Schwartz didn't seem to be anywhere around his livery stable, whose considerable loft was filled with fragrant prairie hay.

We were soon in that loft, kissing and probing. Unfortunately, I still had my corduroy trousers on, which slowed matters down a bit and irked Zenas Clark considerably.

"You'd think it would have occurred to a girl your age why women are supposed to wear skirts," Zenas complained. "How can I get in when you're wearing those damn pants?"

"If you'd let me be for a second I'd be glad to shuck them off," I told him.

He let me be and I stood up and was about to shuck them off, when who should appear out of the hay but my brother, Jackson. He had hay in his hair and he was pointing his pistol at Zenas Clark.

"That's my sister, leave her be, you skunk!" Jackson demanded.

Zenas Clark was so startled at having a gun poked in his face that he temporarily lost his voice and his ardor too. Zenas just sat there, shocked.

"Stop it, Jackson!" I insisted. "Put that pistol down before I box your ears!"

"I'm the deputy sheriff of Rita Blanca—you'll not be boxing my ears," my brother said. "This skunk was about to defile you—I saw it myself."

"Be that as it may, I want you to put that pistol back in the holster I got you," I told him. "I will not be having you shoot Mr. Clark, who happens to be my fiancé."

I was talking to Jackson when I said it, but I was looking at Zenas Clark—one of my little tests of a new suitor was to see how he reacted when I suddenly announced our engagement. It was merely a trick, a test of the suitor's mettle. I had only been enjoying the kisses of Zenas Clark a few minutes, but my sense was he would make as good a fiancé as I was likely to snare in the environs of Rita Blanca.

When I said it Jackson still had his gun stuck in Zenas's face, but when Jackson finally came down off his high horse and put the pistol back in its holster, Zenas's reaction was a snaggle-toothed grin. He grinned, but he didn't speak out, as I expected him to.

"You're not going to deny that we're engaged, I hope, Mr. Clark?" I said, with a touch of the old Courtright hauteur.

"Why, no—I'd be pleased to be engaged to you, but on one condition," Zenas said.

"Which is?"

"Which is that you never wear those damn pants again."

I didn't particularly like the fellow presuming to tell me how to dress.

"And if I should be in the mood to show up in trousers?" I asked.

"I'd be gone so quick you wouldn't even notice," he said.

I saw no reason to take such an absurd threat seriously—if there was one thing I had confidence in it was the strength of my womanly charms.

I rather liked it, though, that Zenas Clark was such a tit-for-tat kind of fellow, much like my cousin Templeton. I can't say that I much care for the type of gentlemen who are overly polite, not that there was exactly a surplus of that species, at least not out here in No Man's Land.

At the moment I couldn't allow myself to dwell on my stimulating possibilities with Zenas Clark because first I had to coax my brother, Jackson, down from Joe Schwartz's loft and get him primed to give a bunch of ten-dollar interviews with the various reporters who were waiting to see him, most of whom were even then getting drunk over in Leo Oliphant's saloon.

I knew that might not be an easy task. Jackson Courtright was not much of a talker at the best of times, and he was very apt to sulk and stall when he felt himself to be on the spot. Besides that, he had been half asleep when he killed the Yazees and his memory of killing might be rather vague.

"Jackson, I want you to tell the reporters exactly what you told me," I instructed, as the three of us were making our way down from the loft.

"I have no idea what I may have told you and I don't care to re-member it even if I could," Jackson said, in that poutish way of his—it made me want to slap him.

"You said it was as if the gun grew out of your arm," I reminded him. "Just say that. It'll make a fine headline."

In fact it did make a fine headline, in many papers: YOUNG DEPUTY SAYS THAT GUN THAT FINISHED THE YAZEE GANG SEEMED TO GROW OUT OF HIS ARM.

But all that came later, because just as we stepped out of the livery stable, two old ladies wandered out of the general store and suddenly began to scream.

"Now what do those old biddies think they're screaming about?" I wondered.

"The lance," Zenas said. "How do you suppose that lance got there?"

I suppose coming from the dim loft into the bright sunlight blinded me, because I failed to see a tall, thin lance sticking up right in the middle of the street. As a result of the screaming various citizens ran out assuming we were under attack—Ted Bunsen came from the jail and the blacksmith from his forge and Hungry Billy Wheless from the general store. Aurel Imlah even came trotting down from his hide yard, carrying a Winchester.

Yet, as far as I could tell, we weren't under attack. When I looked at the lance from a closer distance I noticed a pair of green goggles hanging from it. At least I knew where the goggles came from: my aunt, Hroswitha Jubb.

"Those goggles belong to Ros Jubb," I told everyone. "She does her best to keep dust out of her eyes when she travels in dusty places."

"Miss Courtright's right about that," Zenas declared. "Ros Jubb is never without several pair of her famous green goggles."

"Oh now," Cunningham Calhoun demurred. "I know Ros well and I doubt she'd come all this way for a simple outlaw story."

"She'll be coming—Miss Courtright told us that, Cal," Charlie Hepworth said.

I had already mentioned that we had spotted my aunt Ros, but Cunningham Calhoun's attention must have been elsewhere at the time. He might have been a famous reporter for the *New York World,* but it didn't keep him from missing a lot.

"What if the mysterious Indian left the lance in the street?" Charlie Hepworth asked. "What about that, Cal?"

"If some Indian's done in Hroswitha Jubb, I'd say that's just as big a story as the Yazees," Zenas said. "It might even be a bigger story."

His comment gave his fellow newspapermen pause. Most of them had been meaning to snatch a quick interview with Jackson, and then skedaddle; but if something had happened to the most famous woman writer on earth, then that put a kink in their plans.

"She could have dropped those goggles," Charlie Hepworth suggested. "My missus is always dropping things."

"That Indian hasn't harmed any of us," I pointed out. "Maybe he did find Ros's goggles and returned them the best way he could."

"Oh now! That's a stretcher," Zenas said loudly, annoyed that I made so bold as to interfere with the work of serious journalists.

I was pleased to be able to annoy him a little.

"Ros Jubb looks after her tack," Zenas continued. "If she'd dropped something, one of her sepoys would have picked it up."

"Anybody can lose something, sepoys or no sepoys," Charlie Hepworth insisted. Charlie was willingly yielded a point.

"I wonder if the Indian got Joe Schwartz," Jackson said.

"Why would you think that, Deputy?" Ted asked.

"I hid in his loft all morning and no one came in to feed the livestock," Jackson said.

"It's just one more damn thing to worry about," Teddy remarked. Then he went back into the jail.

"What a fool he is," Zenas stated—it rubbed me the wrong way.

"How dare you criticize our hardworking sheriff!" I told him stiffly.

"Why would you care?" Zenas asked.

"Because he was my fiancé until you came along," I told him. "Just go easy on my old boyfriends until I know you better."

Zenas Clark just grinned.

# 16

I DON'T SUPPOSE there ever was a hero who proved a bigger bust at milking the market than my brother, Jackson. Sit him down in front of a reporter with a notebook and Jackson was about as talkative as a stump. Charlie Hepworth could get little out of him—likewise Cunningham Calhoun. And the rest of the troupe, with their stubby cigars and their whiskey-stained cravats, could get nothing out of him at all.

They all worked at it for the better part of an afternoon while my mulish brother sat on a chair and uttered scarcely a word.

My dreams of riches soon melted away. I possessed only a smattering of the famous Courtright scruples, but even I was not crook enough to charge ten dollars apiece for interviews that didn't really happen.

Once we got better acquainted, I found that, on the whole, I liked the newspapermen. I liked their general messiness and their eagerness to run one another down. Cunningham Calhoun, once he unbent a little under the influence of Mrs. Karoo's rum, told me in secret that Charlie Hepworth was such a bad speller that his paper had employed a spelling expert just to handle his copy. Charlie Hepworth, for his part, told me that Cunningham Calhoun was such a wild fornicator that he had to wear a disguise when he went to New York, to throw off all the husbands who wanted to shoot him, not to mention all the mistresses who wanted to blackmail him.

None of the reporters seemed particularly worried about the Indian, if there was an Indian. Most of them were too drunk to notice the threat posed by this mysterious aboriginal who left a lance in the main street of Rita Blanca with Ros Jubb's goggles hanging from it. What I noticed was that most of them had one-track minds: they couldn't get too excited by the fate of Ros Jubb when they still hadn't closed the Yazee story. The Yazee fight was what they wanted to hear about and they would have preferred to hear it from the hero, Jackson Courtright, but since he had fallen mute they agreed to accept it from me. They didn't acknowledge me in their dispatches, of course: I slipped out of the Yazee story just as my picture had slipped off the cover of my booklet; but that's merely the way of the world, which is a man's world for sure. I remembered to put in the detail that Jackson was barefoot when he shot the Yazees—that was just the kind of detail reporters like, though it was not the kind of detail my brother, Jackson, wanted revealed. He stayed half mad at me for several years because of what he considered embarrassment: it made him seem like a deputy who was so slovenly he couldn't even remember to put his boots on.

I charged the bunch of newsmen a good round of fifty dollars for my trouble, which they considered fair enough. It also rendered them more or less free to leave.

What I learned that afternoon was that I could spin out lies as well as any other yarn spinner. I slipped several fibs into my report and did it so convincingly that none of the reporters ever questioned them.

Then I worked the telegraph like a demon, seeing that all the stories I had just made up got filed with the various august newspapers, while the reporters wandered off to the general store to replenish their stock of cigars.

To my annoyance Zenas Clark had wandered off with his colleagues. I told Aurel Imlah about my aunt Ros and he went loping off with his two Poles to see if he could spot her or maybe track her down.

I myself rarely track down men—I consider it their duty to track me down, if they're interested. But I made an exception in Zenas's case—why should he be allowed to waste time in the Wheless store, reading some dime novel, when we could be finishing what we had started that morning in Joe Schwartz's loft?

As for Joe himself, he had been discovered sleeping off a drunk in his own bed. Jackson fed the livestock for him, which left the field—that is, the loft—clear for Zenas and me.

"I hate to think I've engaged myself to a man who'd rather read than kiss me," I told Zenas when I discovered him with a dime novel in the back of the general store.

Zenas gave no indication of being flustered by the remark.

"Nine days out of ten I'd rather spark you than read," he said, "but this happens to be the tenth day."

I snatched the book away from him—it was yet another dimer about Buffalo Bill. If the picture on the cover looked anything like the real Buffalo Bill, then the famous hunter and scout was a very handsome man—perhaps too handsome to warm to in real life. One of the things that got me about Zenas was those snaggle teeth. They gave him an animal look that was hard to resist.

"You might like Mr. Cody, if you met him," Zenas said mildly. "All of us reporters like him—and the girls just won't let him alone. He's a fine fellow, I tell you."

"I suppose I won't mind being the judge of that, if I ever meet the fellow," I said. Frankly I was bored silly by all this talk about Buffalo Bill.

"Why do you look so sulky?" Zenas asked.

"Why wouldn't I be sulky, sir—I was interrupted in my pleasures and that's a major cause of sulks among us females."

"Okay, let's go buy a blanket and have a picnic."

The comment showed what a sly fellow Zenas was. I had pointed out to him already that hay had its prickly qualities—a quilt or a blanket or even a long coat would come in handy if one planned to copulate in a hay barn.

Cousin Templeton himself had rarely been without a long coat.

Zenas was generous enough to buy the blanket himself, and he was vigorous enough, once we got back to the hayloft, to take most of the sulk out of me. I say most, because copulation, if done right, can sometimes fool a girl into thinking that the fellow she's tupping with is actually nicer than may turn out to be the case.

In this case I insisted that Zenas let me be the rider most of the time. I don't believe he was used to letting girls sit astride him, but he didn't protest. It's a sweaty thing, copulation, particularly in hot weather—I'd rather be on top, sweating on Zenas, than to just lay there like a ninny, letting Zenas sweat on me.

Our night together seemed to go quick; it was the kind of night that builds an appetite—the next morning we were up early and were at Mrs. Karoo's, eating a hearty breakfast, when who should show up but Sheriff Teddy Bunsen. At first I supposed he was following me out of jealousy, but for once I was wrong. He was there looking for Jackson, who seemed to have disappeared.

"He slept in the jail, like he always does, but he ain't in the jail now," Ted informed us. "I thought he might be up here, putting on a feed."

Right away I thought of the Indian—and I got pretty agitated. I didn't want any Indian to get my aunt Ros and my brother too.

Fortunately Aurel Imlah, who had had no luck finding Ros Jubb, had up-to-date information on Jackson.

"I saw him this morning," he said. "Jackson was back of the saloon, gathering up beer bottles and putting them in a sack. I believe I saw him mosey off toward the river, not long after that."

"Why would he gather up beer bottles?" I asked. "Who needs an empty beer bottle?"

"Targets," Aurel said. "He's probably just gone off to take some shooting practice. If I was the deputy sheriff of this town I'd see to it that I got in plenty of shooting practice."

Then I remembered the jackrabbit and the yearling—I had a feeling that Aurel was right.

# 17

I SUPPOSE EVEN experts do need to practice. I was never really expert on the French horn, but for a year or two, I practiced assiduously, to the discomfort of everyone else in the house.

There was no reason why a pistol shooter shouldn't practice too.

Nonetheless, to my irritation, Zenas Clark immediately pricked up his ears. He prided himself on his reporter's instinct, of course—I already knew that. But why did he need to exhibit it at the breakfast table?

"But surely he's a crack shot!" Zenas said. "Why would a crack shot need to sneak around gathering up bottles behind a saloon? He's got half the reporters in America at the moment. What he ought to do is put on a shooting show."

"My brother is a good deputy," I told Zenas sharply. "He's hired to subdue the criminal element in No Man's Land, not to put on expensive exhibitions for a bunch of scribbling drunks."

"He's out of step with the times, then," Zenas said. "Shooting shows are all the rage and there's big money in it, you bet! I suppose a top shot can make fifty thousand a year. If your brother would move east and get in a few contests he'd soon have his fortune made."

Fortunately a fresh plate of flapjacks arrived just at that time—it distracted Zenas's attention for a bit. I hadn't really done a thing to make Zenas suspicious of Jackson's shooting, and yet he was suspicious—I could tell. The more I defended my brother, the more suspicious my fiancé would become.

What I needed was a smooth change of subject, but just at the moment, thanks to all that copulation, all I could do was stuff pancakes in my mouth and feel stupid.

Aurel Imlah came to my rescue.

"If you don't mind my saying so, Mr. Clark, there's another story in these parts that's just about as good as the Yazee story."

"What other story?" Zenas asked. "There's not much that interests readers as much as outlaws do."

"What I was thinking of was the Mountain of Bones," Aurel said. "It's a big hill of buffalo bones about fifteen miles from here. They say there are more than a million bones in that mountain."

"A Mountain of Bones, you say?" Zenas asked. I noticed that he had not been slow in getting his reporter's notebook out.

"How high is it?" he asked.

"About eighty feet at the highest point," Aurel told him.

"A pile of buffalo bones eighty feet high?" Zenas said. "I'd sure like to get a picture of that—maybe Billy Wheless would loan me a camera for a day."

"Oh surely," Aurel said. "I'll be glad to take you."

Mrs. Karoo was looking at Aurel in her usual dreamy way—I supposed they were lovers but I could not yet be sure, and what business was it of mine, anyway?

"Let me interrupt a minute," I said. "Isn't it dangerous to go traipsing off to the Mountain of Bones with this Indian in the vicinity?"

Nobody said anything to that. Aurel just tapped his pipe.

"What about my aunt Ros?" I went on. "Why would the Indian tie her goggles onto a lance and stick it in the middle of the street while nobody was looking?"

"I suppose he just wanted us to know he'd paid us a visit," Aurel speculated. "As far as I know the Indian's never harmed anybody. I think Mr. Clark and I will just skip off and take a look at the Mountain of Bones—it's no riskier than anything else in this part of the country."

It didn't satisfy me, but to a newspaperman like Zenas a Mountain of Bones was a pretty good story, and anyway, when men decide to do something there's not much point in their womenfolk trying to interfere.

"If you ain't back by suppertime I'm going to be worried," I told Zenas, who paid the comment no more attention than if it had been made by a horsefly. It was clear that, having temporarily had his fill of me, he was happy as a lark to go loping over the prairie to inspect a million buffalo bones. The man was so cocky I wanted to kick him, but instead I watched the two of them ride off and headed for the stables myself, meaning to go see if I could find my missing brother.

# 18

LONG BEFORE I came in sight of the Cimarron River I heard the pop-pop of Jackson's pistol. I was astride the big roan horse that had once been Bert Yazee's, and I was plenty nervous—about the Indian, not my brother, Jackson. The last thing I needed was for some giant Indian to jump out of the weeds and grab me.

Jackson didn't look a bit glad to see me when I rode up, and it was easy to see why he wasn't. There was no sign of broken glass anywhere near the log where the beer bottles were lined up.

"Who invited you, by God!" Jackson asked, when I dismounted.

"Jackson, there is no need to blaspheme," I told him. "How many expensive cartridges have you fired off since you hit one of those bottles?"

Jackson made no immediate reply.

"I've never shot a pistol," I mentioned. "I wonder if I could hit a bottle from where you're standing."

"Of course you couldn't," Jackson barked, exposing his petulant side. I suppose many younger brothers have a petulant side.

"Be a sport—let me try!" I insisted.

Reluctantly he handed me the pistol and I promptly emptied it, hitting two bottles out of six. It wasn't crack marksmanship by any means but the fact that I'd at least hit a bottle when he hadn't put Jackson in a fury.

"Goddamn you, I just wish you'd go back where you came from!" he yelled, coloring up.

I ignored this hurtful comment because I realized that Jackson was desperate. How long would it be before some reporter discovered that he couldn't shoot? In no time it would be all over town and then all over the world. Teddy Bunsen would probably fire him, and then how would he pay all the bills he had run up?

Then a hopeful thought occurred to me.

"Specs!" I told him. "Specs . . . I bet all you need is specs."

"Leave me alone, you fool—I can't be wearing specs!"

"Jackson, it's no crime to be nearsighted," I insisted. "Remember how nearsighted Billy Hickok was? He was too vain to admit it and go get himself proper specs, and now he's dead."

"I expect I'll be dead pretty soon myself—at least once I'm dead I won't have to listen to you yap," Jackson declared with some vehemence.

A big sister is only obliged to take so much lip from a younger brother, and I had taken quite enough from Deputy Sheriff Jackson Courtright that morning, so I handed him back his pistol and was soon loping back across the prairie toward Rita Blanca.

I had plenty on my mind too. My famous little brother couldn't shoot, which likely meant his fame would curdle pretty soon; he'd be exposed as a fraud and would likely be out of a job, though, to be fair, Jackson had not been hired for his shooting. Maybe Ted Bunsen would want to keep him around for his skill with the broom and paintbrush rather than the gun.

Jackson was one problem, and Zenas Clark was another. I was enough in love with Zenas that it boded ill for my mood if he decided to leave, and why wouldn't he? He was a reporter—what was there to keep him in Rita Blanca except me?

Aurel Imlah had been kind enough to lure Zenas off on a trip to the Mountain of Bones, but that was a stopgap measure at best.

Meanwhile I had begun to suffer a few doubts about my own morals. None of the Courtrights were prudes but few of them were as oversusceptible as I seemed to be. I had flopped down on top of Zenas Clark on the basis of a very slight acquaintance, and was very likely to do it again once he showed back up. I was in the habit of considering myself engaged to whatever fellow caught my fancy—but somehow Zenas seemed a little more serious as a prospect. Would he want me to leave with him, when he left? Would I go if he did?

On top of that, I had the telegraph office to consider. I was the telegraph lady of Rita Blanca, and though it was a small town, I had an important function to perform. My office might be small, and full of bull snakes, but it was mine and I didn't particularly want to give it up. I was proud of being the only woman telegrapher in the whole of No Man's Land: Charlie Hepworth mentioned that it was so unusual to find a woman telegrapher that he was thinking of doing a story just on me! I liked that, I can tell you—I was already getting tired of watching reporters write up stories about my little brother.

Charlie also mentioned that I was exceptionally speedy.

"I'm in and out of telegraph offices all the time," he told me. "But I've not seen anybody who can rattle the keys as fast as you do."

"And you can even spell!" he added, as if that were the rarest of qualities in a telegrapher.

"I can't spell a lick, myself," Charlie admitted. "The paper offered to provide me with a dictionary, but do I look like the kind of man who would carry around a dictionary?"

As usual, as soon as I got the office open for the day, Bertha and Melba McClendon showed up. They were usually my first customers, the reason being that there were six other McClendon sisters scattered around America—naturally the eight McClendon girls spent the day firing off telegrams to one another, many of which started with me.

This morning, when what I mainly needed was a little time to think, Bertha hit me with a corker.

"So I understand you and Sheriff Bunsen have finally set the wedding date," Bertha said, fixing me with her little henlike eyes.

"What fool told you that?" I asked.

"Mrs. Thomas, down at the general store."

"Mrs. Thomas is a sweet old soul but she can't see, so she makes up rumors," I told Bertha.

"She said you ordered a fine white wedding dress out of Beau Wheless's big catalogue—I often have to refer to that catalogue myself," Melba put in. "I don't know why you're being so discreet about it—we all look forward to weddings down here in Rita Blanca, and I bet you'd make the sheriff a fine wife."

"What we mostly get is funerals," Bertha observed. "A wedding would be a nice change."

That just shows you how hard it is to keep anything secret in a small town like Rita Blanca. The truth is I had decided I might as well keep a decent wedding dress on hand in case someone dandy like

Zenas Clark came along. Billy Wheless lent me the big catalogue and I made my choice and sent my order off. It would probably have taken a while for the dress to actually reach Rita Blanca—if I didn't happen to be in a marrying mood when the dress came, I could just hang it in the closet until some man I could get attached to came along.

It irked me plenty that the McClendon sisters, of all people, found out about my order.

"You two are jumping the gun," I informed them. "Sheriff Bunsen and I have no immediate plans to marry."

"Why not, ain't he steady?" Bertha asked.

Steady as a rock, I thought. But who wants to marry a rock?

# 19

I GUESS EVERYBODY likes to get their name in the papers—I know I do, but the distinction is hard to achieve if you're starting from the vantage point of Rita Blanca. I figured Charlie Hepworth's interview might be my only chance to achieve widespread publicity, so I did what I could to make myself presentable before he arrived. I brushed my hair and donned a frock that would have been considered daring at any cotillion in Virginia.

It may be that I overdid it a bit with my daring frock, because the first thing Charlie Hepworth did when he crowded into my office was drop his pants.

"Charlie, your britches are falling down," I told him, momentarily failing to grasp his intent. I thought his pants were down around his ankles because of some defect in his suspenders, but it took only one glance at his privates to convince me that my theory was way off. He had a serious stiffie working and had obviously crammed into my office with copulation in mind.

"Charlie!" I said, in sterner tones, trying my best to sound shocked.

"Let's hurry up and board the boat of pleasure!" he declared, trying to shove himself between my legs.

"The boat of pleasure—in a desert?" I asked. "You need to be more accurate with your language."

In fact I was hard put not to laugh at the poor man. Charlie's prong was about the length of one of his stogies, after he'd smoked most of it. I'm tall for a girl—at least a foot taller than Charlie Hepworth. Even if I had consented to his embrace—which I didn't—he would have had to climb up on a stool to achieve his goal, and there was no stool handy.

When men turn up crazed with lust and point their peckers at you, the first rule is just not to laugh. Laughing at a man who has offered you the solace of a stiffie is sure to have bitter consequences.

I liked Charlie Hepworth, which didn't mean I had the slightest intention of stepping into the boat of pleasure with him, as he poetically but foolishly put it.

"Can't this wait till after business hours?" I asked him. "Billy Wheless is coming with what looks to be a sizable order. I doubt we'll row that boat of pleasure very far before he arrives."

Charlie, in his rut, had evidently forgotten that there were people on the planet other than ourselves. The fit was on him to a high extent—the notion that mere commercial enterprise might interfere with the enterprise he was interested in caused him to go red in the face.

"Why, the fool!" he said. "What could he want?"

"Oh, I don't know," I admitted. "Maybe he's running low on spittoons, or needs to order several dozen fly swatters. I need him to order some rose water, myself."

"Don't you have a Closed sign you could hang out?" Charlie asked, sounding desperate. "We won't need but a minute."

"Speak for yourself, Charlie," I told him. "On the rare occasions when I row off in the boat of pleasure I require considerably longer than a minute, if I'm to get where I'm rowing toward.

"You better pull your pants up, honey," I added. "Billy's closing in."

Charlie gave up and stuffed himself back in his pants, which were none too clean. The fit was leaving him; soon he was once again a normal reporter named Hepworth.

"Can't blame a man for trying," he said.

"Did I say I blamed anyone?" I asked.

"Why no . . . you didn't," he said, seemingly surprised. "You even called me honey, which was nice of you."

"You might consider getting better suspenders, though," I advised. "And launder your pants a little more often."

Long years ahead, in another place, Charlie Hepworth and I worked together again, but I musn't get ahead of the story.

"When are we going to do that interview you mentioned?" I asked him. The interview, after all, had been the reason for the meeting—though it was only my reason, I now realized.

"Maybe the next time you feel like calling me honey," Charlie said, and then there was Hungry Billy Wheless, with his long list.

# 20

TWO DAYS LATER the big news rush in Rita Blanca was over, and we citizens were forced to wonder if anything would ever happen in the town again. The Indian—if there was an Indian—didn't kill anybody or leave any more lances in our street. Ros Jubb failed to arrive and claim her goggles—Aurel Imlah took another look or two but all he found was one sandal. It might have belonged to one of Ros's sepoys but there was no guarantee that it had. After all, anybody can lose a sandal.

Zenas and I managed to copulate at our leisure a couple more times, but a bittersweet quality had crept into our lovemaking. Oh, it was a fine pleasure to bounce up and down on Zenas in the hayloft, but the facts we had to face were bleak: Zenas didn't love me enough to stay in Rita Blanca, and I didn't love him enough to leave. If we kept on copulating I expect we'd soon make a baby, and I'd be the one to stay home with the child while Zenas went on rambling where he pleased in search of copy. I'd get fat and jealous and Zena would succumb to a girl here and a girl there until I got wind of it, at which point I'd murder him.

So we enjoyed ourselves for two more days and then Zenas crammed himself into the stagecoach with the other reporters—he never shed a tear as he was leaving.

I leaned in the coach and gave Charlie Hepworth a sweet kiss on the cheek.

"Bye, honey," I said, which astonished the other reporters, including Zenas.

Charlie shed the tears that Zenas didn't bother to summon and the stagecoach went bouncing away.

I was still the telegraph lady of Rita Blanca, and very proud of my job, while my brother, Jackson Courtright, the hero of the Yazee fight, took a turn for the worse and became a drunk, for which behavior there was little excuse. Jackson's inability to shoot a pistol accurately was not apt to be discovered for some time, if ever: he could just live out a useful life as a deputy, collaring drunks and now and then sweeping out the cells or giving the gallows a little touch-up with his paintbrush.

I didn't realize that Jackson had taken to drink until I saw him topple down one of the few flights of stairs in Rita Blanca. The stairs were behind Leo Oliphant's saloon; they led to the second floor, where Mandy Williams lived. Mandy happened to be the local painted lady, although she didn't really paint herself much. But she did receive gentlemen callers and she did charge them for certain pleasures. One of the men she received more and more often was my brother, Jackson, the famous spendthrift—a deputy sheriff known to be reckless with his fifteen dollars a month.

I had just eased my last bull snake out of the office for the morning—I was watching him, if it was a him, slide into a hole under a rock when I heard the sound of a falling body and looked up just in time to see Jackson tumble down Mandy's stairs. The fall alarmed Mandy and it alarmed me. I came rushing over and Mandy came rushing down. She was a sorrowful woman with short hair that had never decided whether to be brunette or blond.

Mandy got to Jackson's stretched-out body first and put her head to his chest long enough to convince her that the boy wasn't dead. I already knew that much; I could hear my brother snoring. To say that he reeked of whiskey would be an understatement. He smelled so strongly of liquor that you would think he had taken a bath in it, with his clothes on!

"What's your notion, Mandy—is he usually this drunk when he pays you a visit?" I asked.

"Well, he's never sober when he pays me a visit, Miss Courtright," Mandy admitted.

"You don't need to call me Miss Courtright," I told the young woman. "We're the only two reasonably sensible women in Rita Blanca—if we can't just call one another by our first names, what's the point?"

Mandy Williams saw that I meant it—she favored me with a sweet, shy smile. Being the one whore in Rita Blanca probably didn't provide her with many reasons to smile. I suspect she would have been shocked if she'd known about the kind of things Zenas and I had just been doing in Joe Schwartz's hayloft. Her own practices with her customers were probably sedate by comparison—but I saw no need to go into that, just then.

"I'm just plain Nellie," I told her, with a smile that let her know I didn't look down on her because she happened to be a whore.

"Jackson's about the sweetest fellow in town," Mandy told me. "I saw he was too drunk to do much and tried to make him comfortable on my settee, but before I could get his boots off he ran out the door and fell."

"He's just a boy, Mandy," I told her. "Ever since he got famous he's been under a strain. Maybe the humble life is the best life after all."

That may not have been the most diplomatic thing to say to Mandy Williams, who had probably seen more of the humble life than was good for anybody—but I was just coming to understand that my brother was much too young and immature to be as famous as he was. A single action had made him famous—what we had to do now was figure out how Jackson Courtright could get through the rest of his life just doing the normal things that all of us had to do.

"Do you like Jackson, Mandy?" I asked. The question took the nice young thing aback—maybe, in her profession, it was impossible just to like a fellow. The commercial aspect probably got in the way. And yet I had heard that whores sometimes fall for cowboys and vice versa. I had been more or less managing Jackson's life since he was about three, when I was often called to chase him down. But now I was twenty-two, with ambitions of my own, and I was tired of managing my brother. I would be happy to pass the chore on to a nice bride of some kind, and it occurred to me that Mandy Williams might make a likely candidate, who seemed so sweet and shy. Most women have a little meanness in them, but Mandy looked to me to have only the necessary minimum.

There lay Jackson Courtright, drunk as an owl, an eligible bachelor of seventeen who stood sorely in need of a steadying hand, preferably not his sister's. And there stood Mandy Williams, pretty, quiet, with not much bosom maybe but with a graceful neck and lovely blue eyes. Maybe she was just the bride for Jackson. Maybe—of course this was a long shot—they could even be happy together. Maybe each would turn out to be just what the other needed.

"Mandy, I've got a plan," I told her bluntly. My motto, as I've already said, is act, don't think. "When Jackson wakes up let's tell him you proposed and he accepted."

Mandy Williams's lovely blue eyes got wide.

"Now that's bold, Nellie," she said.

"Only the brave deserve the fair," I told her. It was a tag of poetry I had picked up somewhere.

"I doubt that being married to Jackson could be worse than what you're doing," I told her. "You'd just have one young man to manage, and I bet you could manage him fine."

"Yes, and I could save him some money, to boot," Mandy told me. "I wouldn't have to charge him every time he showed up with a stiffie, which is sometimes twice a day."

"Good point," I said. "I just ordered a fine wedding dress."

"For me?" she asked. "You mean you had this planned?"

"No . . . I ordered it for me, but we're about the same size and my nuptial prospects just went bouncing off in a stagecoach. You might as well use the dress and marry Jackson."

Something like a look of happiness shone in Mandy Williams's eyes for the first time since I'd known her. We two girls had worked up a fine little plot.

When Deputy Jackson Courtright woke up from his snooze, the first thing that he discovered was that he was engaged. To my relief he seemed pleased by the discovery.

"It's about time I got to be the one engaged," he said. "You must have been engaged fifty times—that's not my way of doing things."

"You do like Mandy, don't you?" I asked, a little nervously, once I got Jackson alone for a few minutes. Mandy Williams had gone back up those stairs as sprightly as if she were walking on air. From having nothing but the task of deflating a lot of stiffies in Rita Blanca, she now was engaged to a scion of the Courtrights.

"Mandy, why, she's the sweetest!" Jackson said. "I've been wanting to marry her from the minute I saw her, but I didn't figure she'd have me."

"She'll have you—and it's not because you're a big hero," I told him. "She'll have you because she likes you, and because you're mostly nice."

"Leo Oliphant will just have to find himself another whore," Jackson said—the practical side of things was always quick to assert itself with Jackson.

I walked back to my telegraph office whistling merrily. On the whole I'd managed a nice little plot very well. I'd soon gain a sister-in-law to help me out with my unsteady brother.

I had hardly got back to the office when the line got active and the message read thus:

PLAN TO VISIT RITA BLANCA AFTERNOON THURSDAY NEXT STOP SEEKING ATTRAC-

TION FOR WORLD RENOWNED WILD WEST PAGEANT STOP EAGER TO MEET

DEPUTY COURTRIGHT POSSIBLE EMPLOYMENT STOP WILL REQUIRE NOURISHMENT

FOR HORSE AND SELF STOP WILLIAM FREDERICK CODY BUFFALO BILL

The first thing I thought of was how happy the McClendon sisters would be—their idol was coming to town.

To me, Buffalo Bill sounded like somebody who might need to be taken down a peg, but I soon passed on the news to the McClendon girls, at which Bertha fainted dead away and Melba got the heart flutters and had to fan herself briskly until she got her emotions under control.

It irked me, for some reason. Buffalo Bill Cody wasn't even there, and already he was causing trouble.

# BOOK III

---

# Wild West Days

# 1

AMONG THE COURTRIGHTS I've always been noted for my ability to dislike certain people on sight, before I've even bothered to ascertain whether they smell bad or have false teeth that don't fit or dribble tobacco juice on their shirts or reek of bad hair tonic. Some men possess all those failings and more, but even one will usually cause me to mark a fellow off my list.

I had pretty well convinced myself that this Buffalo Bill Cody was probably somebody who needed to be put in his place. The very fact that Bertha McClendon had fainted at the mention of his name suggested vanity to me. The man might well have an irksome personality. When Thursday came I got ready to be icy and stiff, but then up Bill Cody trotted, on a fine gray horse, beautifully dressed, handsome as a god, friendly as a collie, and all my tough resolves turned into toffee.

Bill Cody was so appealing that I suspect he could have persuaded Eve to hold off on the apple, at least until he had managed to outflank Adam. The whole town turned out to greet him, and he behaved as graciously to everyone as if he'd been a natural prince. Both the McClendon sisters pressed him to sign their autograph books, which he did, with a bold flourish to his script.

Bill was friendly and polite to everybody and yet, now and then, he would look at me and let his eyes rest on mine, as if to suggest that he had come to Rita Blanca mainly to meet me, the telegraph lady, perhaps with romance in mind—but the first words this paragon of men actually said to me were anything but romantic.

"Are you organized, Miss Courtright?" he asked, once the crowd thinned and he had an opportunity to stroll over to the telegraph office.

It was not what I had expected to hear: for a moment I just stared at him.

"You look organized," he concluded, "and on top of that you're far too pretty a female to be left to wither away out here in the sandburs and the wind. I think I better just hire you—we can figure out the details later."

I felt a hot blush coloring my cheeks. "Hire me to do what?" I managed to ask.

"Help me get my Wild West pageant going," he said. "Is your brother that shot up the Yazees hiding somewhere? Sharpshooters are mighty popular now—I'm going to need several once I get my pageant running. Right now your brother's got a high reputation."

"He can't shoot," I said. I thought I might as well spare Jackson the embarrassment of a tryout which would reveal the sad fact to the famous man himself.

Cody looked amused but not surprised.

"So it was beginner's luck, was it?" he asked. I nodded.

"Come out here and stand up straight so I can look at you," he said.

I blushed again—no gentleman had ever summoned me like that.

"My, but you're a beauty," he said, once he'd looked. "I'm not a bachelor by law, but I have the bachelor attitude. Let's enjoy a kiss."

We did enjoy a kiss, a better kiss than I was used to receiving from total strangers.

"I hope we can enjoy more kissing later, in a more private spot," he told me.

"I don't oppose the notion," I admitted.

Then Bill got a thoughtful look—I don't believe our kissing touched him much, deep down. With Bill Cody, as I soon learned, kissing was just the thing that came naturally to mind when he was kissing a pretty girl. Once he'd kissed awhile his mind would soon drift on to other things, as it did that day.

"If your brother can't shoot, then we better leave him in peace," Cody said. "You knew that fool George Custer in earlier days, didn't you?"

"Yes, he was my suitor," I told Cody. "You might be a little more respectful of his memory."

Bill Cody had a way of just looking blandly around as if someone made a remark that lacked interest for him. He ignored any comment that he'd rather not have heard.

"Weren't you sweet on Billy Hickok too?" he asked. "Seems like Billy was always talking about a Miss Courtright and how lovely she was—you lived down in Virginia then, I believe."

"Waynesboro," I said. "And I was sweet on Mr. Hickok, not that that's any of your business."

I suppose being a famous scout gave Bill Cody the opportunity to meet most of the famous people in the West.

"Bill Hickok couldn't see ten feet," Cody remarked. "When we were onstage in our silly little plays Billy couldn't manage to say a single word, but he fired off his pistol once in a while, whenever the spirit moved him. It was loaded with blanks but he shot so close to the legs of the bare-legged actors who were supposed to be Indians that they got powder burns—it didn't sit well with the actors, I can tell you!

"Billy was a fine fellow, though—I miss him," Cody said quietly. I thought I saw a tear in his eye.

I cried a little myself—I missed Billy Hickok too, even if he was more interested in clothes than he was in women. He wasn't a kisser like Bill Cody, but they both had gentle eyes.

# 2

BILL CODY PERSUADED me to close the telegraph office for a while and take a stroll with him down the main street of Rita Blanca. From where we stood, at my office, we could see right through the town, but Billy wanted to make a closer inspection. He held my hand as we walked—I guess holding a woman's hand was as natural to Bill Cody as breathing.

Most people recoil with horror when they're brought face-to-face with the ugliness of Rita Blanca for the first time—I had recoiled in horror myself—but Bill Cody wasn't most people. His eyes actually lit up when he saw our sorry shacks and dusty streets.

"My God," he said. "This place would be perfect for my Wild West setup, once I get it going."

"What are you talking about, sir?" I asked. "All this place is perfect for is getting drunk or getting killed."

"No, I see a blacksmith—you could get your horse shod," Bill said. "And there's a livery stable where the villains in the story could hide until it's time for the big shoot-out."

I saw the man was serious—he actually saw Rita Blanca as the perfect Western town.

"You've got a general store, a big two-story jail, a barbershop, two or three gambling establishments—and there's probably a whore around somewhere."

"No whore," I informed him. "She got engaged to Deputy Court-right yesterday."

"Well, they're easily come by," Cody said.

"Now, Mr. Cody, just slow down," I urged him. "I consider myself as quick-minded as the next girl, but what's this Wild West setup you keep talking about, that you think Rita Blanca's so perfect for?"

Cody looked around, and then gave me a gentle hug.

"I need to wet my whistle before I get into the details," Cody said. "I see a bunch of saloons—which one would you recommend?"

"I have no experience to go on—ladies aren't allowed in saloons, as you should know," I reminded him.

Cody just smiled.

"Wait for me," he said. "I'll just go see if I can purchase a bottle of rye."

We were standing in front of the jail when he said it—I recalled that Sheriff Ted Bunsen was fond of rye. Rather than let Bill Cody wander into a saloon and be gone for hours, I grabbed his arm and walked him toward the jail.

"If it's rye you enjoy I'm sure the sheriff can spare some," I said. "I happen to know that rye's his drink."

Bill Cody was a fresh capture—I had no intention of letting him loose in a saloon, where he would probably be drawn into drunkenness or card games.

Ted Bunsen was half drunk himself when Cody and I paid him our surprise visit, but he graciously managed to find a glass that had only one or two dead flies in it—he soon removed the flies and poured Bill Cody a brimming glass of rye whiskey. It didn't brim for long—Cody drank it off as if it was sarsaparilla, a feat that surprised Ted Bunsen considerably.

"That was quick," he said—coming from Sheriff Ted it counted as witty repartee.

"I am not a mincing drinker," Cody said, holding out the glass. Sheriff Bunsen refilled it and Cody drank it straight off.

"Much obliged, Sheriff," he said.

The jail was rather low-ceilinged—Bill had to stoop a little as he went out the door. Once we were outside in the dusty breeze Cody lit a thin cigar and offered me one.

"No, thanks," I told him. "There are several things you need to learn about me, Mr. Cody."

"Name two," he challenged.

"I don't go into saloons and I don't smoke cigars," I said.

Bill Cody smiled and nodded. "Not smoking cigars is why your kisses are so sweet," he commented—sometimes his tone made me blush. The fact that he said my kisses were sweet left me with the impression that he had made extensive comparisons.

"I suppose it would cost too much to buy this town and move it," he mused, as we were strolling up the street. Whenever we passed a citizen, they'd wave. Just having Bill Cody come to town seemed to have lifted everyone's spirits—including my spirits. His easy good humor was a pleasure to experience.

But the notion that he might buy Rita Blanca was a notion little short of lunacy.

"Buy it?" I said, making no attempt to hide my astonishment. "What would you do with it if you bought it?"

"Sell tickets to it," he said. "If I had it on Staten Island I can guarantee you that that ferry over from New York would be filled with people who would pay cash money to see what a town in the Old West looked like."

Lots of people live in the past, but Bill Cody seemed to be one of the rare few who lived in the future. Here he was in the town of Rita Blanca, a place every one of its inhabitants knew was ugly, and Bill Cody was thinking ahead to a time when people like Georgie Custer and Billy Hickok and maybe the Yazee brothers would be candidates for the museum.

The Rita Blanca I was standing in, getting grit in my teeth, wasn't the Old West to me—it was the only West available. But Bill Cody was sincere, and calm as a banker. He was looking ahead to the day when our ordinary day-to-day lives on the prairie would be—what's the word?—picturesque, like the knights and ladies in King Arthur, or the novels of Walter Scott.

As we were idling around the office Cody suddenly snapped his fingers, as if he just dropped one idea in favor of a better one—the way he did it reminded me of Father.

"Do you suppose there's a reliable photographer in this town?" he asked.

"Hungry Billy Wheless is a fair photographer—he took the pictures of the Yazees," I told him. "What do you need to have photographed, Mr. Cody?"

"Why, Rita Blanca—every stick and stone of it," Bill said. "I'll hire young Mr. Wheless, if I can—he can start at the south end of town and come straight up the street, photographing every single building, back, front, and sideways."

"You are a curious fellow," I told him. "Why would you want to do that?"

"So I can rebuild the town back east and use it in my Wild West pageants," he said. "I'll get some good carpenters and give them the photographs to work from. We'll find some old wood, so the place won't look too new. You have to be authentic when you're putting on shows—particularly when it's history you're selling. The spectators are not going to want spiffy new buildings—I need to convince them that they're seeing the real West."

"That's crazy," I told him. "What are you anyway, a buffalo hunter or an actor? Don't you still have Indians to fight, up there in the north somewhere?"

"There's a few wild ones still out, but it's mainly over for the free Indians," Cody said—he sounded sad about it. "I don't want to kill them, either. I want to hire the best-looking ones for my Wild West pageant.

"Some of the Sioux and Cheyenne are mighty good-looking people," he added.

"You mean you're planning to hire the Indians you were just fighting?" I asked.

"That's right," Cody said soberly. "Right now they're fighting and getting killed, but once I get my Wild West up and running all they'll have to do is pretend to fight. We'll do a fake attack on a settler's cabin, or the Deadwood Stage, and instead of getting killed for their trouble they can be paid cash money."

Then Cody chuckled.

"You look as if you consider that to be a harebrained scheme, Miss Nellie Courtright," he said.

"Of course it's a harebrained scheme," I said. "Pay fighting Indians to pretend to fight?"

"Yep, and pay sharpshooters to shoot and acrobats to tumble and trick ropers to twirl big loops and cowboys to ride broncs and all the rest of the folderol that goes with a Wild West pageant," he elaborated.

"This is making me dizzy," I admitted. "Nobody in their right mind would pay good money to see a place that looks like Rita Blanca. Even Yankees aren't that dumb."

"Sure they are—as soon as something's ended, people will start flocking to get at least a glimpse of what it was like before it was over," Cody said. "It's human nature."

"I'm a human, and it's not my nature," I assured him, but even as I said it I knew my remark was partly a lie. Why read Walter Scott if not to catch a glimpse of what life was like in older times—times that were surely gone forever?

Just then Mrs. Karoo began to ring the lunch bell.

"I hope that means there's some grub to be had, somewhere," Bill said.

He took my hand again and was still holding it when we sidled into Mrs. Karoo's, where he took off his big hat and made his hostess a nice bow. Of course, he was immediately the center of attention, as I suppose he was in just about every gathering he attended. All eyes just naturally seemed to fix themselves on Buffalo Bill, who turned out to possess admirable table manners. He had known Aurel Imlah in former years—the two old buffalo men were soon telling stories about this adventure and that, leaving the rest of us feeling a little left out. The storytelling didn't put much of a break on Bill Cody's appetite—he had two or three helpings of everything and even charmed the two Choctaw girls by saying a word or two in their own language.

Of course, he poured on the charm with Mrs. Karoo, whose cooking he complimented highly, particularly praising the vinegar pie, which he claimed he rarely had a chance to enjoy.

My weakness is men—there it is. My famous susceptibility was just about brimming over by the time we'd finished eating. I would have crawled up on the hayloft with Bill in a minute, but he himself had no such inclination.

"Nellie, what I need's a nap," he mentioned, as we were leaving the table. I suppose the man's own enthusiasm had temporarily worn him out.

"I have to get back to the telegraph office," I told him. "You're welcome to nap in my room—I won't be using it for a while."

His answer was a big, long yawn, followed by a sleepy smile.

I walked him up to my bedroom and even opened the windows for him so he could enjoy a breeze. I suppose I hoped for a kiss, or something, for my trouble, but no kisses were forthcoming. Billy Cody indulged in another mighty yawn and shut the door in my face.

# 3

BEFORE BILL CODY even woke up from his nap, telegrams had started coming in for him from this general or that. I had nearly a dozen wires stacked up by the time Bill came ambling back down the street. I handed him the telegrams but he refused to take them.

"Maybe I'll read them tomorrow," he said. "Right now I need to go hire that photographer and get him started."

"One of these telegrams is from General Crook," I pointed out. From what I had heard, here and there, General Crook was not someone it was wise to ignore, but Cody ignored him anyway. In no time he had Hungry Billy Wheless out taking pictures of Rita Blanca, such as it was.

By the time I closed the office that afternoon I had received a regular bale of telegrams for Buffalo Bill, but the fellow they were meant for was down the street, supervising the big photography project he had launched into with Billy Wheless.

About half the citizenry of Rita Blanca came out to watch this surprising activity, most of whom seemed to share my opinion that it was a crazy thing for anyone to do. The notion that someone wanted to make a replica of Rita Blanca somewhere far away and expect people to pay cash money for a chance to look at it seemed so far-fetched as to be nearly incredible.

And yet it was happening. Aurel Imlah even consented to let his hide yard be photographed—Mrs. Karoo did the same with her rooming house.

"Doesn't this all seem a little odd?" I asked Aurel, who smiled.

"Life itself is odd, Nellie," Aurel said, which was about as philosophical as Aurel allowed himself to be.

"I would never bet against Bill Cody, though," he added. "He's made a go of everything he's tried."

"I got more than twenty telegrams for him," I said. "Some of them are from General Crook. Bill won't even read them, which I consider rash."

"He don't like being bossed," Aurel said. "Bill's always done pretty much whatever he wanted to do, and so far he's gotten away with it."

"I think he may offer me a job," I confessed, a comment to which Aurel Imlah made no reply. If I did accept an offer from Bill Cody it would mean leaving Rita Blanca—I guess Aurel Imlah was the one local I would really miss.

Meanwhile, down the street, Buffalo Bill and Hungry Billy were working their way along, from hovel to hovel. My brother, Jackson, sat on the edge of the gallows, dangling his feet and watching the action, such as it was. Jackson Courtright was the person Bill Cody had traveled all the way to Rita Blanca to interview but so far he had not exchanged more than a few words with Jackson, who, now that Mandy had agreed to marry him, was a deliriously happy man and probably wouldn't have left Rita Blanca even if he had been offered a big wage to do so.

Finally it got too dark to take pictures, though Bill made Billy get a few shots of the wide prairie at dusk. I went down to watch, carrying my sheaf of telegrams, which, once again, Cody refused to consider.

"The good old military can wait," he said and was maybe even a touch annoyed that I had brought the matter up again. I had never met a more confident man—he was absolutely convinced that once he got his Wild West, as he always referred to it, up and going, thousands and thousands of people would be eager to pay to see fake fights. Time soon proved him right, but I was not that interested in the West, myself. I was a lot more interested in kissing or other fleshly activities, a preference that slightly set me apart from Bill Cody, who was determined to get rich or bust.

Just at dark, as Billy Wheless was packing up his camera and photographic equipment, Bill Cody made another of his sly attempts to slip past me into a saloon—moving rapidly, I handed him off at the door.

"Before you go get drunk I need to get a few things straight with you," I began.

"I wonder if Sheriff Bunsen would spare me any more of that good rye whisky," Billy said, not meeting my eye. "I prefer it without dead flies, but if he doesn't happen to have a clean glass I could probably put up with the flies."

So once again we angled across the street toward the jail.

"When you rode into this town you acted like you wanted to offer me a job, but that's the last I heard of that," I told him. "I'm the telegrapher here—if you mean to offer me a job that will take me away, I'd like a chance to train my replacement."

I had already decided that if Cody meant it about the job, Mandy Williams, my soon-to-be sister-in-law, would be my replacement, but I saw no reason to tell Cody that.

Getting a straight answer out of Bill Cody was not the easiest thing in the world, I can tell you.

"You would harass a man about these business details just when he's needing a drink," Bill said, with a touch of petulance.

Then he sighed, as if he were the most put-upon man in the world, instead of the most pampered.

"Get me those goddamn telegrams so I can read them before I get drunk," he told me. "The fact is I'm tired of being a shuttlecock for the military. It's show business for me from now on—but if there should be one more spectacular battle I could help win, it would get such good publicity for the shows that I probably ought to do it. I doubt the Sioux have another big battle in them, but Geronimo's still a menace—I might have to help General Crook try and corner him in Arizona.

"It's iffy, though," he added. "Suppose we can't corner the old rascal—that could produce bad publicity."

"You're not answering my question," I reminded him.

"I do mean to hire you, Nellie," he told me, with a touch of huff in his voice. "I do, but I need to figure out this military problem first. I'd like to scratch up some good publicity but I also need to figure out this military problem first. I'd like to scratch up some good publicity but I also need to avoid anything that might produce bad publicity.

"There is that problem when you're fighting smart Indians," he added.

"What problem?"

"Sometimes they win—ask your friend Georgie Custer," Bill said. "I might bring Geronimo in, but on the other hand, he might bring me in."

"I doubt there's an Indian who could get the best of you, Bill," I told him.

Bill Cody smiled.

"Thousands could get the best of me," he said frankly. "I've been lucky out here on the plains for fifteen years. But it only takes one bullet or one arrow to change all that permanently.

"It's why I want to stop fighting them and start hiring them," he added. "It makes sense, don't you think?"

"I suppose it does, but it's not very daring," I told him.

"Who said I was daring? In fact, I'm the soul of caution," he retorted, before he went into the jail to seek his whiskey.

# 4

WILLIAM FREDERICK CODY turned out to be no easy man to pre-
dict. When he announced that he was coming to Rita Blanca to interview Jackson, I expected him to hire Jackson and attempt to seduce
me. Instead he hired me, showed no interest in Jackson, and seduced
nobody, although I thought I had made it clear when we kissed that I
would not have resisted more serious advances.

After dinner Mrs. Karoo offered him a room for the night but he
told her that he had formed the habit of sleeping out, and he did sleep
out, over by Mrs. Karoo's cistern.

When I found him in the morning he was sitting on a basket, rif-
fling through the telegrams I had made him take the night before.

"Go here, go there!" he said, sounding annoyed. "Track Crazy Horse,
track Sitting Bull. Track the Sioux, track the Cheyenne. Track Geronimo."

Though clearly vexed by the telegrams, he got a merry twinkle in
his eye when he saw me coming—he heaved the sheaf of telegrams
over his shoulder into the morning wind, which soon scattered them
over a wide stretch of prairie.

"It might be more fun, Miss Courtright, to track you for an hour or
two and see where that takes us," he said. Then he laid me down on the
pallet and we kissed more or less to our hearts' content. I say more or
less because Bill's kisses, though fairly passionate, were not as passionate
as Zenas Clark's had been. My susceptibility was acting up again, and Bill
Cody was not unaffected. I could feel his big bullwinkle stiffening up
nicely; and yet the man's mind was not really on the matter at hand.

"If it's more privacy you want you could consider tracking me
down to Joe Schwartz's hay barn," I whispered. "Up there we could
copulate as much as we please."

Bill Cody didn't seem to hear me—he had the habit of not hearing things that threatened to distract him from whatever he really felt like thinking about at the time, which in this case wasn't me, although he did free up my bosom and seemed mighty pleased by the heft and haft of my titties.

"Oh, I expect we should save copulation for when we meet in North Platte," he informed me casually.

"For when we meet in North Platte?" I said—I was more or less stunned. The man had a stiffie the size of a post and he wanted to save copulation until we got to someplace I had never heard of. I wasn't even sure it was a place! And he was idly fondling one of my breasts even as he said it.

"Here's the point, Nellie," he went on—I don't think he noticed that I was as shocked as I was. "I can't afford to be reckless about the generals, not just yet. Some of them are rich, and even if they ain't, they know rich men—bankers and railroad magnates and press lords and the like. I'm going to need some well-heeled investors if I'm to get my Wild West going, and the generals can lead me to the rich men and persuade them to listen."

"I suppose that's true, but why is that a reason to postpone copulation?" I asked him. Here I was, half undressed, and Bill was acting as if he was sitting in a banker's office, explaining the terms of a loan.

Of course, he didn't bother to answer my question. The point, which I only figured out after working for the man, was that Buffalo Bill Cody was a one-thing-at-a-time sort of man. Just at the moment, getting his Wild West going was the first thing on his mind; copulation was way down the list somewhere.

It wasn't that Bill Cody didn't like copulation—I think he liked it well enough, when he could fit it in. I was never his mistress, but for a good many years I was probably the most dependable woman in his life—and one thing I learned was that if any man had an orderly mind it was William Frederick Cody. An aspect of his orderly mind was a strict list of priorities, and on that list copulation probably came in at about seventh or eighth, but no higher. I'd put it just before visits to his tailor—this showed that he did like carnal relations because Cody knew quite well that his splendid appearance was half his act; he did not stint on visits to his tailor. In my long years with him I never saw him appear in public other than beautifully dressed—though he didn't really ever become dandified to the extent that Billy Hickok did.

That morning, though—a young woman half naked on a pallet behind a cistern on the plains of No Man's Land—I had not had time to figure all this out. I wanted him right then and there, and could not hold back tears of frustration when I realized there was little likelihood that I could coax this irritating fellow up in the haybarn to finish what we had started.

"Here's my decision," he said, and he said it with kindness, because he knew quite well that I was, at the moment, a disappointed young woman.

"I'll head for the Yellowstone and give the generals one more month," he told me, wiping away my tears with a fine white handkerchief. "Crook plans to hook up with Terry, so I suppose that's where I'll head."

"You won't get shot, will you?" I asked. I suppose I was more than a little in love with him by this time.

"Why, who would shoot me?" he asked. "No Indian would be fool enough to hang around where Crook or Terry might spot them. I'll carry a few messages and maybe shoot a buffalo or two. Then I'll catch the steamer *Yellowstone* and meet you in North Platte, Nebraska, one month from today."

"What are you going to do about Jackson?" I asked. "He's the hero of the Yazee affair, after all."

"I think we better just leave Jackson here—I expect he'll make a real good deputy," he said.

I suppose I felt slightly wounded, on behalf of my brother.

"Why don't you want him?" I blurted.

"Lacks flair," Cody said in his kindly tone.

Then he looked at my titties again.

"Whereas you've got flair to spare," he said, with a broad grin.

"Maybe more flair than you can handle, Mr. Cody,' I said, still piqued.

"Doubtful, Miss Courtright," Bill Cody said.

# 5

TO THE END of his days Bill Cody looked better on a horse than just about anybody else in the world—it was one of the secrets of his great success in show business. When he mounted up that day and got ready to leave Rita Blanca he looked so handsome and dashing that the McClendon sisters poured forth fountains of tears, and old Mrs. Thomas began to sob as well, although she was blind and had never seen Cody.

Happy as I was to have this dashing fellow admire my young bosom, Bill did just about as many things to annoy me as he did to please me. He seemed to assume that if he just spread a little charm around, pretty soon everybody would be agreeable to doing things his way. In no time, working on that assumption, he had the whole town in a tizzy.

When he got ready to leave he found me at the telegraph office, making a start at teaching my sister-in-law, Mandy Williams, how to operate a telegraph key. Not only was Mandy bright, but she was thrilled to death to have a chance at a paying job that didn't involve dealing with the male stiffie. Still, telegraphy is not something you can learn in five minutes, a fact that Bill Cody, who got at least a dozen telegrams a day, seemed to be slow to learn.

After glad-handing his way around the village and signing a few more autographs, he seemed to be shocked to find me settled in with Mandy.

"I thought you'd be packed and saddled up by now," he said. "What's the reason for the delay?"

"I don't know why you'd think that," I told him. "I have no intention of leaving today."

"But I'm leaving," he said, with a trace of bewilderment on his face—over the years I was to see that look many times in the future. The look appeared when, perversely, life would refuse to align itself with his firm expectations.

"But I hired you—I thought we'd travel together," he said.

"You did hire me, but then you said you planned to chase Indians for a month," I reminded him. "You said we'd meet in North Platte. I see no reason to hurry on up to Nebraska to sit around for a month when in fact I'm still needed here. Surely you didn't expect me to leave Rita Blanca in the lurch in order to twiddle my fingers in North Platte."

"I don't know what I expected, but if I did expect something, it wouldn't happen, not if you were involved," he said. He sounded irritated, though he was favoring Mandy with one of his famous Cody smiles.

"Go chase your Indians, Mr. Cody," I ordered. "I'll be in Nebraska when I'm due."

Bill Cody was not a man who enjoyed arguments. He often got mad but he couldn't stay mad very long. I suppose he thought I'd jump at the chance to be with him every minute, but when he found I wasn't, he merely gave a little shrug and went on to the next thing. In this case the next thing was to hand me a big wad of paper money, which he plucked out of a saddlebag.

"Expenses for you and Hungry Billy," he said. "I believe I've persuaded him to come be the Wild West's photographer."

"I suppose I can put up with Billy as a traveling companion—as long as I don't have to depend on him for directions," I told him. "He's famous for getting lost, you know."

"Uh-oh," Cody said. He had never been lost in his life and probably didn't realize that many prairie travelers spent much of their time in that unhappy state.

"Surely you can find your way to the train station in Dodge City, can't you?" he asked.

"I am expert on the route to Dodge City, but I prefer to avoid the place on account of the Earp brothers," I informed him.

"Those clodhoppers," he said, with evident scorn.

"I suppose they are clodhoppers, but one of them has already proposed marriage to me," I said.

"Marry an Earp? Perish the thought," he said.

"My reaction exactly—however, it does make the matter of traveling through Dodge City a little tricky."

"The young one, Warren, ain't so bad—was it Warren who proposed?" he asked.

"Nope, it was Virgil."

"He would, the skunk," Cody said.

He pondered the question of my relations with the Earps for a while, slapping his leg with his glove impatiently. It was clear that he wanted to be on his way.

"I'll have a word with Josh Teck, the mail rider," he said. "I met Josh in Pony Express days. I reckon he can get you past the Earps."

"He could if he were available," I told him. "But the fact is, Mr. Teck is in Omaha and is not expected to return with our mail anytime soon, which is why it's all the more important to keep the telegraph office functioning properly.

"Without the telegraph office, Rita Blanca would be completely cut off," I emphasized.

"I doubt that would be any big loss," Cody said. "What in hell is Josh Teck doing in Omaha?"

"He's pursuing a lady," I told him simply.

"Josh Teck is pursuing a lady?" Cody asked, in astonishment.

"Why yes, men often do," I reminded him.

"Are you sure this information's fresh?" he asked. "Josh is eighty if he's a day. I wouldn't have thought he possessed the sap to be pursuing women in Omaha, Nebraska."

My information was fresh. I got it from Ripley Eads, the barber, who was Josh Teck's best friend and kept up with his love life, such as it might be.

"You said yourself you were tired of being a shuttlecock for the military," I reminded him. "I only need a week to get Mandy Williams trained up. Then you and me and Hungry Billy could travel together."

"A week in Rita Blanca would be seven days too many," Cody said. He was becoming more irritable by the moment.

"Nobody said you had to spend the whole week in town," I mentioned. "Aurel's about to go on a hunt—I'm sure he'd enjoy your company. Maybe you could even catch the buffalo."

"A white buffalo?" Cody asked, perking up immediately.

"A white buffalo would be quite an attraction at your Wild West," I mentioned.

In fact I had just made up a bold lie, spawned by the fact that *Moby-Dick* was my father's favorite book. If there could be a white whale, why not a white buffalo? Actually the nearest I had come to hearing about a white buffalo was Ripley Eads, the barber, who mentioned that a cowboy had reported seeing a yellow buffalo down on the Big Wichita River, which Ripley seemed to think was in Texas.

It was my inspiration to turn this yellow buffalo the cowpuncher had seen into a white buffalo that Bill Cody might want to catch. My motive was to keep Bill Cody in the vicinity for a few days so I could finish training Mandy—then I could travel with him to the mysterious North Platte. I knew Bill Cody liked me. He admired my bosom and was impressed that I was an organized woman, but there was an out-of-sight, out-of-mind quality about the man that would be folly to ignore. If I let him saunter off to chase around with a bunch of fat generals for a month he might forget me completely. I did not intend to abandon a steady job as the telegraph lady of Rita Blanca in order to be ignored in Nebraska.

So I told my little lie and it certainly caught the attention of my customer, Buffalo Bill Cody. He was looking as excited as I'd ever seen him, and I was the woman who had caused his bullwinkle to stiffen up, though not to much purpose, I had to admit.

"Where's this white buffalo supposed to be?" Cody asked. A minute ago he had been impatient but he was all ears now.

"Somewhere along the Big Wichita River, I believe," I said, leaving the rumor a little vague, as rumors should be.

"Well, that's interesting," he said. "Aurel's always claimed that the country south of the Rio Rojo had not been hunted out."

"So am I right?" I asked. "You would like a white buffalo for your Wild West?" I asked demurely, whereupon I was nearly smothered with Cody's kisses.

"You're so right I'm giving you a raise before you even start, Miss Nellie," he said. "If I had a white buffalo I'd soon be way ahead of all the other shows and circuses that are out and about."

Then he leaned close and whispered in my ear—Mandy had stepped away for the moment, which was sensitive of her.

"Don't yap about this, Nellie," he cautioned. "Don't mention it to anyone. I don't want this prize to get away."

Then he loped off to the hide yard to look for Aurel Imlah.

"He sure looks good on a horse, don't he?" Mandy said. "Are you his mistress yet?"

"No, but I'm trying," I told her.

# 6

BY LATE AFTERNOON the mere fact that Bill Cody had departed Rita Blanca seemed to push the whole town down into the dumps. It was a curious thing, the gift Bill Cody had for making life seem to sparkle. His own spirits were mostly so high that they seemed to lift the spirits of everyone around them.

He was full of jokes and witticisms and could make simple things like eating pudding or pitching horseshoes seem, for the moment, the best fun in the world.

But when Bill left he took his bounce with him. Late in the afternoon, after Bill had left on his quest for the white buffalo, Ripley Ead's shack of a barbershop caught on fire. The bucket brigade was so slow to organize itself that the little shop burned to the ground. All Ripley managed to salvage were his scissors, combs, razors, and a certain amount of hair tonic.

The loss of the barbershop was only one of the calamities that befell Rita Blanca that afternoon.

While the barbershop was burning, a horse thief snuck into the livery stable and stole three horses, fortunately not including my roan.

Then the McClendon sisters' milk cow ate loco weed and began to try to trample the chickens. Bertha liked the chickens better than she liked the cow, so she shot the cow, which displeased her sister Melba, who had the odd habit of taking milk baths.

Throughout the long afternoon calamities continued to occur, most of them as unexpected as snow in August. The blacksmith smashed his thumb with a hammer, and Doc Siblee came down with gout. Pete and Pat, Mrs. Karoo's two Choctaw girls, got homesick and ran off. Two drunks took advantage of the total absence of law in Rita

Blanca—Teddy and Jackson were chasing the horse thieves, of course—to enjoy a shoot-out in the street, in which both were badly wounded and an innocent ox killed. The freighter whose ox got killed was indignant that no lawmen had been there to protect his valuable beast.

Despite these distractions I did my best to field incoming telegrams, most of which, of course, were for Buffalo Bill.

"Gosh, I'm glad I'm not that popular," Mandy said. As a telegrapher she was making rapid strides.

"I like a little time to myself," she added.

Just as we were about to close, Ted Bunsen and my brother, Jackson, rode in, their mission having obviously failed. Teddy rode grimly on to the jail but Jackson, who was clearly in a sulky mood, stopped to greet his fiancée.

"Hi, Jackson," Mandy said. "How's my honey bunny?"

Jackson didn't at first acknowledge this tender greeting, which I confess took me aback. Honey bunny? Mandy seemed to have lost her wits.

"I might be a honey but I ain't a bunny," Jackson told her.

Meanwhile he was glaring at me—it was me he was mad at, not Mandy.

"I guess I know why Buffalo Bill didn't like me," he said, going right to the kernel of his grievance.

"Who says he doesn't like you?" I inquired.

"*I* said," Jackson went on. "He hired Hungry Billy and never spoke hardly a word to me."

I decided not to mention that Cody thought Jackson lacked flair. There had been enough trouble in Rita Blanca for one day.

"It's because I'm short," Jackson concluded. "Tall people don't like short people. I wish I'd shot him, the coward."

"Just because you didn't catch the horse thieves is no reason to stand there talking nonsense," I countered. "Bill Cody is no coward and you couldn't have shot him because you can't shoot straight. If you'd tried to shoot Billy you might just have killed that poor freighter's other ox."

In the course of our lives I've thrown many things at Jackson—a boot, fire tongs, a simple saltshaker. All I had handy on this occasion was a sturdy glass inkwell. Jackson had just dismounted—the inkwell hit him square in the forehead, knocking him flat—deep black ink began to pour over his face and shirt.

No deputy sheriff likes to be knocked down by his sister, with an inkwell or anything else.

"I will arrest you as soon as I get up," Jackson said. "We'll see how you like the inside of our jail."

If Mandy Williams was shocked that I had floored her groom-to-be with an inkwell, she didn't show it. Mandy was a practical girl who immediately realized that Jackson's shirt was going to be ruined forever if she didn't get it into some cold water quick.

"Stand up, I need to get that shirt off you!" she commanded.

"I've got a headache," Jackson informed her.

"I'll be back for you and your headache—first I need to get this shirt under the pump," Mandy insisted.

"But I'll be half naked," Jackson protested, to no avail. Mandy stripped the shirt off him and soon had it under Mrs. Karoo's pump.

The lump on Jackson's forehead wasn't getting smaller, and he was still dripping ink off his nose.

"Go stick your head under that pump, Jackson," I advised. "I regret that I had nothing to throw at you but the inkwell. A stick of firewood would have served my purpose just as well."

"You're still under arrest," he informed me sourly.

I suppose I could sympathize with Jackson's feelings. He shot down the Yazees and became a big hero, but his time as a hero hadn't lasted very long. The newspapermen came and left, leaving Jackson just a deputy, and a short one at that. Then Bill Cody, a big, tall fellow who looked every inch a hero, showed up, exhibited only minimal interest in Jackson, and immediately hired me. This must have caused more than a little frustration—though, in his frustration, Jackson overlooked the biggest fact of all, which was that the comely and practical Mandy Williams had agreed to marry him. It had always been Jackson's tendency to look on the dark side, rarely the bright. Like many brothers he had gotten in the habit of blaming most of his troubles on his big sister—in this case, me.

"Stop glaring at me, Jackson," I said. "If you want to arrest me, let's head on over to the jail, though I won't promise to stay very long."

"I guess Sheriff Bunsen will decide how long you're to stay," he said, rather formally drawing his gun. He didn't quite dare actually point it at me.

"Listen, Jackson, can't you be practical for once?" I urged. "Mandy needs to wash that ink off you. Why don't you let her clean you up and I'll go explain the situation to the sheriff."

"You won't tell it right," Jackson said. "You'll tell it so it comes out my fault."

"But it is your fault," I reminded him. "You're the one who started complaining."

"You're always kissing men!" Jackson declared. "You're always kissing men."

But he seemed to lose interest in his own accusation. He looked so woebegone all of a sudden that I had the urge to hug him, but before I could act on the feeling he put his pistol back in its holster, forgot about arresting me, and walked off to find his fiancée. He even had ink on his pants.

Who would have thought one simple inkwell would spill out that much ink?

# 7

IT HAD BEEN a while since I had paid Sheriff Ted Bunsen much attention—my susceptibilities being what they are, I have a way of forgetting one man when a more interesting man comes along; and even in an out-of-the-way place like Rita Blanca, men more interesting than Ted Bunsen did come along. Andy Jessup, Zenas Clark, and Buffalo Bill Cody all put Ted Bunsen well in the shade when it came to being interesting.

On the other hand, I am not the kind of girl who likes to lose boyfriends. Andy, Zenas, and Bill had temporarily hied themselves off to other parts, but good old reliable Ted could be counted on to be sitting in a rope-bottomed chair in the office of the jail, drinking whiskey that might have a fly or two in it. I decided to slip in and give him a kiss or two, so he wouldn't despair. In fact he was pouring whiskey from his jug to his glass when I came striding in in my forthright way: he jumped about a foot when I surprised him.

"Hello, Theodore," I said. "Deputy Courtright has just placed me under arrest—want to help me pick out a cell?"

"Deputy Courtright might have acted rashly," Ted allowed. "What's the charge?"

"Hitting an officer of the law in the head with an inkwell," I informed him.

Teddy, I believe, was already drunk. He had to concentrate hard on his pouring, and even so, he filled the glass so full that a trickle of rye whiskey slopped over.

"Here, let me drink that down a little, Teddy," I suggested, taking the glass from him. I swallowed off about an inch of violent liquid before I set the glass down and kissed Teddy.

It takes very little harsh liquor to make me amorous.

"The best cells are upstairs," Teddy muttered.

"I hadn't been planning to stay the night but if you could find it in you to be a little friendlier I might change my mind," I said. Then I bit his lower lip, which caused him to jump. It's a good thing I thought to set the whiskey glass in a safe place, because under my guidance Teddy got friendlier and friendlier. We took the glass of whiskey upstairs and, between us, finished it off.

He had shaved off the walrus mustache the week before, which, from my point of view, made all the difference. Who wants to kiss a man with a hedge on his lip?

"I don't think I'm supposed to do this in the jail with a prisoner," Ted remarked as I was trying to work his pants off over his long thin stiffie.

"Theodore, let me tell you something," I said, wiggling his stiffie a little. "The more you talk, the less fun this will be—it's one of those occasions when talk can't contribute much."

Dawn was breaking over the great prairies before Sheriff Bunsen ventured to say another word; and then it was only to mutter about someone named Helen, a slip I noticed instantly.

"Helen, who's this Helen? Is she blond or brunette?" I pressed. But the sheriff of Rita Blanca was in a wrung-out state. All I got from him was a snore.

# 8

HONESTY IS NOT something I wasted much time on—strict honesty, at least—but if I were to be honest with myself I'd have to admit that I'm not wholly free of distressing quirks, one being that the minute I inveigle some gent into actually romping through the night with me I wake up determined to avoid ever seeing that particular gent for a while.

Zenas Clark had been the exception to this rule, and Bill Cody, had he been a little less of a businessman, might have been another. Ted was not an exception, which didn't mean that the demon of jealousy wouldn't rouse itself after a night of restless copulation in a jail cell. Steady old Ted had just happened to mutter the wrong name as he was waking up.

By good luck I only had to walk across the street to discover who the mysterious Helen was. Leo Oliphant was up early, sweeping cigar butts and other debris out of the Whiskey Creek Saloon. He had to sweep around an inert body that happened to be stretched out almost in front of the doors to the saloon. The body looked dead to me, but Leo assured me that the fellow was still drawing breath and sustaining a low pulse.

"That's Joe—he must have drunk nearly a gallon of whiskey last night—and a gallon of my best whiskey will produce a state similar to paralysis. But it finally wears off."

"Do you know a Helen in this town?" I asked, coming right to the point.

"Sure do," Leo said. "She's my wife."

"I didn't even know you had a wife, Leo," I admitted. "Where do you keep her?"

"I don't keep her," Leo said. "Nobody can keep Helen, but at the moment she's up in Kansas City attending her mother, who is poorly. Helen despises Rita Blanca and she particularly despises Sheriff Ted."

Helen Oliphant's relations with Ted Bunsen were a matter I would have liked to hear more about, but I didn't see how I could learn more about it without putting Leo on a track that could only lead to trouble.

"Goodness, Leo, I didn't even know you were married," I admitted.

Leo got a kind of warm look in his eyes—the same kind of warm look that Aurel Imlah got when he happened to be smoking a pipe with Mrs. Karoo.

"I consider myself a near bachelor," he said.

"Don't you miss Helen?"

"Does a dog miss a tick?" he replied.

I suppose life is complicated everywhere, even in a community that was no more than a cluster of hovels in the middle of a big prairie. Why, after a night of vigorous copulation with me, would my longtime suitor Ted Bunsen be muttering the name of Leo Oliphant's wife?

Leo Oliphant had the look of a virile man, to me. He was stocky, black-headed, and usually had a grin on his face.

"Do you think being a bartender makes you cynical?" I asked.

Leo had a deep, vigorous laugh, and my question made him laugh long and loud.

"Yes, to your question, but being a bartender's also made me prosperous," he replied. "Prosperous enough to afford an absentee wife and a long-legged whore now and then."

I walked on up the street. I had the feeling that things might bust out, pretty soon, in Rita Blanca. What I wanted was for Bill Cody to give up looking for the white buffalo, which didn't exist anyway, and squire me out of town before the trouble started.

# 9

BILL CODY AND Aurel Imlah showed up four days later, by which time I had managed to give Mandy Williams a firm foundation in small-town telegraphy.

If there was anything else she needed to know, she would just have to learn it on the job, as I had.

The two hunters returned with no white buffalo, a fact that annoyed Bill Cody no end.

"I guess Moby buffalo got away," I said, to tease him, but I don't think Bill Cody was exactly steeped in Melville.

"We did see a yellow one," he mentioned, "but I don't think a yellow buffalo will play."

I had my valise packed and was ready to leave Rita Blanca at a moment's notice, a fact that didn't escape Cody.

"I see you're ready, that's good," he said. "I hope Hungry Billy's ready too. How many telegrams from generals have piled up by now?"

There were thirty, which I handed to him.

"They're useful for starting fires," he said, stuffing them in a saddlebag.

"You'll be glad to know we ran into Ros Jubb—she said you needed your face slapped."

"What's her present project?" I inquired.

"*Jubb's Journey to Comanche Land* is her next book," he said. "Let's get out of here."

I said a hasty good-bye to Mrs. Karoo and Aurel Imlah and then did the same with Jackson and Mandy. The goose egg on Jackson's forehead was now purple, with streaks of yellow here and there. Cody looked askance when he saw it.

"Did a brick fall on the deputy?" he asked, as we were hurrying into the general store.

"An inkwell accidentally slipped out of my hand," I admitted. "Did you know Leo Oliphant's married? His wife's named Helen."

I was fishing, of course—I wanted to know if this seductress, Helen Oliphant, had maybe laid a snare for Bill Cody too.

"I have little interest in Leo Oliphant or anyone he might have married," he said, in a testy voice.

"Sorry, bite my head off while you're at it," I responded.

He didn't bite my head off but he did have a little pettish fit when Hungry Billy told him that he had decided he couldn't leave.

"There's a passel of work to do and no one but me to do it," Hungry Billy told him. "I can't just go off and leave the store my father built."

"But I need a photographer!" Cody said—then he gave up.

"How hard is it to learn to take photographs?" I inquired.

"Damn hard, if you intend to do it right," Cody claimed. "I had Mattie Brady taking pictures for me—he's the best—but he got so famous that he mostly takes pictures of the president now."

"Give me a month and I'll train up and take pictures for you," I said.

Cody sighed. He did not like the smallest setback when it came to his Wild West. And there was, I supposed, the little matter of propriety in regard to me.

"Now we've got no chaperone," he pointed out. "What if it gets in the papers that Buffalo Bill Cody—a married man—is traveling alone with a lithesome young beauty? Lulu would wring my neck and then she'd wring yours."

"We could just stay to ourselves and not go into towns," I suggested, but Cody wasn't assuaged.

"The Wild West will be family entertainment, Nellie," he informed me. "Performers ain't narrow-minded people—they like their frolics, and you can't get around human nature. For me to travel alone with a lively beauty such as yourself is sure to produce publicity—and the wrong kind of publicity at that."

I realized from the look in his eye that I had gone from being an asset to being a risk—a big risk. He was about to abandon me to protect his shows—I saw it in his eyes. I know Billy liked me but he liked his Wild West better, and would ditch me if he had to to protect it.

I needed to think quick and I did think quick. We were not too far from where Ripley Eads's barbershop had burned down—I could smell the ashes still.

"Let's take Ripley Eads!" I said. "He lost his barbershop. He's got no place to operate. Won't the Wild West need a barber?"

Bill looked at me with admiration—once again I had shown myself to be organized.

"Of course it will need a barber," he said. "Ripley will do fine."

Then he gave me a little soft smile and an appraising look. I believe he liked it that I was quick-minded enough to come up with a chaperone in a flash, in the hope of not being left behind.

Ripley, of course, was as pleased as Bill. He was trying to rent a corner of the jail to cut hair in, but most of his customers had seen the inside of a jail cell from time to time and might not be comfortable coming into one just for the purpose of barbering.

The three of us left Rita Blanca about the middle of the afternoon—I was on my roan and Ripley astraddle our mule, Percy, who had fattened up considerably during his days of easy living in Rita Blanca. Nearly the whole town showed up again to see us off—or rather to see Buffalo Bill off. Nobody cared much whether Ripley or I went or stayed. Bill Cody, of course, was in full fig, wearing one of his fine buckskin suits. Mrs. Karoo cleaned it for him.

The man did like to make a show!

I cried a little bit when we rode past my little telegraph office.

"I won't tolerate much blubbering," Bill said, amiably. "If you are able to work up fond memories of a stinkhole like this, then I can't wait to show you Broadway."

"No, I'm thinking of haircuts," Ripley said. "I suppose play actors are particular about how they cut their hair."

"Not as particular as the Indians," Bill replied.

"Indians?" Ripley replied. It was clear that he had not given much thought to that aspect of his new job.

"There'll be Indians, but not for a while yet," Cody said. "And I expect they'll mostly want to do their own hair."

"I hope so," Ripley said.

"You didn't see the Indian on your hunt, did you?" I inquired. Being out on the barren plains always took adjusting to—part of it was worry that the Indian might appear. What if he was one of those Indians who Cody had said would get the best of him?

"What Indian?" Cody asked.

I explained about the snowstorms and the lance and Ros Jubb's goggles—before I could finish Bill Cody gave one of his big, hearty laughs. He even slapped his leg.

"That's not an Indian, that's just Mickey—he's Frisian," he said. "Mickey likes to wonder around spooking people. I may get him in my Wild West if he'll consent to settling down."

At the time I had no idea what a Frisian was, but I didn't feel like admitting it. Now and then Bill Cody would chuckle a little, as we rode, at the ignorance of people who couldn't tell Indians from Frisians.

I never mentioned the Indian again.

# 10

EXCEPT FOR WHEN they needed to shoe their horses the Earp brothers seemed to live in front of a low dive called the Tascosa Saloon, which was on the main street of Dodge City. They stood there like big black birds of a feather, watching us come. At least the four older Earps stood—the youngest brother, Warren, sat on the steps whittling a stick. He was a willowy youth, maybe a few years older than me. I decided on the spot that if fate put me much in the company of the Earps again I would concentrate my attentions on young Warren.

Cody had no interest in the Earps—that was easy to see. I think he planned to go trotting straight on through Dodge to the train depot.

But Virgil Earp, no doubt still stung by my rejection, came hurrying out to intercept us. I guess Bill Cody concluded that it would be impolite just to ignore the man completely, so he drew rein. Ripley and I did the same.

"Hello, Mr. Earp," Cody said. He wore no pistol but had a rifle in a scabbard under his leg.

"Hello, yourself, Cody," Virgil said. "I see you have an impudent wench with you who considers herself too good to accept the proposal of an honest man."

"I wasn't even aware that an honest man had proposed to Miss Courtright," Bill said, without a glance at me.

"I proposed to her—don't you consider me honest?" Virgil said, in a loud, ringing voice.

"Well, I consider you loud, at least," Cody said. "As I have only seen you twice in my life I have no opinion on the honesty issue."

"Watch your tongue, there's four of us here," Wyatt said. He stepped off the porch and then he wobbled. I believe he was dead drunk.

Young Warren Earp didn't like what his brother had just said.

"Only four, Wyatt—four?" he said. "What do you think I am, a toadstool?"

"Warren, you are not involved in this," Wyatt said. "It's between Virgil and the wench."

"This is Miss Antoinette Courtright of Waynesboro, Virginia," Cody informed them. "'Wench' is not a term she is used to hearing and I don't think she ought to hear it again."

"Oh you don't, do you?" Virgil asked.

Cody didn't bother answering. It was clear he had no fear of the Earps and little interest in what they might think of me or anything else.

Ripley Eads turned white, as if he feared there might be gunplay, but before Virgil could decide whether to risk calling me a wench again, young Warren Earp rose from his seat and dove into Wyatt in a running tackle.

"I am not a toadstool—I'm a full-grown Earp!" Warren said loudly, after he tackled Wyatt.

Not only was Wyatt Earp dead drunk, his little brother was astraddle of him, making it hard for the famous marshal to put up much of a defense. Fortunately for him he had three stout brothers, James, Virgil, and Morgan, who set about pulling Warren off. Even so, subduing young Warren proved no easy matter. He fought like a tiger cat. Once or twice the older brothers thought they had Warren safely under control, only to have Warren twist loose and pounce on his dusty brother, who rose to his knees twice, only to be flattened by a new assault.

"Now this is interesting," Cody said. "The whole of the Earp brethren can barely manage that boy."

The older Earps were all obviously horrified at what was happening. They all seemed to feel that they could not possibly allow young Warren to whip the famous Wyatt, and their embarrassment grew as Warren kept breaking loose and launching new assaults. Being left out of the family count had obviously tapped into a deep pool of temper—and now the question was, who was invincible and who wasn't?

"They're losing prestige every time Warren whops Wyatt," Cody whispered to me. "And prestige might be all that's keeping them alive in a raw place like Dodge."

"Besides that, it's happening in front of an important witness . . . me!" Cody added.

One thing was clear, at least: Virgil Earp now had more important things to think about than calling me a wench. He ignored me entirely and tried to push the conversation to other topics.

"I hear you're working up a show, Cody—where's it going to be?" he asked.

"It's not a show, it's the Wild West, authentic down to the last Bowie knife," Cody informed him. "I'm in the process of assembling stars and heroes now. We may open in Omaha or we may just do a try-out or two in North Platte."

"Anything we could do in your show?" Virgil asked. "Wyatt thinks Dodge City's mostly lost its snap."

Cody laughed—he had a good, deep laugh and he suddenly let it roll out.

"I can't see that young Warren's low on snap," he said. "I see he's a smart boy. I prefer to take my opponents from behind, myself—reduces the likelihood of gunplay."

By this time a crowd had gathered, either to watch the fight or because they'd recognized Cody—easy to do when he was in one of his fine buckskin suits.

Wyatt Earp was on his feet, but he still looked shaky. His brothers James and Morgan tried to steady him but he shook them off.

"I intend to beat the tar out of that young whelp as soon as I sober up," Wyatt remarked, wiping blood off his nose. "And I may beat the tar out of all of you, for not warning me about his sneak attack."

The older brother, James, who was dressed like a bartender and was a bartender—as Cody later told me—was anxious to curb such inflammatory talk.

"Warren's as much an Earp as you," James pointed out. "There was no reason to leave him off the count."

"Mind your own business or go tend bar," Wyatt said. "And shut your damn trap or I'll whip you first."

Virgil and Morgan Earp glanced nervously around, but James Earp didn't glance anywhere.

"I know you're the famous one, Wyatt," James Earp remarked.

"But don't let it go to your head. The sun has never risen on a day when you could whip me."

"Now that's well spoken," Cody remarked in admiration. "I do like a man who can put things crisp like that."

"I'm getting about enough of derogatory comment," Wyatt Earp said, turning toward Bill. "And for my money you're too damn fancy, Cody."

Bill ignored Wyatt's comments completely and turned toward young Warren, who was sitting on a step, catching his breath.

"Can any of you boys ride a buffalo?" he asked.

"Supposing we could, why would we want to?" Morgan Earp asked.

"Money," Cody said. "Virgil asked if there was a place for Earps in my Wild West, and the one thing that comes to mind is the buffalo-riding event. We caught a big bull named Monarch and so far no cowboy's even been able to stay on him for thirty seconds. I'm thinking of offering a big prize for anyone who can stay on Monarch for half a minute."

Warren stood up.

"I can ride anything that's got four legs," he announced. "And sometimes I can even ride critters who have only got two."

Warren Earp was looking right at me when he made that remark.

If Cody noticed Warren looking at me he didn't let on.

In the far distance we hard a train toot.

"Gentlemen, we've got an appointment with the railroad," Cody said, in an amiable voice. "I have a little Indian chasing left to do. In my absence Miss Courtright here will be managing my affairs in North Platte."

"Her?" Virgil Earp asked—he was suddenly reminded of my existence and my impudence.

"Yes, she's a capable manager," Cody told him. "I intend to put her through Harvard sometime when I can spare her."

Then he looked at Warren Earp, who looked loose and lively.

"I admire your tactics, young man," he said. "Anytime you feel like trying to ride my buffalo just present yourself to Miss Courtright and you can have a try. There must be somebody who can ride Monarch—and maybe it's you."

"The hell he'll leave!" Virgil exclaimed. "Who's going to haul fire-wood and clean guns if Warren runs off to be in your show?"

Warren walked over and formally offered to shake hands with me. He stuck out his hand and I shook it firmly.

"Thanks, Mr. Cody," Warren said. "I just might take you up on your offer one of these days."

His brothers glared, but I don't believe Warren cared. I gave him a smile and we rode on to meet our train.

# 11

"I CAN ASSURE you right now that you're safe as a kitten in my house," Lulu Cody informed me as we were laying the table for my first meal under the Cody roof in their big, drafty house in North Platte, Nebraska.

"Billy don't cavort with girls who are smarter than he is," she added. "And I can see already that you're smarter than he is."

In truth it was nothing more than my excellent Courtright pedigree that got me off on the right foot with Lulu Cody, who, of course, was not half a continent away, in Rochester, New York, as Bill had assured me she would be. The first thing we saw, as we were riding up from the depot in a hired buggy, was the stout, square figure of Lulu Cody waiting for us on the porch. Just the way she stood, her hands on her hips, convinced me that Lulu meant business.

"Now look at her! Look at her! No warning!" Bill exclaimed, when he saw her.

He immediately got red in the face. It was obvious that he was highly vexed.

"Isn't she your wife?" I asked. Somehow I was not entirely surprised to find Lulu waiting for us in North Platte, her skirt blowing in the incessant Nebraska wind.

"What's that got to do with the price of eggs?" he asked.

"If she's your wife, why shouldn't she be here?" I inquired.

If anything, Bill Cody had less use for my questions than he had for the wife of his youth.

"Say she is my wife!" he exclaimed. "Does that give her the right to invade every nook and cranny of my life? Can't a man expect a little privacy once in a while?"

"How long since you've seen Mrs. Cody?" I asked.

"I spent a whole week with her no more than eight months ago," he declared, easily managing to feel sorry for himself.

"If you were married to me—God forbid—a week every eight months wouldn't be enough," I told him flatly.

"All right, Nellie—since you're on her side, why don't you drive this buggy home?" he said. "I feel an urge to wet my whistle."

Whereupon he stopped the buggy, handed me the reins, and headed for the nearest saloon.

Ripley Eads was riding with us. I suppose he was one of your sensitive barbers. He sensed trouble about the same time Cody did and jumped out of the buggy as if propelled by a spring.

Both men soon disappeared behind the swinging doors of a nearby whiskey palace, leaving me to deal with the formidable Lulu as best I could.

"Look at them run, the cowards!" Lulu said, when I pulled up.

She was soundly annoyed but not surprised. Lulu was a pretty woman, despite being stout and the tiniest bit bug-eyed. To me she looked French, and it turned out she was mostly French; she was no shrinking violet, and she scared plenty of men badly, but I want to put on record that in the years I worked for the Wild West, I never had a harsh or unkind word from Lulu Cody. Somehow she figured out right away that I was "safe"; that is, I was not likely to become her husband's mistress.

Lulu Cody drew that conclusion at the very moment when I was still more or less musing that I would become Bill Cody's mistress, at some leisurely point when there was no Lulu handy and no pressing business to interfere with our romance. I now realize that I hadn't yet come to terms with the extent to which Bill Cody was all business. Oh, he liked to carouse at the end of the day—indeed I seldom saw him entirely free of the effects of the whiskey he drank—but he was still all business. When I assumed he hired me because he wanted to copulate with me, I was dead wrong. He hired me because I was organized, and also responsible. In the world of shows that Bill Cody was swiftly moving into, the organized man (or woman) was rare, and the responsible ones even more rare. The truth is that Bill Cody had as good an eye for character as he did for horseflesh, and nobody had a better eye for horseflesh than Buffalo Bill Cody.

But that's to jump ahead.

Lulu had an elk roast cooking. As soon as I got my stuff inside, out of the dusty breeze, I hurried into the kitchen to try and be helpful to Lulu and the two stout Finnish girls she employed as household help.

"Give me Finnish girls any day," Lulu told me, handing me a salt-shaker and indicating that my duty was to salt the soup.

"Why Finnish?"

"Because they understand English and I don't understand Finnish," Lulu said. "They gossip in Finnish, which leaves me free to get my work done."

"Now, this is cozy," I said, referring to her bright, warm kitchen, which was rapidly filling up with good smells.

For a moment Lulu looked as if she might cry. She teared up and a tear or two spilled over before she caught herself and bent to check her roast.

"That's right—one thing I can do is make a place cozy," she said. "It's a fine skill, if you ask me, but Bill Cody hates cozy—he flees it like sinners flee the Lord. The cozier I make it, the farther away he wanders."

I knew Lulu was right. My bright efforts to get Bill Cody into a cozy place for romantic purposes had come to naught. Whatever his opinion of copulation, the man was not going to allow himself to be sucked in by coziness.

"Who was that fellow in the buggy with you and Bill?" Lulu asked.

"Ripley Eads, a barber and chaperone," I said.

"I wonder if he does pedicures?" Lulu asked. "I confess I'm rather partial to pedicures."

"It seems unlikely—Ripley's shy," I told her.

The smell of the elk roasting was making me hungry.

"What will you do about Bill's dislike of coziness?" I asked, though it was not exactly my business.

"Do you believe in love potions, Miss Courtright?" Lulu asked.

"Love potions?" The question took me wholly by surprise.

Lulu nodded and took a little bottle out of a cupboard and held it out to me. I had mostly read about love potions in novels—and not the better novels, either. Walter Scott and Mr. Dickens didn't dwell much on love potions.

Lulu unscrewed the top of the bottle and offered me a smell. I took one sniff and immediately got the vapors. The liquid in the bottle was brown, and unpleasantly murky.

"Potent, don't you agree?" Lulu asked. "I got it from a Gypsy. I figure Bill will show up about three hours from now, hungry as a wolf and wanting some strong coffee to do combat with his hangover. Several drops of this in the coffeepot is supposed to do the trick."

I was still struggling to clear my head.

"What trick are you expecting it to do, Mrs. Cody?" I asked.

"It's supposed to make Bill love me again," she said. "He did love me once."

Then, to my dismay, Lulu Cody burst into tears. She stood in her kitchen and sobbed heavily. The two Finnish maids, who must have been used to it, went about their business.

"You see what a crazy old woman I am?" she said, when she had cried herself out. "Love potion from a Gypsy! But I have to try anything, if I want to see my husband more than a few days a year!

"If you were married wouldn't you want to see your husband more than a few days a year?" she asked.

"I certainly would. And if the love potion didn't work I'd try to knock him down with a stick of firewood. I suppose if I hit him hard enough it would keep the so-and-so anchored for a while."

"I've yelled at Bill, don't think I haven't," Lulu said. "But I've never hit him with anything. It would hurt his feelings so."

Here I was, just arrived and already in the middle of the Cody marriage. I tried to think of something good to say about Bill, and all I could come up with was Ripley Eads.

"I might mention that your husband did insist that the two of us not travel together without a proper chaperone—in this case, the barber," I told her.

Lulu waved that one away.

"I told you Bill has very limited interest in smart women," she reminded me.

"Of course he'd hire you. If this crazy Wild West ever gets off the ground he'll need somebody smart to keep up with the payroll and the schedules and such.

"But woo a smart woman? Not likely," Lulu concluded. "Of

course, he likes to kiss every girl he can catch, as far as that goes. But if Bill thought you two needed a chaperone, it wasn't to protect you from him. It was to protect him from you."

I must have been standing there with my mouth open—why hadn't I figured that out?—because Lulu gave a short giggle and invited me to fill my plate.

"No use waiting for Bill," she said. "It'll take him two or three hours to get drunk enough to show himself."

I did as I was told and ate a pile—it was by far the best elk roast that had ever come my way.

# 12

I WAS INSTALLED in an airy upstairs room, with a fine western exposure, and was unpacking my valise and hanging my clothes in a roomy cedar closet when I heard the most awful uproar from downstairs. Many people seemed to be shouting—what they were shouting about I could not determine. I put on my housecoat and went hurrying down. It sounded as if there had been a murder downstairs—I couldn't just stand aloof.

The first thing I noticed when I came into the kitchen was Billy Cody, stretched out on the floor, one hand grasping his throat. He seemed to be alive but his face had a look of stark terror. Lulu had backed into a corner to await developments, and both the Finnish girls were crying out to the saints. A young fellow about Jackson's age was trying to get Cody to sit up.

"What's wrong with Mr. Cody?" I asked Lulu.

"That love potion was supposed to work quick but this isn't how I expected it to work," Lulu whispered.

"I should say not—who's the young man?"

"Danny Mueller, we've been raising him," Lulu said. "Do you think Bill is acting, or do you think he's really sick?"

"How much of that love potion did you put in his coffee?" I asked.

I'll say one thing for Lulu Cody—she didn't flinch from the truth.

"I put in the whole bottle," she admitted. "I am not one for half measures," she added.

I began to feel a little anxious for Bill Cody. One sniff of that love potion had left me feeling vaporish for nearly an hour. I went over to where Bill lay and introduced myself to Danny Mueller, who was plenty worried. Bill Cody was never in his life to have a more devoted friend than Dan Mueller.

"Uncle Bill just took two sips of coffee and fell over backwards," Danny said. "Do you think he's going to die?"

I wasn't confident that he wouldn't, but I did my best not to let my worry show.

"I suspect he just needs to throw up," I ventured. "Let's drag him outside—the crisp air might help."

It was a clear Nebraska night, with many fine stars. We dragged Bill to the edge of the porch and he soon began to throw up in Lulu's flowerbeds.

"She poisoned me, goddamn her!" Bill said, when he could talk a little. "Is that any way for a wife to behave?"

I was not about to admit what I knew. Danny Mueller looked very relieved—he soon went back in to try and calm the Finns.

Even in his weakened state Bill Cody was not dumb.

"You know more about this than you're telling, Missy," he said, giving me a baleful look.

"Your loving wife would never knowingly harm a hair on your head," I told him. "If you neglected me like you neglect her I'd have no compunction about braining you with a poker. But I'm not Lulu. She's of a more gentle temperament."

"Aw, the hell she is!" Bill declared. "You women always take up for one another. I'd say she poisoned me—if it wasn't for my strong constitution I'd probably be dead."

"You've been in a saloon for several hours," I pointed out. "Bad whiskey could have given you an upset stomach. It's bad manners to blame everything on your wife, who is a fine cook. I have never eaten tastier elk, and the rhubarb pie was excellent."

"Shut up, I never said she couldn't cook," Bill barked.

He held one of his hands out, attempting to hold it steady. His hand was shaking like a leaf. He tried it with the other hand—same result.

"You've just got the whiskey tremors," I told him. "Father's hands always shook like that after one of his toots."

"Hogwash," Cody said. "I've been more or less drunk since way back before the Civil War and my hands have never shook like this.

"Lulu poisoned me—but I suppose you'll back her up," he added.

"The woman's crazy about you and you don't even know it!" I reminded him.

"Hard to see why, the way I treat her," Cody said—then he chuckled. Given time, Bill Cody would find the humor in just about anything, including odd situations of his own making.

Then he tried to kiss me but I pushed him away.

"I don't think so—you need to gargle before you start kissing women," I told him.

"I'm leaving tomorrow—I've put off the generals as long as I can," he mentioned. "Surely you can spare a kiss or two for your old boss."

"No sir," I said. "Your own wife's in there pining for the merest touch. If anybody gives you a kiss tonight, it ought to be her."

"Maybe I won't send you to Harvard after all," he said. "You'd probably come back a lawyer and take me to court."

In a few minutes, with no more said, Bill got up and tromped back into the house, leaving me to ponder the ways of man and woman.

Later, as I crept back upstairs, I heard sounds of violent argument from the master bedroom. Cody was yelling—then Lulu yelled awhile—then Bill yelled some more. I was fast asleep before the Codys quieted down.

I suppose every marriage is different. Mother was far too genteel to ever yell at Father; the most she would allow herself, by way of protest, was some heavy sighs. But Mother's heavy sighs probably scared us young ones more than Lulu's howls.

What happened that night in North Platte, Nebraska, proved to be no little fight. For years Bill Cody remained convinced that Lulu had tried to poison him. Long years later, in the course of bitter court proceedings, Lulu finally admitted that she had given Bill the love potion, in hopes of winning back his affection. I don't think Bill was ever convinced it wasn't poison. Mostly, their lives were lived apart. And yet Bill kept buying Lulu splendid houses—in North Platte, in Rochester, in Wyoming, and even in Denver, I heard. There was a sadness to it for both of them, and, I'm sure, for their children too.

But I was only in their lives in a close way for a few years—what did I know?

# 13

I AM NO early riser, I admit. I have always been a sound sleeper, and I awake reluctantly, particularly so if I'm enjoying a good dream. I seem to have plenty of good dreams too—many of them involve kissing cowboys.

On my first morning in North Platte I lingered in the sheets till nearly ten in the morning. I was awake earlier, listening for sounds of trouble, but things seemed to be quiet, with no sounds of argument from the Cody quarters, so I decided to snuggle into the sheets and keep to myself for a while, until I was sure that harmony had been restored to the household.

My little delay was based on the assumption that the Codys had composed their differences, at least temporarily, and might be enjoying a happy connubial breakfast—if a reconciliation was in progress, the last thing I wanted to do was butt in.

But I was hungry and could smell bacon and flapjacks and coffee—sooner or later I was going to have to break into the domestic scene or risk getting one of the headaches I get when I don't get enough food.

So I came cautiously downstairs and into the dining room, where no tender scene—or any scene—was in progress. The big round walnut table was set for one—and I was evidently the one. The two Finnish girls—the northern equivalent of Pete and Pat—began to bring in food, starting with cabbage soup, a delicacy I had never taken with breakfast before. The fact that it seemed to be flavored with oxtail was another little test of my cosmopolitanism. Fortunately the combination worked, but I confess I felt more at home with the eggs, bacon, and flapjacks that followed.

I thought it odd that neither my host nor my hostess was around to get me started on my new duties, whatever they were, but I supposed they must be out checking on their livestock, or something. Maybe Lulu had even coaxed the shy Ripley Eads into giving her a pedicure, though I doubted it.

"Excuse me, where are the Codys?" I asked finally, after I had put away a substantial quantity of food. I thought maybe I'd take a stroll and find out what the town of North Platte looked like.

"Oh, gone!" one of the Finnish girls said, looking distressed.

"You mean gone to town?" I asked.

"No, gone! Gone away!" the other girl said.

"Gone away? Both of them?" I asked, getting an uneasy feeling.

"Both of them—you be our missus now," the younger girl said. Her name was Gretchen and her sister's name was Sigurd, a truth I didn't arrive at until later in the day.

"You mean gone far away?" I persisted, whereupon both the Finnish beauties burst into tears.

I soon began to bawl with them, out of shock, I suppose. I had left my cozy life in Rita Blanca, and now what? I was way up in Nebraska, where I didn't know a soul, and both Codys had deserted me.

I dislike bawling in front of the help—it's the kind of thing that just wasn't done, on our plantation—so I stumbled outside to finish my cry.

Fortunately it was a fine, crisp day—brilliant sunlight, deep blue sky; a passel of ducks and geese were passing overhead. The North Platte River was nearly covered with waterfowl—I remembered that Bill Cody had mentioned that there would be no shortage of ducks where I was going.

Now I was there and the Codys were gone. Fortunately the brilliant sunlight had a good effect—my spirits began to edge up, despite my discouraging start.

They were helped even more by the appearance of Danny Mueller, the young fellow who had been trying to help Bill Cody survive his wife's love potion.

"Hello, Danny—may I call you Danny?" I asked.

"Sure—most people call me Danny," the boy said. He had a sweet, slightly hangdog smile and a cowlick that stuck up whenever he took off his hat.

"I fear I overslept," I told him.

"That's okay," he said. "Uncle Bill and Aunt Lulu were nervous about seeing you anyway.

"It's because they knew you must have heard their big fight," he explained. "Unless you're deaf, you'd have to have heard it."

"I am not an eavesdropper—at least not on a regular basis," I told him. Of course I felt no qualms about eavesdropping in cases of necessity.

"Where'd the Codys go—if it's not a secret?" I asked.

"Aunt Lulu caught a train back to Rochester and Uncle Bill's headed for the Yellowstone River," Danny informed me.

"And when may we expect them back?" I asked.

Danny shrugged.

"Not anytime soon," he admitted. "Uncle Bill said he had a play to do in New York once the generals get through with him."

"What about Mrs. Cody—mightn't she come back?"

Danny looked sad.

"She told me this morning she can't live with Uncle Bill," he reported. "And Uncle Bill still thinks she tried to poison him."

"She didn't—it was just a love potion that evidently didn't work," I told him. "You mean we're looking at months before we see either of them?"

Danny Mueller nodded.

"Well then, Daniel—do you have any idea what I'm supposed to do?" I asked. "Your uncle Bill brought me up here and dumped me. I thought he was starting up a Wild West of some kind and I was to help organize it."

"Oh, Uncle Bill's still mighty keen on the Wild West," the young man assured me. "He means to get it going within a year or two, and meanwhile he told me he wanted you to be in charge of pretty much everything. There's a man at the bank you need to see—and we've got some cattle up on the Dismal River that we're supposed to go and inspect once you get settled."

"Inspect cows?" I asked. "How would I know how to inspect cows?"

Danny grinned—I think he was beginning to see the humor in the situation.

"There's cowboys up there that can help us," he said. "I guess if we see a sick cow they can help us doctor it."

"Wouldn't the cowboys be able to figure that out for themselves?" I asked.

"Maybe, if they're eager to work," he said. "It's mighty bleak up on the Dismal River—the hands might not be eager to work."

"All right—so much for Uncle Bill," I said. "Did your aunt Lulu leave me any instructions?"

"Oh, you bet!" Danny said. "She wants you to look out for good real estate that she could buy cheap—Aunt Lulu's mighty keen on real estate."

I looked off at the plains of Nebraska. Maybe I couldn't see one hundred miles, but I could see pretty far. And everything in sight looked like cheap real estate to me.

"Who's this man in the bank I'm supposed to see?"

"Mr. Applewhite," Dan said. "He runs the bank, although I think Uncle Bill really owns it.

"I'll drive you to the bank if you want me to," he added. "Ladies don't walk much up here in North Platte. The town's kind of stretched out, and Aunt Lulu told me to be sure you weren't bothered by the wrong sort."

"When it comes to an abundance of the wrong sort, I doubt North Platte is any worse than the place I just left," I told him. "But I guess I better comb my hair if I'm going to meet a banker."

"Mr. Applewhite won't like you anyway, no matter how much you comb your hair," Danny said.

"Oh—you mean he's the wrong sort—the sort you're supposed to be protecting me from?" I asked.

Danny Mueller just grinned.

# 14

I HAVE NOT frequented many banks—in Virginia genteel young ladies don't need to—but the few I had peeked into boasted a lot of dark wood and a bit of brass.

The bank in North Platte mainly consisted of Senior Applewhite, a large man with a mole beside his nose. He was too big to fit comfortably in his chair, although it was a large chair, and as Danny Mueller had predicted, he didn't like me, although I had put my hair in a chaste bun and was wearing a modest black dress. It was the dress I used to wear to funerals, during the war years.

"Mr. and Mrs. Cody are our leading citizens," banker Applewhite informed me.

I had no quarrel with that claim.

" 'Spect so," I said.

"That doesn't mean that they are always wise where financial matters are concerned," he went on.

I didn't like him any more than he liked me, so I made bold to interrupt.

"If you're Senior Applewhite, is there a Junior Applewhite somewhere?" I asked.

"Yes, my younger brother, but why interrupt me?"

"Boredom, I guess," I told him bluntly.

Senior Applewhite studied me for a moment.

"William Frederick Cody is a great man, which doesn't mean he is always wise," the banker went on. "He dragged me out of bed early this morning and insisted that I draw up a power of attorney giving you the authority to run his businesses and draw on his funds as needed."

"Probably he was in a practical mood, for once," I said.

"I wouldn't call it practical, young lady—I'd call it the height of folly," Mr. Applewhite said. "What's to stop you from running off with some cowpuncher and taking every cent that Bill Cody has?"

"My sterling character," I told him. "Did you hear from Mrs. Cody while you were waking up?"

"In fact I did," he admitted. "I told her what Mr. Cody had done, expecting her to raise old Billy hell."

"Did she?"

"No, and in fact she said that you might be handling some real estate matters for her," he allowed unhappily. "I have instructions to give you what credit you need."

I sat. Senior Applewhite sat.

"In my opinion both sets of instructions were contrary to sound business practice," he told me. "Why should a slip of a girl be allowed to make free use of the Cody funds?"

"Because somebody's got to pay the help and the bills," I mentioned. "I have no doubt that there will be bills."

"Have you known Mr. Cody long?" the ample banker asked.

"Long enough to know he doesn't flinch from expense and extravagance," I said.

"Are you his harlot?" he asked.

"How'd you like to catch an inkwell in the middle of the forehead?" I responded, standing up. "When I tell Bill Cody what you said I have no doubt that he'll come back here and pound you into blubber!

"And I'll take that power of attorney, while I'm at it!" I said.

"No need, miss, it's safe with us," Senior Applewhite said. He had gone from looking mean to looking scared. The thought that his rude comment might get back to the leading citizen of North Platte, Nebraska, put a different complexion on the matter.

"The document may be safe with you but you're not safe with me, sir—not until your manners improve."

Senior Applewhite handed over the power of attorney meekly enough, and I walked back home and began the long task—not really finished until he closed his eyes in death, of managing the interests of Mr. William Frederick Cody, Buffalo Bill.

# 15

WHEN I WALKED out of the bank in North Platte, after my testy interview with Senior Applewhite, I felt lonely as a lost kitten. I knew no one in North Platte, and no one knew me. For help I had two nice, competent Finnish girls and Danny Mueller, a lonely, half-orphaned boy. I had been entrusted with Bill Cody's power of attorney but had no idea what to do with it. Lulu Cody expected me to buy real estate and to know what real estate was likely to appreciate and what wasn't. I felt as blue as a goose and my hat blew off twice in the whistling wind. A rather good-looking cowboy retrieved it for me after the second blow-off; he acted as if he might like to be my beau but I had too much on my mind to want a beau, just then.

I was frankly put out with the Codys for leaving without saying goodbye or giving me even the merest word of instruction. But once I got back to the big house, I calmed in my thinking a little and poked around until I found the small office where the household books were kept—in fact all the Codys' books were there, whether for the household or the ranch on the Dismal River, or the fat file on the Wild West—that file consisted mostly of applications from circus people who had taken the trouble to send Bill photographs. And when I got around to inspecting the kitchen, which had a fireplace big enough to make a den for a grizzly bear, I found that the Codys had left me a note, or rather two notes.

Bill's note was propped against a jar of marmalade and did not take long to read:

Dear Nellie:
When you visit those cowboys up on the Dismal River remember that

they are lonely men. I advise you to avoid enclutchments as such men have little restraint.

As for the trouble last night, I fail to see the wisdom of staying in a house where I have been poisoned.

I trust you, Nellie Courtright, as I would a daughter. If you stand outside and listen close you will hear the wind call my name . . .

Your fond boss,

Buffalo Bill Cody

He signed his name with a flourish, of course—most of Bill's life might be considered a flourish.

Lulu's note was brisk:

Dear Miss Courtright:

I wish I could have stayed longer. I have no doubt we will be fine friends, someday. There are times when it is not wise for me to be around my husband. His neglect cuts too deep. He says he's leaving but I suppose that's just more lies. Give young Danny Mueller some of the bounty of your warm heart.

Gretchen and Sigurd are fine girls. Don't let them marry if you can stop it.

Erratic as he is, Bill sometimes makes good choices, and he made one of his best when he persuaded you to come work for us. I feel better just knowing you're there to help look after the help.

With all my trust,

Louisa Cody

The notes were not exactly packed with instruction, and nothing was said about when I might see either one of them again, but I had had too good a breakfast to sit around and feel sorry for myself very long.

First I had the girls show me the house—actually a mansion—from basement to attic. The laundry fixings were in the basement, the dining room would seat twenty, and there was nothing in the attic except a few old hampers and a large colony of mice.

Downstairs there was even a billiard table and twelve cues. In Virginia I had rarely been allowed to play billiards—the gentlemen invariably hogged the table. I resolved to learn the game, but this resolve was never fulfilled, although I did find it soothing to roll the billiard balls around and listen to them click.

In the afternoon I applied myself to the household books, which looked simple enough to keep. Then I applied myself to the Wild West files, in which there was a high pile of bank drafts written from every place under the sun. I uncovered an invoice for a diamond necklace Bill had bought from a jeweler in Chicago. I doubt this diamond necklace had been destined to fit around Lulu's sturdy neck. But I had not been hired to preach, and what business was it of mine, anyway? I'm surprised that Lulu Cody hadn't found that receipt—or maybe she had.

For all the record of extravagance that followed Bill Cody like a wagon track, he still—if I was reading the figures right—had nearly ninety thousand dollars sitting in that little shack of a bank in North Platte.

And I held his power of attorney. Despite Mr. Applewhite's low opinion of me I intended to account for every penny of Bill's money that I spent. I did conclude that there was no economic reason to skimp on improvements, plenty of which were needed.

We needed a cat, for example, one with good skills as a mouser—otherwise that aggressive colony of mice in the attic would soon converge on us denizens of the lower floors.

There was a hole in the buggy seat that you could drop a baby through—it was fortunate that we didn't have a baby (though, close observer that I am, I thought I observed a suspicious bulge in the vicinity of Gretchen's belly button).

There being no men around to stir my susceptibilities, I decided to fling myself into action, get the buggy repaired, reduce the mouse population, and find myself a good saddle horse for my trip to the Dismal River. The Rita Blanca roan had worn out my patience on our trip to Dodge City, so I allowed Cody to sell him for me there.

Though I was lonely for the first few nights in North Platte, I was not the sort to stay lonely for long. Ripley Eads often stopped by for supper, and Danny Mueller was always there. Gretchen and Sigurd were passionate domino players—most nights the five of us would either click the ivories or play rummy.

Before a week had passed I had begun to make friends in North Platte, the first and foremost of which proved to be Senior Applewhite. Of course, he had every right to be suspicious of me when I first walked in and snatched the Codys' power of attorney. It was soon clear that he knew more about Bill Cody's love life than I did. He knew about the expensive necklace and the actress Bill had given it to. He was correct to be suspicious of me, but it didn't take much more than a week for me to turn him. I was honest, energetic, decisive, and smart, and Senior Applewhite was not slow to figure that out.

"Bill Cody makes so many mistakes being his impetuous self that it's possible to forget that sometimes he gets it right," Senior said. "And if you don't mind my saying so, he hit the bull's-eye when he hired you."

"I don't mind your saying it—a girl needs encouragement now and then," I admitted.

Senior and I formed the habit of taking coffee in his bank every day or two, and I invariably came away from our coffees better informed than I had been. Senior explained how stocks and interest and bonds and dividends worked. He was just a small town banker but he knew much that I didn't know and needed to. But for the fact that my susceptibilities seldom stir for fat bald fellows, I suspect I would have made Senior Applewhite a beau. He had no wife and drank nearly as much as Bill Cody, but I liked him.

"Nellie, you're just what this town's been needing," he told me, one clear morning. "You've got snap, and not many young women have snap."

Senior got a little misty-eyed when he said it. I think he really liked me, and I suppose he saw that I wasn't likely to want him for a beau.

He was right, but being right just made it worse. I walked home from that coffee feeling a little sad.

# 16

"I DON'T UNDERSTAND the cattle business," I admitted to Danny Mueller, who had kindly consented to accompany me on my inspection tour of Bill Cody's ranch on the Dismal River—the name, I soon discovered, could not have been more appropriate.

It was a cold day, gray and sleety; to my untrained eye the absence of landmarks was total. If Danny hadn't volunteered to go with me I would have got lost and frozen within five miles of where I started out.

"Is there a cabin up there, or are we expected to sleep out?" I asked, a little apprehensively.

"Well, there's a cabin—pretty smelly, I fear," Danny said. "The cowhands don't wash very often, specially when it gets wintry."

"How many cows are supposed to be up there?" I asked.

"I think about fifteen hundred. Uncle Billy's in it with Major North—I think the Major's working in a circus right now. He helps train the trick riders."

As we plodded north, sleet began to freeze on my eyelids. Not only was the icy sleet sticking to me, I was stuck in a situation that didn't make sense—at least it didn't to me.

Every day, back in North Platte, I toted home at least a dozen telegrams for Buffalo Bill Cody, most of them wanting him to come to Chicago or New York or Charleston or Boston, most of them wanting him to be in plays. Even a few weeks in some of those shows would make him thousands of dollars.

So why was he bothering to run cattle on the Dismal River, in partnership with a retired major who was off somewhere training trick riders?

"How much can you make, per cow, in this ranching operation?" I asked Dan.

I believe young Danny, who was as nice a man as you'd ever want to know, was beginning to find my questions just a little tiresome.

Many men soon reach that stage, once I start asking questions.

"Not much right now," Dan admitted. "Uncle Bill says the cattle industry is bad."

"Do you think this sleet storm is apt to get worse? What I don't want to do is ride all day and then arrive in a blizzard so thick that I can't see the critters I came to inspect."

"It's bound to get worse—maybe we better go home," Dan suggested.

"What if your uncle Billy's there when we get home?" I asked. "Do you think he'd fire me for backing out?"

"He won't fire you!" Danny insisted.

I hesitated, I admit. The weather was decidedly uncomfortable, and it was getting more so. I thought of that big fireplace in the Cody kitchen, so bright and cozy. No doubt Gretchen and Sigurd already had a big fire going. It would be nice to be sitting in that kitchen, having a cup of tea with a spoonful of honey in it.

I could almost taste the tea, and the honey.

But I'm a stubborn woman: it would be easy to find a squadron of males who would testify to that. When I set out to go someplace I intend to get there.

Bill Cody had hired me to run his Nebraska operation, which included looking after his cattle on the Dismal River. I didn't know one thing about cattle herds, and the main thing I knew about cowboys was that they were quick to develop stiffies if I let them kiss me much.

Bill Cody had hastily reposed his trust in me. He took one look, decided I was organized, and that was that. In my case, stubbornness probably counted as a big part of what Cody meant when he said organized.

At the sleety moment I just tapped a little deeper into my stock of stubbornness and put away thoughts of the cozy kitchen, the cup of tea, and the roaring fire.

"This weather is bound to improve eventually," I told Danny. "We're not going back."

I think Danny was startled at my decision. Probably he too had been dreaming about the kitchen and the roaring fire.

"What if it gets worse?" he asked. "What if it turns into a blizzard?"

"Have you read much about Eskimos?" I asked him.

"I haven't read much about anything," Dan admitted.

"There's an unpleasant woman named Ros Jubb who's likely to show up here someday. She wrote a book called *Jubb's Journey to Igloo Land*. She says when Eskimos get caught in a blizzard they build a little house out of blocks of snow and crawl in and stay warm."

"But this ain't a snow blizzard, this is a sleet blizzard," Dan pointed out.

I realized I had chosen a bad example, but my decision had been made: we weren't going back. Fortunately I had a thick woolen scarf and adequate gloves.

"Think we'll make that cabin by dark?" I inquired.

"We'll make it by dark," he assured me. "It'll be a shock to the boys."

All afternoon, as we plodded on north with the sleet in our faces, I felt Danny Mueller watching me. He had expected me to do what most young women would have done in our situation: head back to the fire. But I hadn't, and here we were.

Fortunately, just as we reached the icy banks of the Dismal River, the weather, instead of getting worse, got better. To the west we could see a thin strip of pale blue sky.

"I guess we won't have to build that igloo after all," I said. And then I asked him about a subject that was frequently on my mind: Gretchen's belly.

"Gretchen's such a pretty girl," I said. "Think she's got a fellow?"

Danny was horrified by my question—he pretended he hadn't heard me.

"I've heard that Finnish girls are not narrow-minded," I said. "I'm broad-minded myself, which is probably why I get along so well with Gretchen."

Danny looked miserable.

"Nobody's supposed to know," he mumbled finally.

"Maybe not, but from the look of things everybody will know, soon enough."

Danny kept looking straight ahead.

"It's not yours, is it?" I persisted.

Danny jumped so at the mere suggestion of such impropriety that his hat fell off.

"It's not mine," he managed.

"Good," I said.

# 17

"How many years since you gentlemen have washed?" I asked, in an attempt to break the ice once I'd been introduced to the three unfortunate cowboys who had been left in charge of the Dismal River herd.

Their names were Ned, Lanky Jake, and Sam. The first two were stringbeans and silent as stumps, but Sam welcomed the opportunity to complain.

"Why would we wash, abandoned as we are?" he asked.

"Nonsense, you're not abandoned," I said. "Mr. Cody sent me all the way up here to see that things are in good order."

That was a bald lie. It was the welfare of the cattle that interested Cody. The notion that he should worry about three cowboys was the kind of notion that was foreign to his mind.

"We ain't seen Bill Cody since the day he left us with these stinking cattle," Sam complained. "And why would he send a dern girl all the way up here to chouse us?"

"Nobody's chousing you," I told him. "I'm in charge of all Mr. Cody's operations in Nebraska. If you've been doing your jobs correctly you have nothing to fear."

Then Ned decided to contribute two cents' worth of complaint.

"The dern wolves are eating most of the calves," he told me.

"Sometimes they eat the cow too, if she don't hop up and act lively," Sam said.

Meanwhile I was surveying the grimy cabin—in my estimation it was little more than a lice plantation.

"A bear et one of them little yearling bulls," Lanky Jake put in.

Danny Mueller, warming his hands at the fireplace, began to look unhappy.

Finding the cabin had been his triumph, but the news from the north was not good.

"There's too dern many varmints up here," Ned said. "A wolverine et one of my boots."

"Good Lord," I said. "You men are undergoing hazardous duty. I'll be sure to inform Mr. Cody about the excess of varmints."

For supper I had a hard-boiled goose egg, packed by Sigurd, and three biscuits that were a challenge to the teeth. I had already made a decision not to spend the night in the lice plantation.

"I believe I'll bunk outside, if I could be provided with a good roaring fire," I told them. "If you can build one that will keep me from freezing I'll tell Bill Cody you're princes of the prairie."

"No, just tell him we need a good sharp raise," Sam announced.

"I'll table that suggestion until I see the condition of the livestock," I told him. "I'm the company treasurer at the moment and I try to train a fine eye on expenses."

Nothing will tongue-tie a man quicker than a well-spoken woman. Ned, Lanky Jake, and Sam stared at me as if I were a different order of being.

"Where in tarnation did you learn to talk?"

"Virginia," I told them. "How about that roaring fire?"

# 18

I SLEPT, OR at least dozed, in the space between the roaring fire and the back wall of the cabin. Dan Mueller slept inside and got so deep into the lice beds that he practically had to be scalped, once I got him home.

Not long after daybreak we were in the saddle. The prairies had a light dusting of snow.

"According to the books, Colonel Cody and Major North branded fifteen hundred head of cattle in this herd," I mentioned. "How many can you account for at the moment?"

The three cowpunchers, all of whom I had rather come to like, gave the question earnest consideration.

"No idea," Sam admitted. "A count would not be easy to come by, as you'll see."

I did see. The first critters we saw were a small herd of deer—the critters chose to stand and look at us.

Then we saw an idle group of antelope, who scarcely gave us a glance.

But when we came over a ridge and surprised a herd of about forty cattle, they farted, threw their tails in the air, and went racing away. Pretty soon they were over the next ridge and gone.

"A person who didn't know better, such as myself, might get the impression that the game up here is tamer than cattle. Is that the way it's supposed to work on a well-run ranch?"

"There's just the three of us," Lanky Jake pointed out.

"Do hunters ever show up, after all this game?" I asked.

"Oh plenty of dudes come hunting," Sam said.

"Well, if the dudes want sport, why don't they hunt the cattle, since they're a lot wilder than the game?"

This sensible suggestion shocked the three cowboys and Danny Mueller as well.

"They're not supposed to hunt cattle," Danny informed me.

Before I could push my inquiry further we came trotting over a ridge and saw a sight that lodged in my mind's eye so firmly that I never forgot it. A large red cow was sprawled on her side, attempting to calve. She had only got the calf partway out when a pack of wolves attacked, snarling and ripping at the poor half-born calf, splattering blood on the thin snow. The cow was bawling hoarsely, but she had no chance and neither did the calf, who was being eaten just as it emerged into life.

A little further on, beyond the cow, there were a number of coyotes, waiting to help themselves to whatever the wolves left.

As I watched, horrified, the half-eaten calf plopped out and several of the wolves began to eat the cow, who had yet to drop her afterbirth.

I had seen the deaths of several members of my family, but those had been peaceful deaths. The spectacle in front of me was not peaceful—it was terrible.

"Shoot 'em!" I said. "Shoot them!"

The men looked at me strangely.

"No point in shooting them," Danny told me. "The calf's dead and the mother cow's dying. It would just be a waste of bullets."

I was too shocked to accept this passive wisdom. Sam had a Winchester in his saddle scabbard. I jerked it out and charged the wolves, firing as fast as I could lever the gun. I am no markswoman. I didn't hit a single wolf, but I did scatter them, though only for a bit. Then I put the cow out of her misery by shooting her in the forehead at point-blank range. Her hoarse bawling was a sound I will never forget.

Before I even handed the rifle back, the wolves had covered the calf again.

"I'll replace those shells at my expense," I told Sam. "You will not be out a cent."

The men looked at me as if I had gone crazy and they were not far wrong.

"What do you want to do now—I fear it may snow," Ned asked me.

"I want to inspect the cattle—that's my job," I reminded them. "If it snows we'll build an igloo."

The cowpunchers did their best. They got me fairly close to several bunches of cattle, all of which, at least, were healthy enough to run. The snow fell off and on—no igloo was required and it didn't affect our strange inspection. I could not get the bovine Madonna off my mind, or the calf who passed from the womb of his mother to the bellies of wolves without even drawing breath.

Once back at the cabin, Lanky Jake prepared a substantial supper of spuds and beans. Again I slept out rather than risk the close company of lice. That night I dreamed of blood red snow, a dream that was to recur now and then for the rest of my life.

The cowboys were so lonesome for fresh company that they teared up when we left.

I doubt I spoke five words on the trip back to North Platte—and don't ask me what the five words were. It's all a blank in my mind.

# 19

I WAS JUST coming into the hall at the big house in North Platte, stamping snow off my feet so as not to track it in, when I happened to glance down the hall into the big sitting room and glimpsed about the last thing I would have expected to see in North Platte, Nebraska: a young woman practicing ballet! She was a beauty too, black-headed and so pretty in the face and figure that I was in danger of being jealous of her before I even met her. And limber, my Lord! While we watched—Danny had come in too—she stuck one leg straight up, higher than her head. Then she turned and saw us, which produced an immediate blush.

"Don't spy, come in, it's your house," she said, making us a little bow.

"I am Giuseppina," she said, with an accent no different from what an Italian might have.

I heard a chuckle and a tall, lanky fellow in buckskins who came within a hair of being as handsome as Bill Cody ambled up and put an arm around his petite wife.

"Texas Jack Omhundro," he said, shaking both our hands. "And this little wildcat is the peerless Morlacchi."

"It's too much name, just call me Jesse," the peerless Morlacchi told us with a flashing smile.

Of course I had heard of Texas Jack, who was one of Cody's closest sidekicks, both from scouting days and acting days. The two were sometimes rivals and sometimes partners, but no one had told me about the peerless Morlacchi, who would soon become my best friend.

"Excuse my mud," I said, and it was excused. In no time Jesse Morlacchi and I settled into the kitchen for several cups of tea. Every time Gretchen paraded her belly though the room Jesse smiled.

"Who's the poppa?" she asked, when Gretchen left the room.

I shrugged—I had no idea who the poppa was—but I was delighted to have another experienced female to talk with me about such things.

Texas Jack, though he was vastly amused by his pretty wife, didn't hang around long. I think he saw that he might interfere with our girl talk.

"I'll just slide off down to the saloon," he said.

"Just drink beer, no whiskey," Jesse said, at which Texas Jack lifted a fond eyebrow.

"Why do females feel the need to boss grown men?" he wondered. "Bill Cody don't stay around Lulu because she bosses him so. What if I stayed gone nine-tenths of the time, like Billy does?"

"Then you could stay gone ten-tenths of the time and I would get another husband," Jesse told him. She did not appear to be joking.

"He told me Lulu tried to poison him—what do you think of that claim?" Jack asked.

"You know the man—wouldn't you say he has a tendency to exaggerate?" I asked him.

Jesse Morlacchi would sometimes startle the company by flinging her limber leg up beside her head. She did it two or three times, while studying her husband soberly.

"Well, you wouldn't ever try to poison me, would you, Jesse?" Texas Jack asked.

The question didn't seem to interest Jesse Morlacchi—she didn't answer. Texas Jack, looking a little disappointed, went on out the door.

"When he's drunk I make him sleep on the floor," Jesse said. Then she grinned at me in her appealing way.

"I met one of your lovers—he is here," she said.

"One of my lovers?"

"Yes, Zenas," she told me. "He came on the boat with us. If I were single he would soon be my lover."

I suppose I blushed from head to toe because Jesse laughed.

"In a place like this what is there but the beds?" she said.

"Where is Zenas? I need to see him," I exclaimed. Jesse pointed toward the room where she had been practicing. Zenas wasn't there but I found him in a little study of sorts, down a hall. He was as snaggle-toothed and irresistible as ever—we kissed and kissed. Zenas had been scribbling on a tablet when I rushed in but he soon let the tablet fall off his lap.

"I was just writing up a piece about Texas Jack when you came in."

"Texas Jack can wait—I can't!" I told him warmly.

Jesse Morlacchi was right. In North Platte there were mainly the beds.

# 20

Buffalo Bill Cody showed up three days later and immediately had a red-faced fit when he discovered that I was bunking with Zenas Clark.

The fit took me completely by surprise.

"You are my majordomo, don't you realize that!" he said. Then he threw his big hat across the room.

"I'm your what?" I asked. "And even if I am, what's it got to do with Zenas Clark?"

"Newspapermen are triflers," he said. "Triflers!"

"Even if they are, that's not as bad as being a murderer or a horse thief," I responded. "And speaking of triflers, which of the local no-goods is responsible for Gretchen's belly?"

Cody ignored the question. He was bound and determined to make me feel guilty for my attachment to Zenas Clark.

I was proud of the job I was doing for the Codys and had been foolish enough to expect praise for the good organization I had put in place—instead I got attacked because I had a cute little snaggle-toothed boyfriend.

Bill finally calmed down, but only because I burst into tears.

"Oh hush!" he said. "You know you are my favorite darling."

"Favorite darling! I doubt it!" I said, my shoulders shaking.

"Yes you are . . . you are," he repeated. "There's no woman who can hold a candle to you, unless maybe it's the peerless Morlacchi."

Bill dropped that in at the last second, because Jesse Morlacchi was standing in the doorway looking at him coolly.

I guess Bill Cody could not stand the scrutiny of two smart women who were not inclined to overlook dubious behavior on his part.

"I see I am outnumbered and am about to get a licking," he said, picking up his hat. Then he bent over and kissed me three or four times.

"What did I do that was so bad?" he asked, looking as innocent as a lamb.

"My husband better not come home drunk," Jesse said.

"Good Lord!" Cody said. "Can't two old pals even bend the elbow a little, for old-times' sake?"

Neither of us answered. Bill never liked lengthy conversations, so he left.

"What do you think of him, Jesse?" I asked. "When I first met him I didn't think I could resist him but I didn't have to resist him. In fact, he resisted me."

Jesse laughed her lilting laugh.

"Big Billy Cody loves all women—a little," she said. "He makes time for flirtation, but he don't make time for love."

"Doesn't that seem odd to you?"

"Love's just not his interest," she told me. "He meets a pretty girl like you and he thinks he's in love with you for a few minutes or a few hours, but then he gets the chance to chase some Indians or act in a melodrama and he's gone."

Jesse Morlacchi was only four years older than me, but she seemed a lot sturdier—or maybe I mean wiser. Maybe her wisdom came from Europe—I don't know.

"Bill won't really let himself be loved," I said. "If you think about it it's a little sad."

Jesse vigorously disagreed with that statement.

"Not sad at all," she insisted. "Bill is a generous man. When we started acting together we had no costumes—he outfitted us and has never let me pay him back. But don't waste time feeling sorry for Billy. He always does exactly what he wants to do, and he always gets away with it.

"Once he gets his Wild West running he's going to be a big star," she added.

"I can act circles around him, but I'll never be the star William Cody will be—and neither will my husband."

"I suppose you're right."

Jesse shrugged.

"He's America's most glorious boy," she said. "He's the best rider I've ever seen—he just looks right on a horse and he's handsome as a god. Rich people like him and rich people don't usually like troupers—we're too wild for them."

Jesse went back to her practicing and I sat in the kitchen for a while, drinking tea.

# 21

WHEN ZENAS CLARK told Cody he intended to make him the main hero in a book he was writing about Western scouts, Bill eased up on him a little—he never objected to being made a hero, which is not to say that he eased up on me to any noticeable extent. What he wanted was for me to stay in love with him, even if he didn't do much about it; and of course, he wanted me to go on being his efficient, well-organized majordomo.

Before he'd been in North Platte a week I was beginning to wish he'd hurry up and leave. It wasn't because I didn't like him, though. It was just he was more than I was up to dealing with on an hourly basis.

When I told him I thought he ought to sell all those half-wild cattle up on the Dismal River he looked startled.

"Why, did they look poorly?" he asked.

"I don't think so but they're so wild I mainly saw their rear ends. Why keep 'em?"

"Because then I can say I'm a rancher," he said, looking at me as if I couldn't understand the simplest thing.

"Why do you need to say you're a rancher?"

"Because the public will like it," he explained. "Being a rancher's just part of being Western—it goes with being a scout and a Pony Express rider and an Indian fighter. I'll look good on a poster, surveying my vast herds."

I suddenly saw the light. What Bill was really interested in was publicity—regarded in that light, everything he did made sense. He had no objection to whatever normal business I was able to do for him—real estate, or stocks and bonds, a part interest in a grain silo, or any improvement I could make in the royalties from the Buffalo Bill's monthly and other dime novel contracts—but what he really had to have was publicity, and who could blame him? If he didn't get lots of publicity Bill Cody might never realize his drama, which was to get the Wild West up and running. He had to sell himself, and he had to sell the West—otherwise there'd be no show.

"I understand now, I think," I told him—we were in his little office, with files piled all around. "You're a salesman—a pure salesman."

"That's me," he admitted. His hat was off—his hair needed trimming—but then he needed long hair for the posters.

"And you're the smart woman who's going to keep me solvent until I can make it all work."

"I can do it," I said, "but deep down I'd rather we'd had a romance. I don't think it would have been a small one."

My confession didn't surprise him—I think he may have been really flattered, and also a tiny bit sad.

"I don't know—maybe I just wasn't really intended for romance, Miss Nellie," he said.

"I agree, but I can't figure out why not," I said.

In another part of the house Jesse Morlacchi was tinkling a piano and singing a sad Italian song.

"Seems like flirting's about as far as I usually get," Bill said.

The two of us were low for a moment, together. Then Bill stomped off to look at some horses he might buy, and I went back to work.

# 22

BILL CODY WASN'T the only man with a jealous nature—my lover, Zenas Clark, had a powerful jealous streak, as I found out one crisp morning when Zenas caught me chatting with young Warren Earp, who had ridden up from Dodge City to try his hand at riding Bill Cody's big buffalo, Monarch.

In fact I liked Warren Earp, and was glad to see that he had enterprise enough to leave his surly brothers and strike out on his own.

I suspect Warren was a little sweet on me too, which, from my point of view never hurt—but in Zenas Clark's mind Warren's mere presence was tantamount to adultery.

Cody was on the other side of the corrals, watching several cowboys try to get a saddle on the big buffalo. Five cowboys had ropes on him, but so far Monarch was jerking them around at will. If Warren was discouraged by the formidable beast he had agreed to ride, he didn't show it. He had greeted Cody respectfully and was being perfectly polite to me, when Zenas came running up from the big house, his shirt unbuttoned and his feelings in an uproar.

"What do you think you're doing out here with these ruffians?" he asked rudely, grabbing my arm. "Get back in that office where you belong!"

I was shocked. Zenas had never spoken to me in that tone before. I suppose we had copulated so much that he must have come to feel that he owned me.

"Hey, you calm down!" I demanded. "You've met Mr. Warren Earp before, haven't you? He's going to try and ride Cody's biggest buffalo, and I want to see it."

"I'll ride the buffalo, though I admit he is a big scamp," Warren said confidently.

"I don't care what Mr. Earp's going to do with the buffalo," Zenas said. His face was as red as a red flannel shirt. "You get back in the office and do your job."

I tried to disarm Zenas by just looking puzzled and shy.

"This is my job, Zenas," I informed him. "If Mr. Earp rides the buffalo for half a minute I'm to present him with a check and invite him to join the troupe. Besides that, it's my job to work the stopwatch."

I thought if I kept my tone mild Zenas would finally calm down.

In the pen the five cowboys, with Cody's help, finally got a saddle cinched onto Monarch's back. Warren Earp spat and tightened his belt buckle and was about to climb over the fence and go ride the buffalo when Zenas, his temper at a fever pitch by the realization that I wasn't going to obey his order, made the mistake of slapping me.

The slap didn't hurt me, but it was loud. Everybody turned to look, including Warren Earp. I was so embarrassed I froze, but Warren Earp didn't freeze.

"Whoa, now, scribbler!" he said, and clipped Zenas on the jaw, knocking him flat.

Across the pen Cody had begun to look annoyed. He wanted Warren to come on while they had the buffalo more or less under control, which is exactly what Warren did. Knocking Zenas flat had been the end of the argument, so far as Warren Earp was concerned.

Zenas sat up, rubbing his jaw. He looked surprised. Though he had traveled all over the West, reporting on outlaws and killers, it had probably never occurred to him that someone might actually hit him.

"Someone needs to go arrest that fellow," he said, allowing me to help him to his feet.

"What kind of fool are you, Zenas, that you'd slap me?" I asked. "I haven't done anything wrong. Hiring talent for Bill Cody's show is part of my job. Why would you think you had the right to slap me?"

"Because I saw you were keen on that Earp fellow," he said, plaintively.

"That's all?" I inquired.

About that time, with Warren settled into his seat, the cowboys turned Monarch loose. I at once punched the stopwatch I had been entrusted with.

Then I climbed up on the fence and watched the ride.

Warren Earp hadn't been exaggerating when he said he could ride anything on four legs. He didn't control Monarch—nobody could have managed that—but he rode him as easily as if he were rocking him back and forth in a rocking chair. Thirty seconds slowly ticked away, and Warren still rode the brute.

Across the corral Bill Cody began to look worried.

"Get off!" he yelled. "I wanted you to ride him, not tame him!"

Warren swung off and just kept his feet.

Monarch continued bucking until he shed the saddle.

I strolled over in my capacity as majordomo and handed Warren Earp his reward: one hundred dollars in cash. I believe the young man had been expecting ten at most—for him riding a buffalo was no exceptional feat.

But he took the hundred and expressed his gratitude to Cody. He even tipped his hat to me.

In the excitement of the ride I had completely forgotten Zenas Clark—when I looked around he was nowhere to be seen. Warren had left his horse hitched over by the saloon. I strolled along with him, enjoying the morning.

But the more I tried to be friendly, the shyer Warren Earp became.

"That scribbler of yours, he's rude," he told me. "I expect you can do better, if you're willing to look around."

"I may just look around," I said—and I looked right at him, but he didn't turn his head.

"Do you read books?" he asked.

"I sure do—I read quite a few books" I admitted.

"I have yet to read a book," he admitted. "My brothers keep me working most of the time. They prefer free labor."

"Is there any reason why you have to live with your brothers?" I asked. "I'm sure Mr. Cody would hire you at a fair salary if you're interested. Mr. Cody's not easily impressed, but he was impressed with you."

"Wasn't much—I've ridden plenty of broncs that can outbuck that buffalo," he allowed.

"In fact I could hire you myself," I let him know. "I'm the boss here when Mr. Cody's gone."

That startled him.

"A girl can hire people?"

"I sure can," I told him. "It may be that you've worked for your brothers long enough."

This thought clearly took some pondering.

"I guess I should think on that," Warren said. "If I do decide to quit my brothers, what's the next step?"

"My office is in that big house," I said. "Just show up—I'll find a place for you."

Warren Earp smiled a nice smile.

"I've never met a girl with an office before," he said.

"It's just a room with a desk," I told him. "I'm not a princess. I just have a job."

"What would I do, if I came?"

"Be our wrangler. Bill Cody is always buying horses—some for his show, some for his ranch. He needs a professional wrangler to see that the right horses get to the right place at the right time."

Warren studied me for a bit.

"You're not mad because I punched your beau, are you?" he asked.

"No, he had it coming. I would have punched him myself if you hadn't."

Warren considered the matters.

"I never expected to win no hundred dollars, just for riding a buffalo," he said. "I've sure got a lot to think about," he said. Then he mounted up and rode away.

"I guess you kissed him!" Zenas declared, when I stepped back in the house.

"No, Zenas—I didn't kiss him," I said.

Zenas went on glaring at me for a while.

# 23

THE NEXT MORNING Jack Omhundro and Jesse Morlacchi had a loud fight. The rest of us were at breakfast when the fight began. It was such a loud fight that those of us at breakfast stopped to listen. Jesse was yelling in Italian and Jack was cussing mostly in the cowboy tongue. Try though we might, we couldn't figure out what the fight was about, but that didn't mean we didn't enjoy listening. The Finnish girls tiptoed about. Cody looked mildly amused.

"It's lucky Lulu ain't here, or we'd be at it too," he remarked.

Then, suddenly, silence fell, and we all went back to our breakfasts. Half an hour later, while Cody was telling us some yarn involving an old Indian named Rain in the Face, Jesse and Jack came down, looking rosy and cooing like two lovebirds. They promptly consumed a breakfast that would have foundered a hippopotamus.

Later, when the plates had been cleared and the menfolk had gone off, I asked Jesse what the fight was about.

"Nothing—it was about nothing," she said. "It was just time for a fight."

The casual way she addressed it cheered me up a little. Maybe my spat with Zenas was the same sort of thing. Maybe it was just time for a fight. I had my suspicions about how Jesse and Jack made up too. There had been some steady creakings from upstairs that Cody and I tried our best to ignore and, officially, did ignore.

I had the usual bills to pay and telegrams to answer, so I let Zenas alone until after lunch.

I suppose it's a mistake to allow yourself to believe that human beings are consistent. It's normal for couples to have fights, as Jesse had candidly pointed out—and it's also just as normal to get over them and make up. I assumed that's what would happen with Zenas and myself. I didn't like being slapped in public and I wouldn't have liked it much better if it had occurred in private. Still, wrong as it was, I was prepared to forgive him, so I lured him into my boudoir for that purpose. I tried to seduce him—what better way to make up, as Jesse and Texas Jack had demonstrated?—but Zenas just stood there, looking about as friendly as a clam. He just stared at me coldly, as if I were the Witch of Skye, or some other bad witch. He made no move to kiss me, and when I started to unbutton his pants—one of my favorite things to do—he shoved my hand away.

Still, I determined to take a patient course. I was determined to bring Zenas back from whatever swamp of jealousy he had sunk himself in. I tried a little light kiss and he turned his head away. I tried for the buttons again and again he shoved me back, by which time my patience was rapidly wearing thin. I was beginning to get the feeling that something was really wrong.

"Zenas, stop it," I said. "What's wrong?"

"You're in love with Colonel Cody, ain't you?" he charged.

"What are you talking about?" I asked. "Bill Cody's a married man."

In fact the accusation stung me.

"Now, don't lie," Zenas said. "He brought you up here from Rita Blanca—he pays your salary—he lets you live in his house—he even gave you his power of attorney!

"If that ain't love, what is?" he added.

"It isn't love, it's business! Business! That's what it is!" I insisted.

"Bill Cody's only been here three days since he hired me. When he brought me here he promptly left for two months! I work for him! I'm not in love with him."

Zenas wouldn't accept it—he wasn't giving an inch.

"I thought you slapped me because I was chatting with Warren Earp," I mentioned.

"Oh, that oaf, who cares about him?" Zenas burst out. "I doubt that fool can even read."

"He can't," I said.

"I guess Cody kisses you," Zenas went on.

"Zenas, Bill kisses all the girls he meets," I told him. "It's his way of shaking hands—or maybe he thinks it's his duty as a big star. He kisses all the girls—at least all the pretty ones!"

I began to realize that our problem was bigger than I had supposed. Zenas wasn't jealous of Warren Earp, he was jealous of Bill Cody, and Bill Cody was my boss!

Once I thought about it I realized it was something I should have expected. Zenas was a young scribbler, almost unknown, whereas Bill Cody was the most famous scout in the West—one day soon he'd probably be the most famous showman in America.

Besides which, as Jesse Morlacchi had pointed out, Cody was handsome as a god. The plain truth was that I would have been in love with Bill Cody if he'd let me be. And since I was working for him, maybe I still would fall in love with him, sometime in the future.

At least I was beginning to have a better grasp of the problem. Bill Cody had trapped me, just by giving me his trust. I lived in Buffalo Bill's house. I did his work. Even if Bill Cody only showed up in North Platte ten days out of the year, it would still be something that would naturally spook a young man of Zenas's age.

I suppose in Zenas's eyes I was the damsel in the tower, with Bill Cody her knight in armor.

"I'm not in love with him," I repeated, but rather tonelessly this time.

But Zenas had raised a big question and we both knew it.

"If you ain't you will be one day," Zenas said.

He left that afternoon.

# BOOK IV

---

# Tombstone Days

# 1

I STUCK IT out as Bill Cody's majordomo for nearly four years, during which time I sent a mountain of telegrams, wrote a mountain of letters, and signed a mountain of checks, all on Bill's behalf. I subscribed to three financial papers, and I read them, the better to do my job. At my best I managed to keep the Cody enterprises solvent about three quarters of the time. But no one could really control Bill Cody, financially or otherwise. He wasn't indifferent to my expertise. He praised me lavishly and he gave me a big bonus at the end of every year. He continued to smother me with kisses when the mood struck him, which was frequently. But it went no further than kisses, just as I had told Zenas.

Otherwise, of course, he went his own way—went his way to such an extent that I began to dread the mails. Bill would involve himself in a silver mine in Arizona or a tourist hotel in Colorado or a dude ranch in some remote part of Wyoming. I wouldn't know a thing about it until the bills began to come in. There was always a flood of bills—sometimes a tidal wave of bills—and yet, mostly, I was able to pay them promptly because of the big income Bill brought in with his performances. The first Wild West he put on, in Omaha, made plenty of money, even if it was really only a half circus, with a Western skit or two and a lot of trick riding and acrobatics. As long as Buffalo Bill himself was in the arena, on his white horse, waving his hat or busting a few glass targets, the crowd could hardly stop cheering. Warren Earp showed up and promised to ride Monarch again, but this time the buffalo won the contest. Warren Earp was thrown so hard that he was in the hospital for two weeks—Cody let me stay and nurse him, which was nice of him. I offered to hire him again, when he got well, but his brothers had too tight a grip on him and my offer came to naught.

The fact that such a big crowd turned out for the Wild West in Omaha convinced Bill Cody that his idea had been sound, despite the fact that this first effort was imperfect in Cody's eyes. He needed Indians, he needed a stagecoach, he needed a trick roper or two and a sharpshooter with some crowd appeal.

At this time Bill Cody was possessed of boundless energies—he'd work all day and all night, training a horse, auditioning ropers, or doing whatever else it took to improve the program of the Wild West. In only two years, by a process of trial and error, he formed a troupe that was the equal of any that had ever been fired in the Hippodrome or any other arena. Annie Oakley, a petite woman who soon put all the other sharpshooters deep in the shade, became his biggest star—but he found quite a few others. Pretty soon he partnered with a fine manager, Nate Salsbury, to organize the travel and secure the dates, and a press agent named John Burke to stir up interest in the newspapers and bring out the crowd.

All the while, as Bill Cody's Wild West became the talk of America, I sat in my office in North Platte and dealt with the problems of at least a dozen enterprises that Bill had started up or invested in or something. Now and then Lulu arrived and inspected her lucrative real estate. I had been buying up Nebraska at a steady pace, a fact which delighted Lulu Cody. We never had a quarrel. Sometimes Bill would show up, with Jesse and Texas Jack; sometimes Mr. Salsbury and Major Burke, as the press agent was called, would visit between tours. I liked them both but left them to their own devices. I was not fool enough to suppose either of them would be content to take orders from a woman. They ran the Wild West, I ran everything else, and the arrangement worked fine.

When Zenas Clark left my company that fateful day, I realized that I had accidentally trapped myself. Zenas was just the first to see it. I was not Bill Cody's mistress—I was never his mistress—but for several years, there was always the possibility that I might become his mistress if the circumstances were right. Bill was rarely fully sober—when we were together in North Platte there was always the chance that the fever might overcome us. Bill might decide he wanted more than a few kisses, or a look at my titties.

It never happened—but it might have happened. Lulu Cody knew it and chose to leave it alone. Jesse Morlacchi knew it and didn't care. Who did care were my suitors, beginning with Zenas Clark. Zenas had a certain confidence, but not enough to allow him to suppose he could compete with Buffalo Bill. I doted on Zenas Clark, and had from the moment I met him. He was a fine, devilish lover and we might have had a lot more fun if Zenas could just have got Bill Cody off his mind. And yet I couldn't really blame Zenas for feeling as he did. Bill Cody was a force of nature—he was one of the largest personalities of his time. He had done much of what he claimed to have done—been a frontier scout for fifteen years, ridden with the Pony Express, and been under fire from some hot, formidable Indians. He wasn't bogus, and few young men would have felt up to competing with him for a woman or anything else, but especially for a woman.

In North Platte I was the main woman.

Bill Cody left two days after Zenas and I had our fight. Over time I forgave Zenas for his hasty departure, but if he had just waited Cody out we could have had a lot more fun.

It was not the end of Zenas Clark in my life. We would meet again in a distant desert—when we were together we were thick as thick. In a way I was grateful to him even while I was missing him: he did more than anyone to show me what a tight trap I had caught myself in by agreeing to be Bill Cody's majordomo.

# 2

I WAS TRAPPED, in a sense, but fortunately I am too active a woman to accept permanent entrapment. I had signed on with Bill Cody for a term, but I hadn't signed on for life.

You wouldn't think it, but I had even begun to miss Rita Blanca. Jackson and Mandy had not been idle: they had two toddlers, both girls, and another on the way, so, besides missing Aurel Imlah and Mrs. Karoo and my little telegraph office, I was even missing out on being an aunt. I slowly began to realize that I had more that was my own in Rita Blanca than I was ever likely to have in North Platte, where I was a well-kept vassal but a vassal nonetheless.

As the telegraph lady of Rita Blanca I worked for myself while performing a service for the whole community.

In North Platte I worked only for Bill and Lulu—mostly Bill—and I am too independent a woman to spend my whole life writing someone else's letters and paying someone else's bills. Of course, as Cody's representative, I was in the thick of civic life in North Platte, such as it was. I sat on all the councils, advised the Major, headed the school board, had the preacher to Sunday lunch, and did all the responsible things a pillar of the community is supposed to do—it left me bored. Of course, the civic fathers greatly preferred me to Lulu, who mainly gave them the back of her hand. The women envied me, for pleasures I never had, and the men envied Bill, just because he was Bill.

The first person I told, when I decided to quit, was Ripley Eads, my old chaperone, who had prospered greatly in North Platte. He owned a nice little clapboard barbershop and cut so much hair that he had to hire a second barber to assist him. He had married a lively little Cheyenne woman and was in the process of developing a sizable family.

"Ripley, do you ever miss Rita Blanca?" I asked, with my usual directness.

"Nope, can't say I miss the place," Ripley said succinctly.

"I miss it. I'm thinking of quitting Cody and heading back."

Ripley looked stunned.

"Quit Cody?" he asked. "Why?"

"Boredom," I told him. "The fact is that I'm bored."

"But you're said to be the highest-salaried woman in Nebraska, which is a good old state, in my opinion."

"It may be a good old state, but I'm leaving it," I announced. "Since we're old compañeros, me and you, I thought I'd ask your opinion."

"Which you got."

"Yes, which I got, and it's about as useful as a mud sandwich," I told him.

Then I went straight to the telegraph office and sent Cody a cable giving sixty days' notice. He was in San Francisco at the time, and the troupe was rolling in money, from all reports. Jesse Morlacchi wrote me, mentioning that they had sold four thousand dollars' worth of tickets in one night, which is fine box office in anybody's town.

Of course, when Bill Cody got my wire he went through the roof and immediately sent me this wire:

DEAR NELLIE YOUR TELEGRAM WAS A BITTER BLOW STOP YOU HAVE ALWAYS BEEN MY FAVORITE DARLING STOP I LOVE YOU LIKE A DAUGHTER STOP IF THE PAY IS TOO LOW I'LL RAISE YOU STOP PLEASE RECONSIDER STOP COMPANY PROSPERING LOVE BUFFALO BILL

I immediately wired him back:

DEAR BILL I LOVE YOU TOO STOP BUT I'M LEAVING NORTH PLATTE IN FIFTY SEVEN DAYS STOP DO NOT BOTHER UPBRAIDING ME BECAUSE MY RESOLUTION IS FIRM LOVE NELLIE

Two weeks later he stepped off a train in North Platte. He hadn't told me he was coming but I was not surprised. He did his best to sweep me off my feet and got red-faced and flustered when it turned out that my resolution was firm. The man, of course, was very used to getting his way.

"But, Nellie, you're all I've got," he declared, several times. "You're my steady anchor. Without you I'll be ruined in a week."

"Tosh, all tosh," I told him. "You've got Mr. Salsbury, who's a capable man."

Then the fool pretended to cry—he'd mastered the trick of crying on demand in his acting life. If so, he hadn't learned it well, because he wasn't really crying—he snorted into his handkerchief while pretending to boo-hoo.

"If you can't act any better than that I'm surprised people come to see you," I told him. Even Gretchen and Sigurd were amused by his weak performance.

"Oh, folks don't come to see me because I can act," he said, giving up on the crying. "They come to see me because I'm Buffalo Bill."

Then he dropped the histrionics and became the friendly man who had won my affection three years ago in Rita Blanca.

"I suppose the real trouble is that you can't find a suitable boyfriend, living way out here," he said.

I didn't bother lying.

"You're right, I can't find a suitable boyfriend," I admitted. "Give or take a cowboy or two, I might as well be a nun."

"It's because they all think you're my gal—am I right?" he asked.

It irritated me to admit it—but of course it was true.

Bill Cody looked me in the face for a very long time. I believe he was trying to decide whether to let himself fall in love with me. There we were, a private pair, in a big house full of comfortable beds. He kept looking at me and I began to feel that maybe this was the day—maybe the man was finally going to seduce me. He had already kissed me several times. My susceptibilities had begun to stir. Would he take the final step?

"Oh, Nellie, I think we better not," he said, "though you're the peach of peaches and the fairest of the fair."

I was disappointed, but I held my tongue and didn't reproach him.

"I'm a better friend than anything else, Miss Nellie," he said, in his fondest voice.

Then he sighed a heavy sigh.

"You're right to leave—I just hope you'll allow me to call on you from time to time, in big emergencies," he added meekly.

"What I need, you see, is a friend for life," he added. "I reckon that's you, if it's anybody."

"It's me, Bill," I said. "You'll find me a steady friend."

Then Bill did leak a tear or two, a genuine tear or two, and I did the same.

Then and there Bill Cody wrote me out a check for two thousand dollars—no small amount of money in that day and time. We exchanged a good tight hug and that was that.

# 3

YEARS LATER, WHEN I started writing my popular romances for the ladies' magazines, I learned about the suspense and how you're supposed to keep the reader guessing about certain matters until the very end. Who gets the girl is the main thing you try to leave up in the air as long as possible, since that's apt to be the one thing the reader really wants to know.

But I wasn't yet a writer when I left North Platte, and my normal tendency was to blurt out everything and let the feathers float where they may.

I worked out my full sixty days, got myself packed, booked our train for Dodge City, and made provisions for a wagon and horses to await us there. Cody assigned Lanky Jake and grumbling Sam, the Dismal River cowboys, to escort me back to Rita Blanca. Jakey and Sam fully approved of me because I had managed to sell that worthless cow operation, whereupon the third cowboy, Ned, disappeared, but he crossed my path again many years later, when I was making a sightseeing trip to Death Valley.

Jakey and Sam had been working for me in North Platte anyway, tending Bill Cody's diverse and unruly menagerie, which included buffalo, elk, antelope, longhorn cattle, and even a llama. Nobody liked the llama and the llama liked nobody.

Of course the town gave me a big send-off: there was a farewell dinner in which most of the civic fathers got drunk and wept all down their white shirts when they tried to make speeches about how much I had contributed to the growth of North Platte, Nebraska.

Bill Cody had showed up for my farewell dinner, of course. He made a long speech about how brilliant I was, and what a treasure.

Then the band played and Cody and I waltzed all alone on the stage.
He was wearing his best white buckskin suit, and looked fine as ever.

When the waltz was over and the cheering quieted down Bill
clapped his hands and a little brown man about the size and color of
one of Ros Jubb's sepoys came tripping out carrying a velvet box on a
satin pillow. He made a deep bow and offered the box to me.

I got mighty nervous.

"Oh my Lord, what have you done now, Bill?" I asked.

Bill bent and kissed me tenderly—there were tears in his eyes. One
of his most winning attributes was his ability to get swept away by his
own showmanship.

"It's the Duleep pearl," he told me. "It's the largest pearl in the
world and I'm giving it to you because you're my favorite darling!"

I opened the box as carefully as if it contained a cobra. But there
was no snake, just the lustrous white pearl. I couldn't at first believe
that such a thing of beauty could be mine. It was large enough to be a
pendant and hung from a tiny silver chain. Bill slipped the chain
around my neck and there I stood, wearing the Duleep pearl. The
crowd was as awed as I was—they fell silent for a second—until I
whirled on Bill Cody and gave him a big smacking kiss, at which point
the crowd went wild.

So I had my farewell party—by the next morning, when I actually
left, both Cody and the town of North Platte had gone on about their
business. Cody had ridden off to the Red Cloud Agency, to try and persuade the old Bad Face to lease him some Indians for his Wild West.
Ripley Eads was cutting hair and the blacksmith was shoeing horses. A
young couple at the depot busied themselves with flirting. Only my
two Finnish maids actually came to see me off. Little Pickle,
Gretchen's son, waved me bye. Fame is brief, unless you're Annie Oakley, Bill Cody, or one of the world's natural stars.

When we got to Omaha later in the day I was surprised to see my
picture on the front page of the Omaha paper. There I stood, wearing
the Duleep pearl, and there was Buffalo Bill, with his arm around me,
looking pleased as punch. Tears came to my eyes. I suppose I did love
Bill Cody, in my way, and now he was gone to lease some Indians
while I headed back to Rita Blanca. Would I ever see that handsome
man again?

Lanky Jake and grumbling Sam were mighty impressed to discover that they were traveling with a woman who had her picture on the front page of the Omaha paper.

"Hope old Jesse James don't read the Omaha paper," Jakey said.

"I thought Jesse James was from Missouri," I said. "Why would he be reading the Omaha paper?"

"Jesse, he does watch the railroads," Sam mentioned. "If he gets wind of that big jewel he might try to rob us."

"Oh, fiddlesticks," I said. "He won't try to rob us."

For once Sam was right and I was wrong.

Later that day, as we bore down on Kansas City, Jesse James boarded the train and tried to rob us.

"Cough up that pearl, Miss Courtright," were the first words he said.

# 4

"Over the years I suppose you've acquired some facility in boarding trains, Mr. James," I said, since there he was in my compartment, accompanied by two ruffians, both of whom could have used a shave.

"Yes, I have—but the goddamn trains are getting faster all the time," Jesse James lamented.

"But not so fast yet that you can't catch them, obviously," I said.

I had hastily sent my two escorts back to the cargo room, in order not to provide Jesse and his gang with any excuse to shoot them.

This greatly disappointed Jakey and Sam, both of whom had bought new pistols just before leaving North Platte. My fear was that if they brandished their weapons Jesse would immediately cut them down.

He was a small man, nervous and rather greenish in color. He did not look friendly. Cody told me that he had been a violent killer from an early age. I could have kicked Bill Cody for being so foolish as to advertise to every outlaw who could read a newspaper that I had the Duleep pearl. But it was too late to kick him.

Fortunately, Sam had spotted the outlaws racing beside the train, which gave me time to size up the situation and send the cowboys away.

"But Mr. Cody sent us to guard you," Sam protested.

"You are guarding me," I assured him. "You're just guarding me from the cargo car."

Cody had provided me with a sleeper, of course, which is why Jesse James found me so easily. Fortunately, I am cool under pressure and I was cool as ice in this emergency. Before Jesse found me I snatched the Duleep pearl out of its box, rubbed a little salve on it, opened my legs, and slipped the pearl inside myself. Then I sat back and opened my book—it was Mr. Hawthorne's *The Scarlet Letter*—I was trying to figure out why those old Yankees came down so hard on mere adultery. I had only read a sentence or two when Jesse strode into my compartment and demanded my pearl.

"Cough it up now, no trouble," he repeated.

"Why do you have that greenish look, Mr. James?" I asked. "Could it be that you smoke the green pipe?"

I meant opium, of course. There was plenty of it available on the plains in those days, particularly among the railroad crews. The thousands of coolies who had been brought in to build the railroads didn't like being without their opium.

"What are you talking about?" he asked, but I thought I had seen a fleeting look of guilt across his face.

"Opium," I told him bluntly. "It can leave people looking a little greenish."

Jesse James was shocked—somehow I had divined his secret.

"It's for the toothaches," he admitted, with a shy look. "A horse kicked me right in the mouth when I was fourteen and I've suffered from toothaches ever since."

His ruffians were not interested in their boss's toothaches.

"This ain't a church social, Jesse," one reminded him. "Get her to cough up that pearl."

"He's right," Jesse said. "Hand it over and there'll be no trouble."

I held out the little silver chain.

"Would you be content with this expensive chain?" I asked.

In fact I didn't like the chain and meant to get it replaced eventually.

Jesse, looking puzzled, took the chain but continued to frown and point his gun at me.

"We mean business, Miss," he said. "We want the pearl."

One of the ruffians, who later showed up in my life a second time—he was bartending then in Tombstone—began to rifle through my luggage, a liberty I resented. I had spent half a day packing my things according to an orderly system so I could find a clean undergarment, if I happened to need a clean undergarment.

"I'll thank you to leave that luggage as you find it," I said. "Only a ninny would leave a rare pearl in a suitcase."

"Then where is it, damnit?" the ruffian asked.

"In my vagina," I said bluntly.

"What?" Jesse stammered. He looked shocked, almost terrified. The ruffians just stood with their mouths open.

It was a gamble on my part. The three of them could have held me down and extracted the Duleep pearl quickly enough. I had thought of swallowing it, but what if it stuck in my throat?

What I banked on, putting it where I had, was that these were country train robbers. Neither Jesse James nor his brother Frank had the reputation for raping that was the case with Bloody Bill Anderson and some of the other Southern gangs.

I don't mean to suggest that Jesse James wasn't mean. He was mean, but killing mean, not raping mean. I don't think he wanted anything to do with my vagina; perhaps he'd never even heard the female privacy called by its right name before.

I just sat there, looking Jesse James square in the eye. Mention of my vagina stopped him dead, which just goes to show that words do have their power.

"Let's shoot her," one of the ruffians suggested. "That'd show her."

"Let's don't," Jesse said. He stuck his pistol in his belt and looked at me again.

"That pearl's probably paste anyway," he said—he actually tipped his hat to me as he was leaving.

"I'd be sparing with the green pipe, Mr. James," I advised him. "The green pipe can get you in trouble."

"It's just the toothaches," he said.

Not three years later I read in the paper that Jesse James had been shot down while standing on a chair, straightening a picture. The railroads had a considerable reward on him by then, which no doubt tempted the shooter.

What I remembered about him was his greenish hue, and the fact that he wanted no part of my hairy grotto, Duleep pearl or no Duleep pearl.

He was not the only man to have a fastidious side.

When Jakey and Sam showed up they were in a glum state. Jesse James had confiscated their new pistols.

"Never mind, boys—I'll rearm you in Dodge City," I assured them.

"If the dern Earps don't kill us first," Jakey said.

Jakey rarely looked on the bright side of things.

# 5

To my astonishment the first person I saw when we disembarked in Dodge City was Warren Earp washing a pig. Warren looked much as he had when I got him out of the hospital in North Platte, after the buffalo ride. But the pig was a real sight. It was so big it could hardly walk. If I had been asked to guess its weight I'd start my guessing at around a thousand pounds.

The pig was standing calmly at the watering trough in the communal corrals, and Warren was soaping it and giving it a good scrubbing. The pig seemed to enjoy the scrubbing—it never moved or so much as twitched.

"Hello, Warren Earp," I said, giving him a big hug. "I did not expect to find you involved with swine."

"It's Lord Angus's prize pig," Warren told me sheepishly. He was in his undershirt and some old pants. Warren Earp had long possessed an easygoing charm.

"Who is Lord Angus and what's the point of a prize pig?" I asked.

Warren smiled. I felt sure he liked me, but he showed no interest in Jakey and Sam, who removed our luggage from the train and trudged off to the livery stables to pick up the rig and horses that Bill Cody had reserved for us.

I could see that Dodge City had suffered a sharp decline since my last visit. Several houses had fallen down, several more were leaning, and there were very few cowboys to be seen.

"Lord Angus owns Wyoming, or most of it," Warren said. "I have no idea why he wants a pig so big that it can barely walk, but I'm sending it to Chicago for some big fair they're having. Lord Angus wants him clean.

"He's supposed to win the blue ribbon," he added.

"Won't he have time to get dirty again, between here and Chicago?" I inquired. Washing a pig in Kansas and hoping he'll stay clean all the way to Chicago seemed a dubious proposition.

"He'll have a private car," Warren informed me.

"I've heard enough about this pig. Are you married yet?" I asked.

"I ain't," Warren admitted. "And my brothers all moved out west."

That was a surprise. Most of my memories of Dodge City involved the coarse Earps.

"Out west—isn't this west?"

"Used to be, when the railroad stopped here," he said. He stood back a step or two and inspected Lord Angus's pig.

"But the railroad don't stop here anymore—it goes clear to California," he added, as if I would never have occasion to read the newspapers or concern myself with the railroads.

"Is that where your brothers went—California?" I asked.

"No, just to Arizona. I suppose you've heard about the silver boom."

I had heard about the silver boom. In fact, thanks to me, Bill Cody had been one of the first investors in the Arizona silver mines, and it was among the few investments Bill could claim that hadn't gone bad yet.

"Do you think this pig is clean enough to win a blue ribbon in Chicago?" Warren asked, with a shy grin.

"I told you I was tired of discussing this pig," I reminded him. "Have you ever been kissed by a real girl? If not, I'm planning to kiss you, later in the day."

I suppose most men don't like to be asked direct questions about that sort of thing—many simply decline to answer, which was Warren Earp's method. He had a little goad with a sharp point on it, which he used to get Lord Angus's pig in motion toward his private car.

I'm female enough not to enjoy being abandoned for a pig, but it was a fine bright morning, so I thought I might as well visit the Tesselincks at their print shop where my little *Banditti* book had been run off. But the print shop, when I got there, was closed—it looked as if it had been closed for years. Most of the window had been broken out—all I could see, when I peeked inside, was lots of dust and many mouse droppings.

It had only been four years since I had passed through Dodge City with Bill Cody—then it had been a thriving place, but it wasn't thriving now. Buildings that had once housed thriving businesses were boarded up now. Even the saloon had only two horses hitched out in front of it. I had been in fine spirits when I stepped off the train but the sad, dilapidated state of the town was making me gloomy in a hurry. It was no wonder the Earp brothers had left, all except Warren. It occurred to me that Lord Angus's prize pig was probably worth more than the whole town of Dodge City, which was a good reason to load up my luggage and get out of there. If Warren Earp had showed a little more enthusiasm I might have lingered, but Warren was shy with girls and probably always would be. With nothing to do but look at boarded-up buildings, I soon got to thinking about how short life is and how quickly places and people just go down.

Dodge City had been one of the most famous towns in the West. Bill Hickok had played cards there, and so had Bat Masterson and a lot of other famous Western gents. It had flourished: there had been three hotels and at least six or seven saloons; there had been whores and gambling and rowdy cowboys fresh off the trail and full of sap. All gone, the cowboys, the hotels, the whores.

I guess Jakey and Sam felt the same way I did; when I got back to the livery stable the wagon was loaded and the horses saddled.

"I thought this place was supposed to be lively," grumbling Sam grumbled.

"We've been here two hours and nobody's even shot off a gun—it's a big disappointment," Jakey said.

"You got to see one Earp—Warren," I told them. "And you got a good look at Lord Angus's prize pig that's expected to win the blue ribbon in Chicago."

"What kind of a job is that for an Earp? Washing a pig?" Jakey asked.

I didn't bother to answer.

# 6

I AM NOT, in the main, an anxious woman. Generally, if I run into a problem, I fix it—or at least I try. Lack of regular and satisfactory copulation is one thing that is likely to make me anxious; it was a fact that there had been a sad shortage of dependable lovers in North Platte, which is one reason I didn't mind leaving the place. One thing that's held me back from marriage was the fear that I'd impulsively marry myself off to some dolt, only to discover that he didn't provide me with regular copulation. I considered the sad example of Lulu Cody, a woman who was lucky if she saw her husband six weeks a year.

Thinking about how easily life can slip down got me into such a lather of worry that I snapped and snarled at Jakey and Sam so viciously that both of them stopped even trying to converse with me. We made a silent camp, ate a silent supper, and slept a mostly silent sleep, although Jakey would snore.

I was in no easier mood the next day. I felt as if I needed to cry, but I couldn't really find anything to cry about until we came in sight of the old, muddy Cimarron River. Then the dam inside me suddenly burst and I cried a river of my own tears, to the deep consternation of Jakey and Sam.

"You fools, I'm just sentimental!" I yelled at them, while catching my breath.

Indeed I was so sentimental that I nearly caused the wagon to turn over in the river, although it was an easy crossing place.

"You will cry, I guess, if we lose all this kit!" Jakey yelled.

I realized both my escorts were exasperated with me—not without reason.

"I'll make it up to you!" I yelled—and once my cry was over, my spirits suddenly soared. I hugged both the cowboys—to their relief—and promised them big bonuses once we arrived in Rita Blanca, which we did near sunset on a fine prairie day. By the time we reached Joe Schwartz's livery stable I had come home to a place that was much as it had been when I left to work for Cody.

My brother, Jackson, had grown stout and sported a mustache, Teddy Bunsen was still sheriff and still gloomy, Aurel Imlah's beard still looked as if a bird or two could be nesting it, and Mrs. Karoo still smiled serenely at her dinner guests. Hungry Billy Wheless had added a photography gallery to his general store. He filled it with pictures of cowboys and buffalo and horses watering at dusk and longhorn cattle and even the occasional Indian who happened to pass through.

The Yazee raid museum was still there, though, with Hungry Billy being so busy, it bore a neglected air.

The best new thing, of course, from my point of view, was my two curly-haired nieces, Jean and Jan, who were as yappy as I was; they were soon following me everywhere, much as their hens had followed the McClendon sisters, who were still as passionate about Buffalo Bill Cody as ever.

After my nieces, the next most interesting addition to the population was a woman barber, by name Naomi, an olive-skinned woman of sizable girth who had had herself a little barbershop built. Naomi came from the Bible lands somewhere and had a son called Little Pita, who was just the age of my niece Jan. The cowboys had been reluctant to let Naomi shave and trim them at first, but she wielded the smoothest razor in No Man's Land, besides being a high-spirited woman in a place where there weren't many. She soon won over the cowboys and the freighters and anyone else who happened to be passing through Rita Blanca. The cowboys came to like Naomi so much that they fell into fisticuffs over who got barbered first.

Naomi and I soon became fast friends—she was as frank as I was. Sometimes, at the end of the day, we'd walk over to the river together, trailed by Jan, Jean, and Little Pita, and sit and watch the water while the tots got muddy. One of the things Naomi and I were in complete agreement about was the desirability of regular copulation. Since the tots were safely out of earshot I started the discussion by lamenting that local prospects seemed rather thin on the ground.

Naomi rolled her big eyes and smiled her seductive smile.

"I've always been lucky, when it comes to men," she allowed.

"If you're so lucky, who are you tupping with now?" I asked. Much as I liked Naomi I felt a tiny prickle of jealousy. I wanted to be the one who was lucky, when it came to lovers.

"My Aurel," Naomi cooed—and the prick became a sting, if not a deep one. I had always found Aurel Imlah attractive, but had just assumed he loved Mrs. Karoo. I guess Naomi had tested that assumption and found it to be false.

"They are brother and sister," Naomi said, when I mentioned Mrs. Karoo.

Just then three muddy tots came racing into our laps.

"Pita ate my mud pie!" Jean complained. Little Pita did sport a rather muddy mouth, but Naomi showed no alarm.

A little later, with the sun just setting, we all walked home.

"I am big—I like a big fellow," Naomi admitted. "Aurel is big, if you know what I mean."

I suppose I did know what she meant, but with the three tots scampering around I saw no need to elaborate on the matter.

# 7

I HAD NEVER supposed that my brother, Jackson, would turn into much of a husband, but I was wrong. His tots crawled around on him like little possums. My sister-in-law, Mandy, looked as if she had a good-sized pumpkin in her belly—soon there'd be another to crawl around on Jackson.

One thing hadn't changed for the better about Jackson: he was still hard to talk to.

"Is Teddy Bunsen going to sit there being sheriff his whole life?" I asked.

"I don't know—why?" Jackson asked.

"Because you've been a deputy about long enough, don't you think?" I said. "It's high time they made you sheriff."

Jackson looked startled—evidently the possibility that he might be sheriff someday had never occurred to him.

"But if I was sheriff, what would Teddy do?" he asked.

"Now that's wrong thinking—unambitious," I told him. "If you're going to live your life in a little hole like this, then the least you ought to settle for is the office of sheriff."

Jackson and Mandy had a nice enough life, by their standards; but Jackson and I were more or less the last of the Courtrights, a proud family. Few Courtrights had been content to spend their lives at the deputy level. Whatever his feelings on the subject I wanted more for Jackson than he wanted for himself. I wanted him to be sheriff. I knew he was a good deputy, arresting many drunks, and helping to keep the public order. Still, I wanted more—and wanted Jackson to want more.

"I'm not like you, Sis," Jackson pointed out, as we were enjoying a filling meal of fried okra, turnip greens, mashed potatoes, and a small wild turkey that had fallen to Jackson's gun.

"Apparently not," I admitted. "I guess I got what's left of the ambition in the Courtright family. Father never had much, that I can recall."

"Father was a gentleman," Jackson remarked, as if that explained everything.

"Father was a gentleman and you're a good deputy," I said, wondering why the Courtright men were so dull.

"What about you, Nellie?" Mandy asked. "Will you really stay with us?"

I suddenly realized that the answer was no. I wouldn't stay with them—not long. It was fine to come home to Rita Blanca, which, as Bill Cody had noticed, was the perfect Western town. But soon enough, my days would start hanging lifeless. Even if I secured a little copulation it wouldn't be enough.

"I suppose I'm too ambitious, Mandy," I told her. "I need some hustle."

I don't think I had ever admitted that to myself in quite such a blatant way before. After all, I had been running Bill Cody's businesses for over three years. Pretty soon I'd get in the mood to run something else.

Mandy was looking at me seriously.

"I hope you don't want more from life than there is," she said solemnly.

Then Jean and Jan jumped in my lap, smelling young.

"I probably do, Mandy," I said. "I probably want more than there is."

# 8

I HAD BEEN back in Rita Blanca about two weeks, and was already seriously considering moving on, when the deacons of the community ganged up on me one morning and got me to agree to be the mayor of the place. When the whole passel of them cornered me in the little telegraph office, all dressed in their best clothes, I could tell something serious was afoot. Ted Bunsen, who had become a deacon himself, came right out with the offer.

"We need a mayor," he said. "The job's yours if you'll take it."

"I'm flattered, folks—but why me?" I inquired, after they had finished describing the desperate situation they considered the town to be in.

"You're organized!" they said, like a chorus.

I suppose I was, and I suppose it showed, since that had been the first comment Bill Cody had made about me, when he showed up more than three years back.

Somehow hearing it again, from my old town mates, made my heart sink a little. Would I always just be the organized one, in any community I settled in? Why couldn't I be the beautiful, adventurous one?

"We need you to find a reliable schoolteacher and get a school going," Hungry Billy mentioned. "Your own brother's tykes will need schooling soon, and there's plenty of other tykes running around without their ABCs."

"Yes, and we need to find a preacher and get a fire wagon of some kind," Joe Schwartz said. "Dry as it's been this whole town could burn if a big prairie fire headed this way."

When I asked if they had a salary in mind they all looked nervous, since it must have been obvious just from the way I was dressed that Bill Cody had been paying me a lot more than they could afford. But they hemmed and hawed and came up with the low figure of four hundred dollars a month, which was one hundred dollars more than I had been expecting. It was a solid salary and left me with no real reason to turn the deacons down.

"I accept, but for six months only," I told them. "I've been feeling some pretty strong wanderlust lately—it may be that after I get things organized here I may want to strike out and see the world."

They all looked pleased as punch at my acceptance, so we shook hands all around, though my old beau Teddy Bunsen made so bold as to kiss me on the cheek. The look in his eyes suggested that under certain circumstances he might try to do better. Would I give him the chance?

# 9

BILL BONNEY—or Billy the Kid—got off on the wrong foot with me faster than I could snap my fingers, and here's how it occurred. I was in my office, scribbling on a novel I had decided to call *The Good Deputy,* when I glanced down the street toward the jail, where the good deputy himself, my brother, Jackson, was standing outside talking to a tall youth who had just dismounted from a not particularly impressive nag. Pretty soon Ted Bunsen came out of the jail and walked over to where the two men were conversing. It was a rather blowy, dusty day, but the two lawmen and the stranger were well accustomed to dust, as anyone needs to be who lives out on the plains.

Then the three men, seemingly amiable, walked across the street toward the general store, where they were soon joined by Hungry Billy Wheless, who hurried out to shake the stranger's hand. Then they all wandered around in the street for a while, pointing to this thing and that. It occurred to me, as I watched, that the stranger must be asking questions about the Yazee raid. At once Jackson pulled out his pistol and swung his arm, more or less as he had on that fateful day when the Yazee brothers met their end.

That sort of thing was always happening in Rita Blanca. A cowboy or two would ride in and want to see where the big fight had occurred. Gawkers like this young stranger were just the kind of people Bill Cody meant to sell tickets to, once he got his model of Rita Blanca up and going.

For a time I stopped paying attention and went back to my scribbling, but in fact I had managed to rough out only a paragraph—in the story my hero and his family were proceeding up the Missouri River by boat, accompanied by Bill Hickok and some thirty immigrants, most of whom would be lucky to last a year—when who should come flying up the street but my nieces, Jean and Jan. Neither of them was much taller than a low-slung pig, but they were racing at top speed. When they finally got there and jumped into my arms they were so out of breath they couldn't speak. I could feel their little hearts fluttering when I hugged them.

"Billy the Kid," Jean gasped.

"Billy the Kid," Jan chimed in. "Ma said tell you."

"Okay, you told me, many thanks," I said, giving the stranger a little stronger scrutiny. From what I could see he could have been any stranger off the trail, but I thought I ought to go take a closer look—who knows but what I might be able to fit this famous young killer into my *Good Deputy* somewhere? The tykes wanted to send a few telegrams to an imaginary rabbit they were corresponding with, but I lugged them out, one under each arm, and carried them with me down the street.

Billy the Kid had a rifle, none too new, which he liked to lean on as he talked. He wore an old black hat that didn't fit his head, and sported a dusty jacket that his long arms stuck out of about a foot. A small pistol had been casually stuck in his belt. Evidently Hungry Billy had been given permission to photograph him—the big camera was being set up as I approached. Jean and Jan, shy all of a sudden, wiggled free and raced off to find their mother. Young Mr. Bonney was nearly as snaggle-toothed as Zenas Clark; on Zenas I found it appealing but in the case of the Kid it wasn't.

The group of men had been chatting away, but of course that stopped when I walked up. In the course of history I suppose we gals have shut down millions of conversations, just by showing up.

Nobody said anything for a moment, and then Ted Bunsen decided it might be his responsibility to introduce me.

"This here's Nellie Courtright, she's our mayor," Ted said.

"Mayor?" Bill Bonney said, with a rude guffaw. "The way I hear it she's Bill Cody's heifer," he said, at which point I walked up to him and slapped his face, not gently.

"I'm nobody's heifer," I told him bluntly. "If you can't be respectful you can leave."

Bill Bonney looked startled and took a step back. Close up he looked young, and he was young. Probably he had never been close enough to a woman to be slapped by one before.

"You don't need to be touchy, missy," he said. "It was only a poor joke."

"I'll decide what I need to be touchy about," I said. "I doubt you would have made that remark if Mr. Cody had been here."

"Well, he ain't here, is he?" the youth said. "Anyway, I withdraw the remark."

"Sis, lay off," Jackson said, which was a mistake. "Billy just wanted to know about the Yazee shoot-out."

"Don't be instructing me, Deputy," I warned him. I expect my face was red—I have always been quick to react to insult. Bill Bonney's face got red too—he had misjudged how much trouble his casual remark would get him into.

I decided to let them all escape, so I motioned to Billy and showed him exactly where I had been standing when the Yazees bore down on us. He seemed grateful for my tolerance and sort of awkwardly tried to work his way back into my good graces by parading his gunfighter's expertise.

"The Yazees had never been bested, so they got cocky," he said. "I've seen it happen before."

He spoke as if giving us a lecture.

He marked off where each of the horsemen had fallen and walked out in the middle of the street and paced around.

"They didn't bother to spread out," he said. "That's what gave the deputy his chance. If they'd come at you twenty yards apart I doubt the deputy could have got more than two of them. Bunching up like they did was foolish behavior. They didn't bother to study their move, so now they're dead."

Billy kept glancing at me, and with every glance he seemed to shrink a little. Probably the last thing he had expected to encounter in Rita Blanca was a talky woman mayor. He seemed to be relieved when Hungry Billy took charge and posed him for some tintypes. Hungry Billy was mighty excited—he planned to be selling those tintypes for years.

Bill Bonney held no attraction for me, but I soon enough stopped being mad at him and mellowed sufficiently to invite him to lunch at Mrs. Karoo's.

Perhaps it was the writer in me. Here was one of the most famous characters ever to come out of the American West. I wanted to get to know him a little better. I thought I saw some slight menace in his eyes, but what I mainly saw was a rough boy who had had no steady upbringing. His manners were crude—probably his spirit was too. I doubt that he had much opportunity to be anything but crude.

That said, it became clear that he was a kind of specialist when it came to gunfights. He spent nearly three hours muddling around the Yazee sight—Hungry Billy showed him the little Yazee museum and didn't even require him to pay the quarter.

After lunch, which he consumed even more rapidly than most of Mrs. Karoo's diners, I got him to accompany me back to the telegraph office, where I conducted what I believe to be the longest interview Billy the Kid ever gave. I made it into a pamphlet, and over the years, it outsold my *Banditti* booklet, though not *The Good Deputy* when that best seller finally came out.

"What's the main thing about being a gunfighter, Bill?" I asked, at the end of the interview. We had, by then, got on easy terms.

"Being willing to shoot people, that's the main thing," he told me.

"That's it?"

"Sure," he said. "A lot of folks talk about shooting people, but then when it comes to it they don't."

"But you do?"

He smiled—the smile had some sadness in it.

"I do," he said. "I do."

"I hear that conditions are unsettled in Lincoln County," I mentioned. I knew that that vast New Mexican county was where Billy's reputation had been made.

"It's wild right now," he said. "Wild. But I suppose it will quiet down when somebody finally kills me."

I confess I was shocked at the casual way he alluded to his own death.

"When somebody kills you?" I said. "So you expect it, then?"

He didn't answer, but he looked at me as if he thought I must be slightly dense.

When I mentioned that I had known Wild Bill Hickok, Bill Bonney let a wistful look come into his eyes.

"He was a gent, I hear . . . a real gent," he said.

"That he was," I said.

"I wouldn't mind being a gent and dressing fancy," Bill said. Then he grinned. "If I live that long."

Billy rode off about dusk on his unimpressive horse. I guess you could say he was just one more tourist, who had ridden all the way from Lincoln County to see where a famous gunfight had happened. The most famous killer in the West had visited the perfect Western town. Bill Cody would have made an exhibit of it, if he'd had the time.

I was just on my way to Tombstone when news came that Sheriff Pat Garrett had shot Bill Bonney down.

It was the biggest news anywhere. Billy the Kid, dead! Dead as Custer, dead as Hickok, dead as the Yazee gang!

Looking back on it I wish I'd asked that wild sad boy to stay for supper.

# 10

GENERAL W. T. SHERMAN didn't have too much to recommend him—at least not to me, who had been brought up to admire the elegance of Robert E. Lee—but at least there was no hem and haw in him. He got right to the point. Before I even knew he was in the vicinity he rode right up to the mayor's office, which was also the telegraph office and my writing room, and rapped on the windowpane, although there was a big Closed sign hanging not an inch from where he rapped.

This occurred at about eleven o'clock in the morning, when it was, as usual, windy.

I was scribbling on *The Good Deputy* and had finally got my characters off the Missouri River—they were now well lined out along the Santa Fe Trail and I was trying to decide what calamity to visit on them next. I considered a buffalo stampede, a prairie fire, a plague of grasshoppers, all of which could easily have occurred over that vast stretch of country. But in fact, though the travelers were certainly due a fresh calamity, I felt more like writing a love scene, though love scenes always raise the issue of plausibility. Could my heroine, Marcie Jones, wander off from the party, encounter a handsome Pawnee youth, and exchange a few passionate kisses—or would it be more likely that she would begin a liaison with the blacksmith's helper, a stripling I had decided to call Jasper? I had about decided to go with the blacksmith's boy, reasoning that I could always conjure up a handsome Indian a little later in the story, when General Sherman rapped. He had three soldiers and a pack mule with him.

I opened the window and gave the man a frosty look.

"If you can't read that sign, then you need specs," I told him.

"I have specs," he informed me. "I read the sign. Then I looked in the window and there you were. I think it's about time you opened up and did your duty.

"I'm General William Tecumseh Sherman," he added, reaching into his coat pocket, from which he extracted three messages and handed them to me. I saw that they were written in a neat and legible hand.

"I am not in the army and do not enjoy being ordered around," I told him, "but I'll send your telegrams and then I'll thank you to honor my sign."

The general, a sharp-featured man, looked in and spotted my tablet.

"I suppose you are writing a book—most women are, these days," he commented.

"If I am there's no need to discuss it," I pointed out.

"If I remember right you used to work for Buffalo Bill Cody," he said. "I've heard you were starchy and I see it's true. But I have no leisure for jawing. Do you know where Esther Karoo lives?"

"Yes—in the house with the hedges around it."

It was the first mention I had had of Mrs. Karoo's first name.

General Sherman looked around, spotted the house with the hedges, and surveyed the rest of the town without much interest. One of his worn-out soldiers was asleep in the saddle, a fact that the general didn't miss.

"Shake that fool, we can't have a slumbering cavalry," he said, though without much heat.

"I seem to remember there was a shoot-out here," he mentioned. "The Yazee gang, wasn't it?"

"Correct—my brother, Jackson, shot all six of them," I said.

"That's mostly luck, I expect," the general remarked.

Then he gave me a long look.

"I've met a few Courtrights," he said. "I suppose you're the prize of the lot, or this town wouldn't have made you mayor."

"They made me mayor because I'm organized," I told him.

"Uh-oh," he said, with a trace of a smile. "If I didn't have seventeen forts to inspect I'd sit under a tree and watch you be mayor for a day or two."

"You might if you could find a tree," I observed.

General Sherman looked startled.

"There is that," he admitted. "I keep thinking I'm in Tennessee, but I'm not, am I?"

Brisk as he was—at least, that was his reputation—he seemed reluctant to go.

"An organized woman is a fright to the mind," he said, and then he tipped his hat to me and rode up to Mrs. Karoo's, where he stayed about an hour. The soldiers were allowed to dismount—in a blink all three sat down and went fast asleep.

In my family—some of whom lived in Atlanta—General Sherman was regarded as the blackest monster on the planet. He didn't seem a monster to me, but then I was not at war with him.

On his way back down the street General Sherman gave my office a wide berth, but he did stop at the jail. Pretty soon Jackson and Ted Bunsen and Hungry Billy were walking over the shoot-out site with him. His sleepy soldiers even perked up and took an interest. Hungry Billy even managed to get the general to pose with Jackson and Ted for a photo or two, after which the general and his three sleepy soldiers and his pack mule rode off in the direction of the seventeen forts he meant to inspect.

About a week after General Sherman paid us a visit, Sheriff Ted Bunsen showed up at my office and proposed to me one last time. Of course I was scribbling on *The Good Deputy*. It looked as though my heroine, Marcie, might be pregnant by that blacksmith's boy, whom I pictured as a large youth with sturdy thighs.

I myself had yet to be pregnant, which I understand to involve some discomfort such as early vomits and the like. Very few pregnant women turned up in the fiction of the day—particularly not pregnant women who had not bothered to get married—so I knew I was writing a daring passage (daring enough that the preachers would preach against my book) and I wanted to concentrate and push my narrative all the way to the birth of the babe; but I looked up and there was Teddy. He hadn't rapped on the glass, as General Sherman had, but there he stood, good old Ted, a beau of sorts, if rather a dull one.

The life of women is mostly interruption—at least that's how I experienced it. Father used to interrupt me freely, asking me the meaning of a word, or how much water had accumulated in the rain gauge, or if I thought the milk cow was going dry.

Zenas Clark, when I first knew him, thought nothing of interrupting me for no better reason than that he wanted to poke his stiffie in me. If I had known how sparse such attentions would get to be I would have opened my arms to Zenas every time—in later years, I mostly did.

"What is it now, Sheriff?" I asked brusquely.

"It's our engagement—is it still on?" he asked, in his normal nasal voice.

"Well, you'll have to let me think, Theodore," I said firmly. "The last time it was mentioned was before the Yazee shoot-out, which occurred way back in eighteen seventy-six, as I recall. Then I worked for Bill Cody nearly four years, which brings us well into the eighteen eighties. That's how I figure it."

Ted did some hasty mental calculations but didn't say anything.

"That's a good long engagement," I pointed out. "I suppose the main question is whether we still want to attempt marriage with one another."

"If that's the question, then what's your answer?" he asked.

"I'll be frank, Theodore," I said. "I am loath to commit myself to the married state until I've sampled the quality of our copulation, which is an act we've accomplished only once and that was a while ago.

"We could hike off to some private spot and have another go at copulating," I suggested.

Teddy was still beet red.

"I fear I've forgotten how to go about it," he admitted.

"Oh, honey," I said. He was so hopeless I found I almost loved him.

Teddy stood as if planted.

"Ted, if it was that hard to do, the human race would have died off long ago," I reminded him.

"What about the sin part?" he asked, his blush fading a little.

"That's just preacher's talk," I told him. "A couple that's been engaged as long as we have deserves a modicum of copulation, I suppose."

"How do we start up?" he asked.

There's such a thing as too hopeless, but I was in a tolerant mood that day.

"First we find a private place," I said. "Then we lock the doors, so my nieces won't surprise us—you never can tell where those rambling tykes are apt to pop up. Then maybe we'll start by kissing again."

He had not, as I recalled, been a bad kisser.

"Then when you get a nice big stiffie we'll commence in earnest," I answered him.

"The jail's pretty private," Ted told me. "I've turned loose all the drunks, and Jackson's gone off with Aurel to try and locate that bunch of mules that ran off two nights ago."

"Perfect," I said.

Actually, the scarcity of copulation was encouraging me to describe it pretty frankly in *The Good Deputy*. The preachers would be beside themselves when they read what I had Marcie do with a cowboy who couldn't wait.

"You run along to the jail and I'll be right behind you," I told him. "Here come the McClendon sisters—as soon as I've dealt with them I'll come to the jail and slip in."

Off the man went, and I did deal with the McClendon sisters, who merely wanted to wire some money to a derelict brother. For some reason their hens decided to follow me instead of the sisters, but I discreetly gave one of them a firm kick, which outraged them of course but prompted them to leave me alone.

In no time I was in the jail, where, remembering that I was mayor, I decided to throw caution to the winds—I suppose I rather rushed Ted Bunsen, my old sock of a beau. He was right to admit that he was still a virtual stranger to even the rudiments of copulation. I can't abide clothes at such a time and soon had mine scattered hither and yon over the office, which shocked the sheriff a good deal, I fear. He himself was reluctant even to take down his pants—he thought unbuttoning a button or two would suffice but I disregarded propriety and yanked his pants down myself. Even then copulating with Teddy was no sure thing—he seemed to have no inkling as to how to find the entrance to the cave of joy. Tired of waiting—why can't the fool find it?— I put him in with my hand, and then later, after an eruption and a nap, I put him in again and had some fun myself.

Somehow we forgot to lock the back door. While we were sprawled about, wondering what came next—I saw nothing wrong with thirds, myself—the back door suddenly opened and a small, friendly-looking Mexican man stepped in. He wore a big yellow hat and he was carrying an old broom.

"Sorry, Señor Ted, I forgot I borrowed this," he said. He sat the broom down, bestowed a nice smile on me, and left.

Teddy was so shocked at being caught with his pants down that I feared he might have a stroke.

"That was Mexican Joe," he informed me.

"Theodore, I would never have guessed," I said.

# 11

THE VERY NEXT day Ted Bunsen showed up at my office and broke off our long engagement, an action which did not particularly surprise me.

"All right, Teddy, you're off the hook as far as matrimony is concerned, but where does that leave copulation?" I asked him.

"We can't be doing it in the jail," he informed me. "Too many interruptions."

"How about Joe Schwartz's hayloft?" I proposed.

That possibility seemed not to have occurred to Teddy—like I said, there's such a thing as too hopeless.

"Or we could find a nice spot out on the prairie somewhere and enjoy ourselves on a blanket—would that suit you?" I asked.

Teddy was silent for a long time. I don't think it had occurred to him that copulation might be possible pretty much anywhere, if both partners were willing and able.

"I need to think about it all," he said.

"Okay—you wander on off and leave me to get on with the town's business," I told him. "I didn't really want to marry you anyway!"

Ted looked relieved.

"I prayed to the Lord, Nellie," he said.

"And what's the Lord's opinion?"

"I'm supposed to stay a bachelor, that's the gist of it," Ted said.

"For once I agree with the Lord," I told him. Then I shut my window, put out my Closed sign, and got on with *The Good Deputy*.

Privately I had already concluded that Ted Bunsen wouldn't do as a husband, even if he dared to risk it. He might come to want me enough, but I don't think he would ever come to like me enough for it to work. Pleasure scared him, and if a man is going to be scared of pain and easy pleasure then why waste time with him?

Fortunately for me, before I had time to get sad about my rejection—which it's possible to do even if you have very little liking for the man who did the rejecting—a fresh possibility appeared in the person of Andy Jessup, the good old Skivvy Kid, who passed through Rita Blanca with five scruffy fellows who claimed to be geologists. Andy was guiding them down to the Cherokee country, where they planned to prospect for oil.

"Oil?" I asked, when I got Andy off by ourselves. "What kind of oil?"

"Do I look like a scientist?" Andy asked. He still had his sweet smile—it wasn't backed up by very much heat but it still was a mighty appealing smile.

"I'm just curious," I told him. "Bill Cody always claimed there was a big future for oil, if it's the right kind of oil. I suppose it's useful for greasing wheels and such."

I found it hard to take much interest in oil, but years later, when Zenas and I were living in California, some of the biggest oil strikes in history were made on Cherokee land. Then I remembered Andy and those five scruffy men. One or two of those old Cherokees got so rich they even bought mansions in Beverly Hills and were able to parade around in fancy motorcars, all because of oil.

I was always glad to see Andy Jessup when he showed up, which was often during my last months in Rita Blanca; with Cody retired to the stage, Andy had become the leading guide to the southern plains. He made friends with Quanah Parker and some other big Comanches and was able to take scientists and rich dudes across the reservation with no trouble from the residents.

I had a big sweet spot for Andy and cried many tears over his death—he was shot down by an ordinary drunk in Abilene, Kansas, for no reason whatsoever except that it was Saturday night and the drunk felt like shooting off his gun. Andy was in a hotel, standing at his window admiring a lightning storm that was moving across the prairie—the drunk's bullet hit him square in the head. They say he was dead before he hit the floor, which I hope is true because no sweeter fellow ever walked the earth.

We never quite found the moment to become lovers, Andy and me. There was some kissing now and then, but we'd always get to laughing about some joke and let the kissing peter out. Andy traveled: I guess he was gone when I was in the mood for him, and there when I wasn't—though that doesn't sound right either. The fact is we were meant to be chums, not lovers, and somehow squeaked through without hurting one another's feelings very bad.

When I think of Andy now, from the high hill of my age, I still remember him coming up to the telegraph office in his long johns—my young darling, the Skivvy Kid.

# 12

To hear Zenas Clark tell it, Tombstone, Arizona, was paradise on earth. I suppose Zenas believed it, because he came all the way to Rita Blanca to talk me into helping him with a newspaper he had started up called the *Tombstone Turret*.

Zenas still had his old snaggle-toothed appeal, and he must have been getting in some practice with somebody because he was even better at copulation than I remembered him being. On the whole we made a lively couple, which didn't quite remove all my doubts about that wild community.

Rumor had it that the Earps ran the town now and the death rate from gunfire was seldom less than a man a day.

"That's exaggerated," Zenas insisted. "It's seldom more than three or four a week."

"Three or four a week does add up, though," I countered. It made Zenas sulk a little; he hated to be argued with.

"The sun shines every day out of a clear blue sky," he tried.

"I got plenty of freckles now—why would I want more?"

In fact I even had freckles on the tops of my bosoms, which Zenas could see for himself, since we were naked in my bed when we had the conversation.

"Did I mention that Tombstone has four fine hotels?" he said, grasping at straws.

"I don't care about a bunch of hotels but I do care about your worthy prick," I told him, "so I'll think about it and maybe join you in Tombstone in the near future."

"Why not now?" he wanted to know.

"Because I'm the mayor," I reminded him. "I promised them six months and I mean to give them six months."

"But you'll come, won't you, sweetie?" he pleaded.

I tickled him in a sensitive place—I wanted his worthy prick to do its job again.

Later, the job finished, I decided I might as well go to Tombstone; I told Zenas I would come as soon as my term ended, in one month. Then I shocked him by announcing my intention to travel over land. I had developed no fondness for trains.

"Good Lord, travel over land, in this day and time!" he protested. "You'll get lost and never be found."

"I suppose Jakey and Sam can guide me well enough," I told him. My old cowboy friends were up in Dodge City, wasting their time running a livery stable.

At mention of Jakey and Sam, Zenas boiled up and had a fit.

"They'd only do it because they're sweet on you," Zenas insisted. "If I catch them I'll pound them to a pulp."

I've seen too many male fits to take them seriously, especially Zenas's, which usually only lasted about as long as it takes to boil water.

"Of course, they may harbor some affection for me—I hope so," I told Zenas.

"But I'm not sweet on either one of them. I plan to be chaste in my travels, chaste as a nun."

After the tupping we'd just done, the thought of me chaste as a nun became, for Zenas, a term of amusement.

"Chaste as a nun," he'd say, if we were about to attempt copulation.

"As I understand it the boom in Tombstone is based on silver," I said. "What happens to us and our newspaper if the silver peters out?"

"It won't—there's a mountain of silver," he insisted. "And there's copper and maybe gold. Before you know it, Tombstone will be as big as Denver."

I wasn't convinced, but I was in love with Zenas by then, and agreed to move to Tombstone when my term as mayor ended in only one more month.

I suppose my doubt about the likelihood of the boom lasting forever made Zenas a little doubtful himself.

"Look at it this way, Nellie," he said. "If the boom does fail we'll be just that much closer to California."

"Smart thinking, honey," I said.

# 13

It was with many a pang that I took my final leave of Rita Blanca: somehow I felt that I had grown up there. Being its first telegraph lady, and then its mayor, had helped make me a responsible young woman. I had never been one to suffer fools gladly, but the main thing I learned, in the end, was not to insist on too lofty ideals. If you want to be part of a human community you have to suffer fools—patiently, if not gladly—and you must practice civility as best you can. There were normal people, like the McClendon sisters, and great driving fools like Bill Cody, but the tribe of human beings is never likely to be crowded with Aristotles.

I served, in the end, six months and a day as mayor of Rita Blanca. Nobody was happy to see me go. Tears were shed and speeches made. A kind of band played and everybody danced, right down to my little nieces, who were short-legged but nimble. I got hugs and kisses from everybody except Ted Bunsen, who confined himself to a handshake. He had still not quite recovered from having been twice seduced in his own jail. Mexican Joe, his crime forgiven, showed up and played the trombone.

Well, they say it takes all kinds—a dubious maxim if you ask me. My guides, Jakey and Sam, were the impatient kind, on this occasion. Some fool had convinced them that there was so much silver in Tombstone that you could pick up nuggets in the street—and if you were not content with nuggets you could wander out into the desert and find chunks of silver the size of goose eggs. Naturally my escorts were eager to get going, before someone else found all those.

We finally departed Rita Blanca just after lunch—Aurel Imlah had hunted long and hard and secured just enough buffalo liver to make a fine repast, which Esther Karoo, old friend of General Sherman's, cooked to perfection.

I had purchased an excellent black pacing horse for my trip to Arizona. I waved, and the citizens of Rita Blanca waved back; soon it got a little dusty and I could just make out the hedges around Esther Karoo's house. Then the town was behind me, though my past wasn't, not quite. I planned to stop for the night at our old Black Mesa Ranch, which we reached in time to see a flaming sunset light our way into the vast West.

I had meant to spend the first night at our old family place, but once I got there I found I didn't want to. I was a future-looking woman—the past had no grip on me yet. I spent five minutes by the sad little patch of family graves. The roof of the old cabin had fallen in, and the barn was more or less no barn. Passersby had helped themselves to most of the lumber, and why wouldn't they? Even the beam that Father hung himself from was missing.

Jakey and Sam, of course, were still impatient. They saw themselves as millionaires already, a piece of rank credulity that irked me, I suppose. But I kept quiet. We all of us have our unrealistic hopes. And Jakey and Sam, though well aware of my quarrelsome nature, had agreed to take me on a long and uncertain journey.

We made our first campfire close to the Cimarron River—geese were calling and ducks were quacking most of the night. I had picked up a copy of my little *Banditti* booklet at Hungry Billy's store and I read it to the boys before the firelight faded. I suppose the narrative gripped them—they didn't say a word or make a sound. When I came to the killing of the six Yazees, their eyes got really big.

"Why, your brother Jackson's a famous man," Jakey said. "A man who can shoot like that could probably get in a show and be rich. Why would he stay in Rita Blanca when he ain't even been made a sheriff?"

"Because he's a good deputy, that's why," I told them.

I didn't mention that Jackson Courtright's skill with the pistol had been a onetime thing.

# 14

THE FIRST THING I witnessed as Jakey and Sam and I rode along the main street of Tombstone was Wyatt Earp, whacking a fellow on the head with a big pistol. I rode right up to the scene before I quite realized that a violent confrontation was taking place. Perhaps it was some form of arrest, though I didn't see any badge on Wyatt. I had already noticed that the town didn't suffer from any shortage of Earps, because Virgil and Morgan were taking the air—which was hot—on the porch of one of the big hotels Zenas had hoped to impress me with. The hotel was the Cosmopolitan, which seemed to me an odd name to give to a hotel in a rocky place where most of the inhabitants seemed to be living in tents. I suppose people can name hotels to suit themselves.

Wyatt Earp drew back his arm to whack his victim again when he happened to notice that I was riding past, with Jakey and Sam.

"Oh hell!" he said. "Not you!"

"What a charming welcome, Mr. Earp," I told him.

At this point his victim dropped to his knees, groaning quietly.

"Now you shut up, Frank—I barely tapped you," Wyatt said. "Get on down to the jail—I'll be along in a minute."

"What'd the poor fellow do?" I asked.

"Why would that be your business, Miss Courtright?" he asked. Wyatt hadn't shaved, and did not appear to be entirely sober; but then full sobriety in Tombstone was a rare thing, as I soon found out. He wore the same dingy black coat that he had sported in Dodge City—his brothers Virgil and Morgan were similarly attired.

"I'm the new reporter for the *Tombstone Turret*," I informed him. "I'll be writing up arrests and murders and court proceedings and the like. Since I'm here I might as well start with this fellow Frank. What did he do? I'm sure the citizens of Tombstone will be glad to read that speedy justice has been served."

The cowboy named Frank managed to get to his feet, though he was still distinctly wobbly.

"Justice?" he said. "You expect justice from an Earp?"

Then he staggered off, holding his bleeding head.

"Frank McLaury is a stagecoach robber and a cattle rustler and so is his brother Tom," Wyatt declared. He stuck his big pistol back in his belt. "And so are the goddamn Clantons and some others. Any whacking they get is well deserved."

"Cattle rustling?" I said, in surprise. "All we've seen for the last fifty miles are rocks and rattlesnakes. Where would a cow find anything to grass on, in this desert?"

I was to learn that there were plenty of cattle in the area, and abundant grazing near the Mexican border, but I didn't learn any of this from Wyatt Earp, who sneered at me unpleasantly.

"You ought to have married Virgil when you had the chance," he said. "Now he's married, and so is Morgan. And I'll thank you to leave Warren alone. The last thing that boy needs is a bossy wife."

"You are remarkably rude, Mr. Earp," I told him—then I rode on down the street to the office of the *Tombstone Turret,* a three-room house in which a lot of ink got splashed. But Zenas, who was not ink-free himself, came running out and gave me a big kiss. Jakey and Sam, who evidently didn't care for the sight of people kissing, wandered off to wet their whistles. Both had been excited by the abundance of saloons—indeed, so far as I could see, except for a small photography shop, a gun shop, and a general store, there was nothing much in Tombstone but saloons. The four hotels themselves were mainly just saloons with a few bedrooms attached.

"I just saw Wyatt Earp pistol-whip a fellow he claimed was a stage robber and cattle rustler," I told my inky lover.

Zenas just grinned.

"Stage robbers abound," he said, "and there's no shortage of cattle rustlers either."

While Zenas was stabling my pacer at a big livery stable called the O.K. Corral, I set about getting my kit off our pack mule. It was really a job for Jakey and Sam, but they had been polite and put up with my sulks and rampages all the way from the muddy Cimarron River to the dusty San Pedro, so I decided to leave them to their carousing—they'd earned it.

The mule—it was our same old Percy, no longer a youth—tried my patience but I finally got the kit off and Zenas showed up and helped me get it out of the street. Before we could get it inside we heard a general yelling from the direction of the Alhambra Hotel, about a block away.

This time it was Virgil Earp who was doing the whacking—his victim attempted to hit Virgil with a rifle barrel but Virgil was the more experienced pistol-whipper. He soon gained control of the rifle himself and whacked the young victim yet again with the barrel of his big pistol, which ended the fight. Virgil collared the fellow he was struggling with and dragged him off toward the jail.

"That unfortunate is Ike Clanton," Zenas informed me. "The Earps and the Clantons are bitter enemies."

"I doubt that the Earps have any other kind of enemies," I surmised.

"Virgil's the town's marshal," Zenas informed me. "He has three deputies but he only uses them to herd in the drunks. If there's serious fighting to be done he calls in his brothers, or else Doc Holliday."

I had read that Doc Holliday had been a dentist down in Texas or somewhere, but I didn't keep up with outlaws unless they tried to rob me, as Jesse James had, so I knew few particulars about Mr. Holliday and for the moment didn't care to learn more.

But I had come to Tombstone to be a reporter for the *Turret,* and also to spend some time with Zenas in what Jesse Morlacchi called "the beds."

"I've been here twenty minutes and seen two men arrested, both by Earps," I mentioned.

Zenas didn't comment—he had tried to lift my trunk, which was as heavy as if it had been filled with cannonballs. I had to help him wrestle it through the door and back to our room.

"How much of a crime needs to be committed before you want me to report on it?" I asked. I had been mostly bored by my ride across country and was eager to get to work. I think it irked Zenas a little that I was so businesslike. He wanted me to organize his office and help keep him solvent, but he also wanted me to drop everything and flirt with him when he felt like flirting.

"Couldn't we just do it before we get into the business problems?" he asked.

I suppose I had been slow to notice that he had a certain look in his eye and a certain bulge in his trousers.

"Well, aren't you the bold one," I said, giving his stiffie a squeeze. "I suppose we do have a little catching up to do."

The back room was the bedroom, where we did a little hasty copulating. If anything, I was impatient. I had just arrived in Tombstone and my businesslike nature would assert itself.

"There you are, my sweet," I said brusquely, when Zenas spunked.

What I really wanted to do was get out in the street and find out what was really going on between the rustlers—if they were rustlers—and the Earps. It could be my first story for the *Tombstone Turret*.

# 15

AN HOUR OR two later in the day I was standing in the front room of the *Turret* when Ike Clanton, the accused rustler that Virgil Earp had pistol-whipped and jailed, came wobbling down the street toward the O.K. Corral. Since he had to pass right in front of our office I decided to step out and make his acquaintance. Rascal and rustler though he may have been, I mainly liked Ike Clanton and mostly got along with him well.

He even looked glad to see me when I stepped out and introduced myself.

"Why hello, Miss Courtright—got any cocaine?" he inquired. The sun was bright in the street—Ike had to squint to make me out. Actually we did have a bit of cocaine in the office—mixed with cool water it made a good headache remedy. I supposed, from the lump on his temple, that Ike Clanton had a headache.

"I believe we do—come on in," I said, leading Ike into our inky domicile.

The ink put him off a little—I suppose he was a bit of a dandy.

"A man could easily get smudged in a place like this," he commented. Zenas chuckled.

"I'm the new reporter for the paper, as well as being Mr. Clark's fiancé," I informed him. "What did you do to cause Marshal Earp to whack you with that pistol?"

Ike gave a bitter laugh and swigged down a glass of well water with a little cocaine in it.

"I complained about that damn Wyatt beating up my friend Frank McLaury for no reason at all," he said. "But even if I hadn't complained Virgil would have whacked me anyway. Just walking freely in the street is crime enough for the Earps, whom I don't suppose you've met."

"Oh, I met the lot of them in Dodge City years ago," I told him. "Mainly I find them coarse, though I exempt Warren from that judgment."

"You're a kind little lady or you'd call them worse than that," Ike said.

"I used to run the telegraph office in a place called Rita Blanca—I doubt you would have heard of it," I volunteered.

"Oh, I've heard of it," Ike said. "That's where some lucky deputy laid out the whole Yazee gang, if I'm not mistaken."

"You're not mistaken—my brother was the deputy."

"I wish he were here, then," Ike said. "I'd have him go shoot every last Earp except Warren.

"Though if Warren should get in the way I can't promise much," he added.

I got my reporter's twitch when he said that.

"Are you suggesting there's going to be a battle, Mr. Clanton?" I asked.

"Not if they don't crowd us," he said. "If the Earps will let us be I imagine we'll just go home."

"Who's us?"

"Why, the Cowboys," he explained. "Myself and my younger brother Billy, and Frank and Tom McLaury, and one or two other fellows who might want to get in with us.

"The Earps just better leave us alone," Ike added.

Then he thanked me politely for the headache remedy and went on up the street toward the O.K. Corral.

Zenas was quick to explain that the Cowboys, capital C, were just a loose gang of border ruffians who robbed stages and rustled Mexican cattle and generally made themselves a nuisance, not only to the Earps but to pretty much anyone who happened to be traveling in the region between Tombstone and the border.

I gave it all some thought.

"This place is shaping up to be wilder than Dodge City, or Rita Blanca either," I told him.

"It's a lot wilder," he admitted. "Hardly a day goes by without a shooting or two, and some of the time it's the Earps who start the gunplay."

"Does the place have a coroner?" I wondered. "I like to be precise when I file my reports."

"We have a coroner and a judge and a magistrate," Zenas assured me.

"Do you think the Cowboys really mean to fight it out with the Earps anytime soon?"

Zenas just shrugged.

"It all depends on the moods," he said.

"Moods?"

"The Earps' mood—the Cowboys' mood.

"Maybe the Cowboys will just get on their horses and go home," Zenas said. "If they'll just ride off I expect the Earps will let them go."

I peeked out the window, cautiously. If hot lead started flying I wanted to be in a position to dodge it.

Down at the Earps' end of the street I didn't see a soul stirring; but I looked the other way and saw five men milling around in the general vicinity of the O.K. Corral. The man Wyatt had beaten was standing by a horse, but no one seemed to be in any hurry to depart.

In fact Ike Clanton seemed to be riled up. I couldn't hear what he was saying, but he was gesticulating angrily. Then the whole group ambled across the street and disappeared—they were on the other side of the photography shop, which I had not yet had time to visit.

"Since you spoke of moods, I might just mention mine," I told Zenas. "Mine's what you might call a nervous mood."

Then I looked down the street toward the jail again and nearly jumped out of my skin, because in the street that had been empty a moment earlier, here came the Earps, plus a skinny stranger that I suppose must have been Doc Holliday. They were all wearing dingy black coats. Wyatt and Morgan had big pistols in their hands. Virgil Earp held a walking stick. It was windy enough that Doc Holliday had to keep adjusting his coat, under which I thought I saw a shotgun.

"Zenas, the Earps are coming—do you think we ought to warn the Cowboys?" I asked.

Zenas ran to the window, took one look, and pulled down the shade.

"This office just closed," he said. "Let's hide under the desk."

# 16

OF COURSE, ZENAS had done the prudent thing—pulled down the shades, locked the door. But my reporter's temper was up—I could not bring myself to crouch under a desk at such a time. From deep in my memory rose once again the charge of the Yazee gang—all I could think of was to get out in the street and rescue my brother.

To Zenas's dismay I unlocked the door and dashed out—I even took my tablet, which would be a poor weapon if I were challenged.

The Earps had come level with where I stood. The Earps ignored me, though Doc Holliday gave me a quick glance. Just then a short man wearing a badge came out and tried to stop the Earps' advance—but they hardly paused.

"That's the county sheriff," Zenas explained. He had popped out behind me, hoping to drag me to cover.

"I don't think they listened to him," I said. Then I noticed that Zenas and I were hardly the only solid citizens in the street. The photographer, Camillus Fry, whom I had not yet met, was standing there with a black cloth over his arm—I suppose he had been making a picture when he sensed the menace. More than a dozen other citizens were just standing in the street gaping; they had blank, trapped looks on their faces—all of them were mobile, and yet they didn't flee. I had seen that look before, in Rita Blanca, when a cyclone was bearing down on the town—we all knew we ought to run and hide, and do it quick, and yet we didn't move. Fortunately the cyclone just missed us.

The Earps, with Doc Holliday on their right flank, continued their advance, despite the fact that they had no accurate notion of where the Cowboys had gone. The Cowboys' mood or rationale I can only guess at. They were somewhere on the other side of the photography shop, perhaps feeling muddled, with no clear notion of what ought to happen next. They may well have all been outlaws—but were they fighting men? The Earps, of course, were fighting men and not much else. If gunplay should begin, it was highly likely that there would be fewer Cowboys when it ended.

"Nellie, bullets are going to fly," Zenas warned. "We ought to get behind that wagon if you won't hide under the desk."

He was dead right, of course, but I was too stubborn, or maybe too curious to consider anything of the sort. I wanted to see the fight, if there was one; and I wanted to be the first one to write it up, as I had written up the Yazee charge in my *Banditti* book.

I didn't have long to wait—suddenly the Earps and the Cowboys bumbled into one another. The latter had been ambling out toward the street, not really expecting it to be so full of Earps.

Probably the Earps supposed that they could easily stare down the Cowboys, as they had stared down so many of their kind. But this time, the two groups were too close together for the staring down to take effect.

"You're all under arrest!" Virgil said loudly, at which point Frank McLaury made a motion in the direction of his gun but didn't really pull it.

"Hold on now, I don't want this!" Virgil Earp said—but whether he wanted it or not, he had waited too long to stop it, because two gunshots rang out almost as one.

Unfortunately I was directly behind Wyatt and Morgan Earp—I couldn't plainly see who those two were shooting at, nor who was shooting at them, if anyone was. I *think* Wyatt and young Billy Clanton may have exchanged shots—I also think Morgan Earp fired at least one round at Frank McLaury before the shooting became general.

Though I twice heard a bullet's whiz I remained rooted in the street, and so did everyone else who had chosen to watch the fight.

Ike Clanton, who did not seem to be armed, came running up to Wyatt and took his arm. I suppose he hoped to call everything off, but if so, his timing was sluggish. Wyatt yelled something at him that I didn't hear, at which point Ike hurriedly left the fracas and ran into the photography shop, not to be seen again for a while.

Both the McLaury brothers attempted to hide behind the horse, but the shooting made the horse restive, so that tactic didn't work. Suddenly there was a yell from Doc Holliday, who poured both barrels of his shotgun—borrowed from Wells Fargo, I later determined—into Tom McLaury, who soon ceased to inhabit this life.

Another young man, unknown at least to me, detached himself from the Cowboys and followed Ike Clanton into the photography shop, whose owner, Camillus Fry, stood not ten feet from me, still holding his black cloth.

What occurred in the middle part of the battle, which I suppose went on for at least ten minutes, is something that has never been satisfactorily explained—not to me, anyway. I was there, but I can't explain it myself. The horse milled around, dust was kicked up, guns went off with some regularity, and yet, so far, only Tom McLaury had actually fallen. Not to this day would I claim to know with absolute certainty who was shooting at whom, or with what results.

"I got him!" Morgan Earp called out at some point—but I don't know who he got, if he got anybody.

"They got me!" Doc Holliday called out about the same time—but he still seemed to be firing away with his small nickel-plated pistol. If Doc got anybody, other than Tom McLaury, I don't know who it may have been.

Then I saw Virgil Earp fall over, followed, a minute or two later, by Morgan, who went down heavily.

That left only Wyatt and Doc Holliday standing—Frank McLaury having sunk down in the street. He died within the hour, and so, to my sorrow, did handsome young Billy Clanton, who asked to be remembered to his sisters as he lay bleeding in the dust. A doctor got there in time to pump two shots of morphine into young Billy, but it didn't save him.

Billy Clanton was a sweet-seeming, curly-haired lad, and polite at the finish. I knew neither of the McLaurys nor young Billy either, but later, thinking back on it, I suppose he had just come to town to help his brother and had no intention of getting into dangerous gunplay with the Earps. With him went whatever promise his short life held.

The locals later speculated about the O.K. Corral shoot-out quite a bit. Some thought forty shots were fired—others put it at thirty.

I was not counting gunshots, but I can't recall that I saw anyone reloading their weapons so I suppose those reports are just exaggerations. When I published my little booklet, *Death at the O.K. Corral,* I ducked speculation about the number of bullets fired.

Wyatt Earp walked away from the shoot-out unscathed; not so his brothers. Virgil was shot in the leg and Morgan across the shoulders. Both of them had to be carted back up the street in a wagon. Doc Holliday proved to have only been grazed on one hip.

The short sheriff with the badge—Johnny Behan, he was called— actually tried to arrest Wyatt Earp for murder, an attempt that Wyatt indignantly rejected, though he did promise not to leave town.

As for us humble citizens, our reaction was much like the reaction I remember from Rita Blanca, when all the Yazees lay dead—we all just milled around, blank and numb and useless for the rest of the day. Zenas got drunk and I got drunk with him. Copulation was neither suggested nor performed. The hand of death had spared us, but it didn't spare the McLaury brothers, or sweet young Billy Clanton.

I felt, for a time, the relief that comes from surviving a catastrophe. I was alive though others were dead. Being alive felt good.

But I couldn't sleep a wink that night for thinking about what seemed to have been a pointless slaughter.

"What kind of community have you brought me to, Zenas?" I recall asking at one point.

"I expect it will be settling down once the boom's over," he said. But I could tell he had been thinking along the same pessimistic lines as I had.

Probably some kind of arrest had been planned when the Earps set out along that street to face the Cowboys. But the arrest went wrong; three men died and three more were injured. And that was just what could happen on one sunny afternoon in Tombstone, Arizona.

"It might be that this place has a little too much snap," I suggested to Zenas, as we were staring at our supper.

"Maybe it does," he agreed.

# 17

THE NEXT MORNING I was out early with my reporter's tablet, trying to track down witnesses to the big shoot-out at the O.K. Corral. Actually, the big shoot-out had mostly occurred across the street from the stables, but the combatants had moved around some, and locating the fight at the O.K. Corral was close enough, I figured. Zenas had already cranked out a one-sheet paper in big caps announcing the slaughter, and people were snatching them right off the press as if they were ten-dollar bills—the report was brief and short of details but at least the names of the dead were included.

But I wanted to dig a little deeper for a follow-up story, which is why I was out early, but gathering solid information about the combat did not turn out to be easy. The fact was that I had arrived in Tombstone only hours before the crisis. Many of the citizens turned out to be dried-up, taciturn types who had no interest in talking to a yappy young woman they had barely met.

I was scarcely out the door before here came Jakey and grumbling Sam, both obviously the worse for a night of hard drinking—both had already concluded that Tombstone was no place for honest cowboys.

"I guess this is gamblers' heaven, but we ain't gamblers," Jakey said. "It's wilder than Dodge ever was."

I gave them their wages and a bonus and a hug apiece, plus a little cocaine for their headaches. I felt a pang of sorrow when those fine boys rode off. If I had had any sense I'm sure I would have been going with them, out of this violent desert and back to the calm of the plains.

But I had Zenas to think of, and our newspaper, and am anyway just too stubborn to give up on something without giving it a big try.

I worked my way down the street, asking questions, but solid information was hard to obtain. One old miner, with a foot-long beard and a pick over his shoulder, gave it as his opinion that the Earps were to blame for it all.

"You can't go far wrong blaming an Earp," the old fellow avowed. "I suppose before they quit they'll kill us all."

Then I had what I suppose was a piece of luck—I spotted Doc Holliday sitting by himself in a rather spindly chair outside the Cosmopolitan Hotel. He still wore his dingy black coat but had not bothered to don a shirt. He was smoking a cigar and coughing after every puff—but he kept on puffing. If he was much worse for the shoot-out it didn't show.

"Mr. Holliday, could I speak to you for a moment?" I asked politely.

From inside the hotel I heard the loud voice of an angry woman—I have no idea what she was mad about but she was loud. The sound caused Doc Holliday to bunch his shoulders slightly.

"Hell, yes, I'll talk to you, miss," he said. "I guess I'd rather be shot for adultery than for missing my aim at a goddamn spittoon, which is what Kate's so mad about."

"I don't consider this quite adultery," I told him, rather taken aback.

"You don't, but Katie will if she sees us chatting," he assured me.

"Oh, is Katie your wife?" I asked.

"More or less," he said. "The damned woman has ragged me about enough—and it's barely sunup," he continued. "If she assaults us I may just shoot her."

"No, don't do that," I urged. "It seems like the community absorbed quite a bit of shooting yesterday, which is what I want to ask you about," I told him.

Doc Holliday favored me with a rather thin smile.

"Shooting's an everyday occurrence in this part of the country," he said. "Just because there was an excess yesterday don't mean there won't be a healthy sprinkling today."

I felt sure the man knew what he was talking about.

"I'm the new reporter for the *Tombstone Turret*," I informed him. "I'm trying to get a clear perspective on that shoot-out yesterday up by the O.K. Corral."

Doc looked at me with real amusement for the first time.

"You want to get a what?" he asked.

"A clear perspective," I said. "What I can't understand is how such a terrible set-to occurred right in the middle of a settled community."

"Where might you be from, miss?" Doc asked.

"Waynesboro, Virginia, originally," I told him. "More recently I've resided in North Platte, Nebraska, and Rita Blanca, which is a town in No Man's Land."

"Oh, dern!" Doc said. He stood up and firmly shook my hand.

"You're that gal who keeps books for Bill Cody, I believe," he said. "And didn't your brother mow down the Yazees?"

"Correct," I said. "What about assisting me with my perspective?"

Doc gave a hearty laugh followed by a cough. He coughed so hard the blood rushed to his cheeks.

"Oh well," he said, when he stopped coughing. "I suppose it was a fairly lively fracas. Virg and Morgan got pretty shot up but I escaped with a grazed hip."

"And three men got killed—let's not forget them," I reminded him.

"Only three—are you sure? I had it in mind that it was four—are you sure it was only three?"

"Quite sure," I said.

"I told Katie it was four, now she'll rag me for bragging, I suppose," Doc said. He obviously was more worried about the reaction of the woman called Katie than he was about what happened at the O.K. Corral.

"I had a toddy or two before Virgil Earp asked me to participate," he mentioned. "I am only a fair pistol shot when I'm drunk, so I told Virgil I'd go if he could loan me a shotgun."

"Which he loaned you?" I said.

"No, Wells Fargo loaned it to me," he said. "I suppose they hoped I'd shoot a few stage robbers and make life easier for the men who carry their payroll.

"It's damned dangerous work, carrying payrolls," Doc told me, undoubtedly a solid opinion, because the driver of the Bisbee stage was killed that afternoon.

"I thank you for that information," I told him, "but what I'm most anxious to know is why the fight started in the first place."

Doc Holliday looked plainly disconcerted.

"What started it—now that stumps me," he admitted.

Then he thought for a while, even going so far as to furrow his brow.

"I guess we expected to run a bluff on them, like the Earp boys generally do," he said. "I suppose the bluff didn't take, this time. I know we were all mad as hell at Ike Clanton."

"Why? What did Ike do to get everyone so mad?"

"Have you ever met him, miss?" Doc asked.

"Just briefly."

"He chatters, you know," Doc said. "I've told him to shut up fifty times and yet the man still chatters. Wyatt told him to shut up just yesterday, but it's like telling the damn sun not to shine. Ike will hold it in for a few minutes and then the damn fool will start chattering again."

"So three men are dead because Ike Clanton is a blabbermouth?" I asked.

Doc shrugged.

"I imagine he was the first killed," he said.

"Why, no—he wasn't killed at all," I informed him. "He left the scene early, on Wyatt Earp's advice."

"Good God, now that *is* a disgrace," Doc said. "You mean we shot up all that ammunition and didn't even kill Ike?"

"You didn't kill him—I suppose he left town," I said.

"I feel rather foolish," Doc said—and he did look rather abashed. "I suppose I was more drunk than I thought. The least we ought to have accomplished is to have killed Ike."

He sighed.

"I guess it will have to wait till next time," he said, standing up. He flipped his cigar into the street and turned to go inside, putting a finger to his lips as he went.

"Katie's quieted down," he whispered—"maybe I can slip inside and get a shave."

# 18

LATER IN THE DAY I was lucky enough to meet Kate Holliday, better known as Big-Nosed Kate, and I'm glad to say that she was perfectly pleasant to me. It's true that her most prominent feature was her nose, but we can't all be born beauties. Katie Holliday was a generous woman who was mainly doing her best to keep her sick husband alive.

I think Katie liked me, but she had slept through the whole O.K. Corral affair and had nothing to contribute to the record.

In fact, though yesterday's fusillade of shots may have caused everyone in earshot to conclude that all hell was breaking loose, it was strictly a one-day ruckus so far as daily life in Tombstone went. Ruckuses involving guns were just part of civic life in Arizona's great boomtown.

The one person who might have given me a clue as to what set the Earps off—my young friend Warren Earp—had been helping drive a herd of cattle to Tucson that day. When he finally returned, a week later, other problems had arisen. Warren had so much to do that I doubt he ever wasted a thought on the O.K. Corral combat.

None of the older Earps would talk to me—as a clan they were still furious I had rejected Virgil's proposal of marriage. Wyatt himself was rude as rude on the few occasions when I ran into him. The only time he ever came into the newspaper office was to place an ad to assist the recovery of a mule he claimed had been stolen from him. He offered the not exactly princely sum of five dollars for information leading to the return of the mule.

"Only five dollars, Mr. Earp?" I said, as I took down the information. "Do you think anyone's likely to trouble themselves about a mule for such a modest sum?"

"Do I look like a spendthrift?" he said. Then he walked out. Those were the last words Wyatt Earp said to me for something like thirty-five years, until I happened to encounter him on a movie lot in Hollywood. Mr. D. W. Griffith was making one of his Westerns—I had done the scenario and Wyatt was there as a firearms consultant or something. When I went up to him and introduced myself he looked blank. I tried a few sallies: mentioned Dodge City, Rita Blanca, Virgil Earp, Warren Earp, Bill Cody, Tombstone, Ike Clanton, and the O.K. Corral, but it was only the mention of Ike Clanton that caused his eyes to light up with a dark light.

"The damned rascal, he got away from us that day!" he said, echoing Doc Holliday's sentiments.

Of course, Ike Clanton did a good deal more than get away from the ruckus at the O.K. Corral. The next day he charged Wyatt and Doc with first-degree murder. They were jailed for a while, but they had a smart lawyer who soon got them off. But Ike and the Cowboys refused to leave it be. A few weeks after the O.K. Corral, Virgil Earp was shot down while crossing the street. He lived, but lost the use of his left arm. A sensible family would have left for safer climes at that point, but not the Earps. Morgan made the elementary mistake of playing billiards with his back to a glass door, through which he was efficiently shot and killed.

Wyatt, with the help of Doc Holliday, swore vengeance and got vengeance. Various of the Earps' sworn enemies soon bit the dust—so many that even Wyatt soon realized he had overplayed his hand, as far as Arizona went. The only thing for him to do was leave, so he left. He and Doc were soon established in Colorado—efforts to bring them before the bar of justice did not succeed.

Meanwhile killings in and around Tombstone continued at a steady pace. The Earps, or for that matter, the Earps *and* the Cowboys, contributed only a modest element to the general lawlessness that prevailed in the area. The deadly Apache leader Geronimo was still out at this time, but folks in Tombstone didn't even have time to worry about Geronimo. It got so bad that Zenas wouldn't even hear of me riding a stagecoach to Benson or Bisbee, much less Tucson, to do a little shopping or buy a load of newsprint or anything.

The truth is, I was just as anxious about him. Rita Blanca, day to day, had never been as dangerous as Tombstone was.

I wrote up my little booklet about the shootout at the O.K. Corral, expecting it to fly out of the office, as my little *Banditti* book had. Now, of course, it's just as great a rarity as the *Banditti,* but at the time it hardly sold at all. People were moving into Tombstone or hurrying out at such a rapid rate that the O.K. gunfight was soon mostly forgotten. I stacked the unsold copies of my booklet in a shed—the next time I went to look, the pack rats had got most of them, which accounts for the rarity. The Earps eventually drifted off to other parts of the West— Virgil became a peace officer in California, Wyatt ran a saloon up in Alaska, and I soon completely lost track of sweet young Warren.

When the chatterer Ike Clanton was shot dead while rustling cattle a few years later, Big-Nosed Kate, whose name by then was Katie Elder, sent me an obituary from the Tucson paper that didn't even mention that Ike had been the cause of a big shoot-out in Tombstone when it was at the height of the boom.

Zenas and I ran the *Tombstone Turret* for two more years, by which time the mines were beginning to flood and the boom was ending. The big hotels were empty and the tent dwellers were gone. Geronimo finally came in, with his little straggle of warriors. The gunfire petered out, but so did customers for the *Tombstone Turret*. Our thoughts were turned more and more to California, where the air was said to be so soft.

One day out of the blue a telegram came offering to sell us a magazine called *California Skies,* whose mission was to extol the beauty of everything under those balmy skies, from the tall timbers to the border with Mexico.

I had inherited some money by that time, and Zenas had one or two rich aunts to call on. Without thinking twice we bought the magazine, moved to Santa Monica, and so far as Tombstone went, felt lucky to have escaped with our lives.

# Book V

---

## California Days

# 1

IT WAS ODD that my lovely, snaggle-toothed Zenas Clark had cared to start up a newspaper in a desert—odd, because the great waters of the world were his first love. Born in Chicago, he grew up on Lake Michigan, he used to say. No sooner had we taken possession of our offices in Santa Monica than Zenas had bought a boat. The offices of *California Skies* were on Ocean Avenue, so that day in and day out, year in and year out, Zenas could look at the water.

We had a fine burst, Zenas and I. Our six lively girls emerged year by year: Belle, Beverly, Bettina, Bess, Beulah, and Berrie.

We had a big shingled house two blocks in from the Palisades. The magazine prospered, and Zenas's rich aunts kept dying, which enabled Zenas to buy bigger and bigger boats, the upshot of which was that—mostly as a stunt—Zenas and four of his sailing friends decided the time had come to sail around the world.

Although I had my misgivings, I was not the kind of wife to put a stop to an adventure like that. I fell in love with Zenas Clark because of his adventurous spirit—it was a little late to try and make him into a settled, salaried man.

The four around-the-worlders set off from San Pedro, with myself and the B's, as we called the girls, and the families of the other bold sailors all gathered at the dock, with plenty of press available. Everybody wished them luck and waved heartily—if stupidly, in my opinion. They had named the boat the *Nellie C.*

They made it to Tahiti in good health and great spirits; at least, that's how it seemed in the pictures they sent back.

Neither the men nor the *Nellie C.* were ever seen again—not by us at least. The great waters hold them somewhere: at least, that's one theory.

It wasn't *quite* the end of Zenas Clark, though, because two years later two Portuguese sailors turned up at the offices of *California Skies* with a little coffee-colored boy—our little Benjy!—who was Zenas's son by a Polynesian beauty, I guess, and a boy of such buoyant spirits that he was soon loved by all. The sailors wept when they handed him over: he grew up the darling of the household and the office, merry as the day was long.

I confess I held back a little, at first, wondering about Zenas. Maybe he wasn't being rocked in the bottom of the deep—maybe he had just got tired of running a magazine in Santa Monica. Maybe, on another island somewhere, another Benjy was being conceived. But I didn't get on a boat and go looking for him. If Zenas and I agreed upon anything it was that chastity was a negative virtue which shouldn't be allowed to impede positive, vigorous people.

Zenas's disappearance didn't long impede *me,* of course. I was attractive, rich, and free—as the editor of *California Skies* I got asked to all the balls and events, and I went to them all, trailing my girls after me. Men came and went: bankers, railroad magnates, architects, high-born crooks, and of course, once the movies came along, lots and lots of actors. I saw no reason to tie myself formally to any of them, so I didn't. My girls grew to become belles in their own right, popular at every soiree. Belle herself had the best business head of anyone in the family, so I eventually put *California Skies* in her hands—frankly, I felt that if I had to edit one more article on Yosemite I might choke. But the magazine grew until it was a huge operation with a staff of forty. I think Belle might have been swamped had it not been for the arrival of rowdy Charlie Hepworth, the old newsy who had taken such a fancy to me long ago that he had tried to fornicate with me in my telegraph office in Rita Blanca.

Charlie was cigar-stained and inebriated as ever, but he did know the journalism racket, so Belle and I made him general manager, which worked well for all concerned. Randy old Charlie ran the magazine efficiently and had an abundance of skirts to chase in his off-hours.

"I still carry the torch for you, though, Nellie," he told me, from time to time, with a certain light in his eyes.

"I know you do, Charlie, which is why I don't intend to put my virtue in jeopardy by crowding up in a telegraph booth with you."

Then we shared a big laugh.

Once I had the magazine in steady hands I decided it was time to do something about the big pile of manuscript that I had continued to scribble on between crises of one kind and another.

This was my book *The Good Deputy*, which, once I forced myself to read through it, didn't seem half bad. By this time I was running a household of some twenty souls: my girls, their beaus, a troop of maids and gardeners and governesses and music teachers. My girls grew up speaking Spanish readily but I wanted them to have French and also some acquaintance with the arts.

It was on the whole a lively household—we had moved up into the Beverly Hills by then—but not, on the whole, a household very conducive to authorship. So I rented myself a cottage in Pasadena and set about making my manuscript into a book. By good luck I succeeded: my book became the biggest best seller since General Grant's *Memoirs*.

Well, the rich get richer, I suppose. Mainly in *The Good Deputy* I had just written about a heroine much like myself, who rambled all over the West, as I had. The book sold four million copies—not right off, but eventually—and it was translated into several languages I had never even heard of.

After that I reigned, for a time—though Virginia-born, I became the queen of California. I opened fairs, made speeches, gave dinners for whatever kings and potentates happened to pass through southern California—and once the movies cranked up, many did.

Of course, I knew Mr. Griffith and old man Zukor, who seemed old even when he wasn't—and Charlie Chaplin and Mary Pickford—and the upshot of it all, once *The Good Deputy* was published, was that I got asked to write scenarios, a trade at which I proved rather adept. After my vast novel it was a relief to write something short, like scenarios, that I could knock out in maybe twenty minutes.

So the years sailed on and the Old West, the West of Dodge City, Rita Blanca, and the O.K. Corral, quickly receded into myth. Over in Victorville, California, Western films were being rolled out by the dozen. I even wrote a couple myself, though I never took the trouble to visit Victorville.

And then, late in 1916, a telegram came that shook me to my core: it was from Bill Cody, and the message was simple:

/

NELLIE I'M DYING STOP COULD YOU COME AND SEE YOUR BILL

Could I come? Would I come? Two hours later I was on a train to Denver.

# 2

I NEVER REALLY lost sight of Bill Cody, nor he of me. In a way I suppose you could say Bill Cody was my lodestar. To lose Bill would have meant to lose a part of myself—the dreaming part. Once every month or two he'd send me two dozen roses—I sent him back champagne, or maybe a fine cognac.

I read of his triumphs in the great capitals of Europe. The old queen came out of mourning to see the Sioux dance. Little Annie Oakley took Paris by storm. Four kings and a crown prince rode in the Deadwood Stage. The show ran for months on Staten Island, just as Bill had predicted—it hosted millions at the big Chicago Exposition of 1893.

I knew, too, of Bill's troubles and humiliations. He tried to divorce Lulu and failed. He sold the Wild West at various times to various people, some of them nice, like Pawnee Bill, and some of them not, like the old press lord Harry Tammen of Denver, who was doing his best to make an event of Cody's dying.

I found Bill Cody in a common hotel room in Denver. He still had that great handsome head, and wonderful smile. Other than his clothes, all that was in the room were his pistol and a bottle of whiskey. When we embraced there were tears in his eyes, and in mine too.

"Bill, is this cheap room the best they can do for you?" I asked. "Why don't you just go home?"

He smiled a wry smile.

"Not up to arguing with Lulu," he said.

"All right—then I'm going to move you to a suite. I'm not rich for nothing."

I soon had him installed in the best suite in the hotel, which seemed to pick his spirits up a little.

Handsome as he was, Bill looked bad. He had not lied—he was
dying. All the gear he had to move was his pistol, his whiskey bottle,
and a shirt or two.

"I ought to shoot Harry Tammen," he said. "He sold everything I
owned at sheriff's auction—including my horse, Isham."

Then came the old broad smile.

"Of course, half of it was Pawnee Bill's, so there's another man who
will always hate me," he said.

I had met Pawnee Bill, whose real name was Gordon Lillie, and I
knew that though such a betrayal would enrage him, he would never
hate Buffalo Bill.

"Bill, you've been a rascal!" I said. And then I broke down and
sobbed.

"But none of us will ever hate you," I assured him, when I got my
sobbing under control. "Gordon will forgive you, as we all have."

"Do you know why I brought you here, Nellie?" he asked.

"Why? I suppose it was to say farewell . . . what else, Bill?"

"It's more than that," he said. "To me you'll always be the sassy
telegraph lady I first laid eyes on in Rita Blanca."

His eyes filled again—I didn't rush him.

"I want you to be the one to telegraph the news of my death," he
told me. "The UP's holding an open wire. There's a key right in the
hotel, set up specially for you. The governor himself had it put in."

"Why, Billy," I said. "I'm so flattered. But I haven't struck a telegraph key in years."

"Nellie, it's just four words: 'Buffalo Bill Is Dead!' " he told me. "I
want you to be the one to send the news off to the world."

"Billy, I'll try, but I need to practice," I insisted.

"So, go practice. But leave the whiskey," he said.

I did go practice. The manager had kindly set up a little desk in a
kind of closet—if Charlie Hepworth had been there he would have
laughed. In a closet that small I'd have little chance of escaping him.

When I got back to the room Bill looked pretty sunken. He said
Johnny Baker, the sharpshooter he had half raised, was on his way
from New York.

It looked to me as if Johnny Baker had better hurry.

The winter dusk falls early in Denver—shadows soon fell on the

Rockies. The whiskey bottle was empty. Bill looked out the window at the great West he had helped build.

"It was a wonderful spree, wasn't it, Nellie?" he said.

"Oh, Bill—it was," I said.

I took his big hand—still warm, but the hand of a dead man.

I allowed myself a private cry and then I marched downstairs like the telegraph lady I had been and sent off to the world the news that a great Western spirit had passed from among us.

Within the hour regrets came from President Woodrow Wilson and the king and queen of England.

Johnny Baker arrived, late by two hours. Annie Oakley sent a fine tribute. The world weighed in. And I went home to Los Angeles, heartbroken. I had lost my truest friend.

# 3

BILL CODY DIED in January but wasn't buried till June, the reason being that Harry Tammen had sweet-talked Lulu Cody into burying Bill in the wrong place; not in the town of Cody, Wyoming, which was named for him, but on the rocky knob called Lookout Mountain, outside of Denver. I didn't go, mainly from fear that I might kill that black-hearted Harry Tammen. I understand that several of Bill's old girlfriends showed up, as befits a prince of men.

I sent Lulu a card of sympathy and later held a luncheon for her when she showed up in California. After all, for most of her marriage, she had been left to be lonely, which eats at a woman. Two years later my brother, Jackson, died, of a tumor of the bowels. He was still deputy sheriff of Rita Blanca, which, of course, by then was a part of the state of Oklahoma. Ted Bunsen was still his boss—he had had no other deputy—but I suppose Teddy Bunsen must have picked up the pace, because he married Naomi, the lady barber, and had nine children. My nieces, Jean and Jan, had grown up and gone to live in Chicago, where Mandy had settled after Jackson died.

I went to Rita Blanca for Jackson's funeral—about the only thing that had changed was that the town now had a water tower. My long-bearded friend Aurel Imlah had turned a wagon over on himself while crossing the Cimarron. He drowned, though he had made that very crossing over one hundred times.

Esther Karoo had gone to live among the Choctaws but Hungry Billy Wheless still ran the general store and the little Yazee museum. My little *Banditti* booklet was in the thirty-eighth printing.

After Jackson's death I took a world tour and then came back and settled into my big house in Beverly Hills. Nellie Clark was still a name to conjure with, in southern California. I gave money to the library, helped start up an opera company, dabbled in real estate, wrote scenarios for various and sundry, and usually tried to have a man of some sort handy. I knew Goldwyn and Mayer and Schulberg and most of the big movie moguls—at least, I saw them at parties.

But I was a little surprised when the pugnacious Louis B. Mayer, whom I knew very slightly, called me up one day and told me that MGM was making a movie about my early years in Rita Blanca. It was called *The Telegraph Lady* and the lovely Lilllian Gish had been engaged to play me.

"Hold on, Louie," I said. "What makes you think you have the rights to my life?"

I don't think he liked being called Louie—anyway, he barked right back at me.

"Because you did a scenario for D.W. Griffith in nineteen oh six," he told me. "We bought it, we're doing it, and all I called you for was to invite you to the set."

You know, he was right. I *had* done a scenario for Mr. Griffith, a fact I had completely forgotten. Scenarios flew thick and fast in those days; most of them died speedy deaths. The last thing I expected was that *The Telegraph Lady* would surface again.

Of course, what Louie B. Mayer really wanted was a little publicity—it's the lifeblood of the movies, after all. So I allowed him to send a big white limousine on the appointed day. We stopped by the office and picked up Charlie Hepworth, the only man in Los Angeles, probably, who had actually *seen* Rita Blanca in its prime, and off we went to Ventura, or thereabout, where they had found a little stretch of California prairie and built their movie Rita Blanca on it.

They say that what the movies are really selling is magic—seeing the Rita Blanca that MGM made would have convinced me, had I needed convincing, which I didn't, of course. Zenas and I had moved to Los Angeles in 1883—we saw the movies come in from the ground up, you might say; but even so, walking through the set of Rita Blanca was something special—it was like walking through my youth—and I suspect Charlie Hepworth may have felt the same. There was Beau Wheless's general store, and Joe Schwartz's livery stable, where Zenas and I had first enjoyed one another. There was even hay in it!

And there was Ted and Jackson's jail, with the gallows that Jackson had painted on his first day of work as a deputy, so many years ago. They had even built Mrs. Karoo's house, and Aurel Imlah's hide yard, and Ripley Eads's barbershop, and Leo Oliphant's saloon.

When I asked the head carpenter how they got it so accurate he smiled and pulled out a stack of about one hundred photographs—to my astonishment I realized that they were the very photographs Buffalo Bill had had Hungry Billy make, so Bill himself could set up the perfect Western town somewhere, once he got his Wild West going, which he had. There's nothing the research people on a movie can't find, if you set them to looking.

How I wished Bill Cody could have been there, for the main idea had been his, and he had had it long ago. He had figured out first what others had figured out later, which was that the thing to do with the Wild West was sell it to those who hadn't lived in it, or even to some who had. Just sell it all: the hats, the boots, the spurs, the six-guns, the buffalo and elk and antelope, the longhorn cattle and the cowboys who herded them, the gunslingers and the lawmen, the cattle barons and the gamblers, the whores, the railroad men, and the Indians too, of course, if you could find them and persuade them, as Cody had.

Charlie Hepworth, a big talker, was unusually silent as we walked around—I believe it sobered him a little to see how easily the distant past could be brought back in perfect detail. When the company broke for lunch Miss Gish joined us under a big arbor that had been thrown up. I had met her before—we chatted about actors. Of course, she thought Charlie Chaplin was the greatest man alive, and Mr. Griffith second. Photographers were busy snapping us as we talked.

After lunch, during which Charlie, who was tongue-tied around actors, took in a bit of grog, we wandered over for one last look at the telegraph office where, I guess you could say, I made my name.

Of course, in real life, the Yazees were dead before I even set foot in the Rita Blanca telegraph office, but in my scenario I had adjusted the facts sequence a little. In the movie Lillian Gish is made to rush out with an old buffalo gun of some sort and come to the aid of my brother, although the buffalo gun misfired and the actor who played Jackson still got to kill all the Yazees.

Charlie Hepworth was staring at the reconstruction of my old telegraph office with misty eyes.

"What are you thinking about, Charlie?" I inquired, though I already had a notion.

"You know exactly what I'm thinking about," he said.

"Just let me remind you that no one invited you to drop your pants on that occasion," I said.

"Oh, Nellie, stop your yapping!" Charlie said, with a sudden sad look in his eyes. "A man can have his dreams," he added, with a sniffle or two.

"I didn't mean it that way, Charlie," I said in apology—in fact I was not sure how I had meant it or why I even said it.

We stayed for most of the afternoon, watching them choreograph the Yazees' wild charge. Stuntmen did the charge several times—nobody wanted to risk an expensive actor falling off in such a melee and getting hurt.

The photographer took a few more shots of me with Lillian Gish, and then Charlie and I got back into the big white car and purred back toward Santa Monica. When I dropped Charlie at the office he stood on the sidewalk for a moment, looking sad.

"Hey! What's the matter with you, young fellow?" I asked—in fact I was nursing a sadness of my own, the cause of which I could not quite pinpoint.

Charlie Hepworth thought about it for a moment, the sea breeze blowing his sparse gray hair.

"I guess I won't be seeing that picture, when it comes out," he said.

"Why not, Charlie?"

He shrugged. "Once is enough to live your life through, ain't it?" he asked.

I wanted to get out and hug him, but Charlie turned and stumbled off.

*The Telegraph Lady* came out and was the hit of the year. Of course, I was invited to the fancy premiere—but I didn't go—and I was never tempted to see that picture.

For once that well-known liar Charlie Hepworth had said something true.